She fit into his arms
made to order, Do

Her warm, womanly frag
tantalizing scent of her blood teased his senses even as it awakened his hunger. He spoke to her mind and then he bit her lightly, just enough to break the skin, just enough for a single taste. It sizzled through him, more potent than hundred-proof whiskey, more desirable than anything he had ever tasted. Though sorely tempted to take more, he sealed the tiny puncture, then lifted his head and quickly wiped the memory from her mind.

When she smiled up at him, he knew he was lost.

It was after midnight when Dominic took her home. He kissed her deeply before saying good night, acutely aware of her gaze on his back as he walked to his car.

He was in more danger than he had ever been in his life, Dominic mused as he turned to wave at Maddy.

And so was she.

Other titles available by Amanda Ashley

A WHISPER OF ETERNITY
AFTER SUNDOWN
DEAD PERFECT
DEAD SEXY
DESIRE AFTER DARK
NIGHT'S KISS
NIGHT'S TOUCH
NIGHT'S MASTER
NIGHT'S PLEASURE
NIGHT'S MISTRESS
NIGHT'S PROMISE
NIGHT'S SURRENDER
IMMORTAL SINS
EVERLASTING KISS
EVERLASTING DESIRE
BOUND BY NIGHT
BOUND BY BLOOD
HIS DARK EMBRACE
DESIRE THE NIGHT
BENEATH A MIDNIGHT MOON
AS TWILIGHT FALLS
TWILIGHT DREAMS
TWILIGHT DESIRES
BEAUTY'S BEAST
A FIRE IN THE BLOOD
HOLD BACK THE DAWN
ENCHANT THE NIGHT
NIGHT'S ILLUSION

Published by Kensington Publishing Corp.

ENCHANT the DAWN

AMANDA ASHLEY

ZEBRA BOOKS
Kensington Publishing Corp.
www.kensingtonbooks.com

ZEBRA BOOKS are published by

Kensington Publishing Corp.
119 West 40th Street
New York, NY 10018

This book is a work of fiction. Names, characters, businesses, organizations, places, events, and incidents either are the product of the author's imagination or are used fictitiously. Any resemblance to actual persons, living or dead, events, or locales is entirely coincidental.

To the extent that the image or images on the cover of this book depict a person or persons, such person or persons are merely models, and are not intended to portray any character or characters featured in the book.

If you purchased this book without a cover you should be aware that this book is stolen property. It was reported as "unsold and destroyed" to the Publisher and neither the Author nor the Publisher has received any payment for this "stripped book."

All Kensington titles, imprints, and distributed lines are available at special quantity discounts for bulk purchases for sales promotion, premiums, fund-raising, and educational or institutional use.

Special book excerpts or customized printings can also be created to fit specific needs. For details, write or phone the office of the Kensington Sales Manager: Kensington Publishing Corp., 119 West 40th Street, New York, NY 10018. Attn. Sales Department. Phone: 1-800-221-2647.

First Printing: September 2022
ISBN-13: 978-1-4201-5163-3
ISBN-13: 978-1-4201-5164-0 (ebook)

10 9 8 7 6 5 4 3 2 1

Printed in the United States of America

To Beverly Clemence,
who, more than thirty years ago,
encouraged me to find a publisher.
I'm so glad I listened.

Prologue

At the sound of a stag's horn, twelve Knights of the Dark Wood gathered in a circle beneath a bright yellow moon. Save for a gentle breeze that stirred the leaves of the trees and the hems of their hooded cloaks, utter stillness surrounded them.

More than twenty-five years had passed since the death of the Elder Knight known as Paul 9, who had been killed at the hand of Quill Falconer. A new Elder Knight had been appointed to take his place. For a time, every Knight in the country had sought the life of Falconer, but the vampire had taken his witch-wife, Callie, their twin son and daughter, and fled the country.

Tonight, the Brotherhood had met to pledge their loyalty to the Elder Knight who had been chosen to succeed Lucian 32, who had briefly replaced Paul 9.

It was no easy task, being the leader of the Brotherhood. The Elder Knight made policy, administered punishment, made sure rules were obeyed and that the members never forgot the sole reason for their existence—the complete and utter destruction of the Hungarian vampires.

As the horn sounded a second time, a stoop-shouldered

man clad in a long, white robe strode into the center of the circle. Staff in hand, he made a slow turn, his steely-eyed gaze settling briefly on each man present. "We are here tonight to remember the passing of Lucian 32, who died peacefully in his sleep a fortnight ago. By a vote of the Counsel of the Brotherhood, Gregory 73 has been chosen to wear the mantle of the Elder Knight. His name has been sent to every member of our community throughout the nation. All have taken a solemn oath to give him their loyalty and their allegiance. Gregory 73, come forward."

A tall man clad in a black robe stepped into the center of the circle. He was lean and well-muscled, with thick brown hair and penetrating brown eyes beneath heavy brows. Lowering his hood, he bowed his head.

The white-robed Knight handed the staff to Gregory 73, then placed his hands on the Elder Knight's head. "This quorum, representing the combined number and strength of the Brotherhood of the Knights of the Dark Wood, hereby swears its allegiance to you, Gregory 73, and to none else. Will you, from this night forward, dedicate your life to the mission of the Knights of the Dark Wood? Will you do all that is required of you, and swear fealty to our cause, which is righteous and just?"

"I will." The Elder Knight's voice, filled with power and authority, echoed through the Dark Wood like thunder.

"So let it be written," the white-robed Knight declared. Drawing a jewel-encrusted dagger from beneath his robe, he made a shallow cut in the newly ordained Elder Knight's palm. And then he did the same to each Knight present. One by one, they clasped hands with the Elder Knight, mixing their blood as a symbol of their loyalty.

The white-robed Knight cut his own palm last of all. Clasping the Elder Knight's hand, he declared, "By our blood united, we renew our oath to destroy the devil-spawn known as the Hungarian vampires, as well as any and all other supernatural creatures, and to shield and protect any and all humans from their evil."

As one, fourteen voices rang out in the night. "We do so swear!"

Gregory 73 sat in his cell within the Knight's temple, staff in hand. It was a small, simple room, yet it held the necessary furnishings—a sofa and small table, a comfortable bed. A stout oak chest held his clothing, his now useless invisibility cloak, and what few personal belongings he possessed. His first order of business was to find and execute the witch who had betrayed them—Ava by name. She had destroyed the power of their cloaks, which had shielded their presence from the Hungarian vampires. She had also removed the enchantment from the medallion each Knight had worn to alert them when vampires were near.

He had overheard the Brotherhood lamenting the fact that the witch, Ava, had betrayed them, even as they discussed their urgent need to locate a new witch ally, and to destroy Quill Falconer. Gregory quite agreed. The whole Falconer family was an abomination. None more so than Quill, who had mated with a mortal woman, an act every true Knight looked upon with repugnance. Unlike Transylvanian vampires, Quill's ilk were capable of mating with human females. Destroying the Hungarian vampires before they could procreate with female mortals had been the primary mission of the Brotherhood of the Knights of the Dark Wood for a thousand years and more.

But Gregory had his own reasons for wanting the vampires dead.

He smiled faintly. Though the Knights did not yet know it, there was already a witch in their midst. Gregory had kept his ancestry hidden from everyone, including the previous Elder Knight. But now his moment had come. No one hated the Hungarian vampires more than did he. The creature known as Quill had murdered his father, but now, at long last, Gregory would have his revenge.

Quill Falconer might be out of his reach. But the vampire's son was in New Orleans.

Still, Gregory was not yet ready to reveal the truth of what he was to his fellow Knights. To that end, he needed to find another witch—one to do his bidding until he was ready to reveal his ancestry. And he had the perfect sorcerer in mind.

Wand in hand, he chanted the words of summoning.

Gregory 73 reared back as an enormous black vulture appeared before him. He stared at the hideous creature, the shiny wings, the wicked talons, the slash of white on the bird's head. Lifting his left hand, Gregory waved it in front of the vulture, from right to left, murmuring, "*Rivelare*," as he did so. Power filled the room as the name of the man who had been bespelled appeared in the air. "Jasper!"

The bird bobbed its head up and down, its black, beady eyes focused on the Elder Knight's face.

Gregory shook his head. "Who's done this to you, my

old friend?" Unleashing his dark magic, he walked around the scavenger. "Ava." Gregory spat the name. "Interfering old crone."

Murmuring the words of an ancient spell of unmaking under his breath, he walked around the vulture—three times to the left, three times to the right—and then struck the bird with his wand.

Multicolored ribbons of smoke erupted from the tip of the wand, swirling around the vulture, and when they settled, the warlock known as Jasper stood in the bird's place, stark-naked and shivering from head to foot.

Wrapped in a thick, woolen blanket, the warlock huddled in a chair, a cup of strong black coffee cradled in his hands as he related the events that had led to his enchantment, how the witch known as Ava had rescued Quill Falconer from a Transylvanian vampire, destroyed the vampire's coven, and turned Jasper into a hideous creature along the way.

Gregory nodded intermittently. He had heard the stories, had followed Quill's doings for centuries.

"How can I thank you for undoing that hideous enchantment?" Jasper asked. "Ask of me whatever you will and I will see it done."

"Yes, you will," Gregory said. "Whatever and whenever I say."

Jasper shivered as the Knight's power rolled over him.

"Fail me and what Ava did to you will seem like a blessing in comparison."

Jasper swallowed hard. He might be a powerful warlock, but he was no match for the Elder Knight.

"After you are fed and clothed, I want you to renew the enchantments on the invisibility cloaks of my Knights, and then you will fashion new medallions that will alert my people to the presence of vampires. Can you do that?"

"Yes, my lord." He would do it or die, of that Jasper had no doubt.

Perhaps being a vulture hadn't been such a bad thing after all.

Ava Magdalena Langley woke abruptly, all her senses alert. Sitting up, she stared into the darkness as she felt a shift in the universe. She honed in on the magical signature that had awakened her, knew a moment of dread when she realized what it meant. Black magic was afoot in the Dark Wood. A new Elder Knight had assumed the mantle of leadership and, unlike the last one, Gregory was a wizard, and one to be reckoned with. Dark power swirled around him as he cast an ancient spell of undoing.

Rising, she went to the bedroom window and peered into the distance. To mortal eyes, there was nothing amiss.

But for those who had eyes to see, black magic rode the wings of the night.

Chapter 1

Claret prowled the back streets of New Orleans, her thoughts not on prey but on the Hungarian vampire who had destroyed her companions and thwarted her at every turn. The vampire whose blood she had tasted and longed to taste again with every nerve and fiber of her being.

Quill Falconer. Even after more than a quarter of a century, she hungered for his blood. She had searched from east to west and north to south looking for him, but to no avail. He had taken his woman and his children and left the country. Twenty-five years and still she could not forget him—the taste of his blood on her tongue, the texture of it, the smell. The power.

Quill was incredibly powerful, as was his witch-wife, Callie, damn her to hell.

Claret lifted a hand to her throat, remembering the last time she had seen the vampire. He had been her prisoner then, hers to savor at leisure, until a powerful witch came to save him.

Once freed, Quill had destroyed the members of her coven and very nearly destroyed her as well. She had been at rest when he came for her. They had struggled, fangs and claws rending preternatural flesh, until he wrapped his hands around her throat, but his own blood, blood she had consumed, had given her the strength she needed to break his hold and vanish from the room. She had not seen him since.

But she had never forgotten him, and she never would. Someday, she thought, someday she would taste his blood again.

She paused at the sound of footsteps coming her way, thoughts of Quill momentarily forgotten as a young man rounded the corner ahead.

Anticipation stirred deep within her.

Dinner was about to be served.

Dominic Falconer strolled through the streets of New Orleans. He had always wanted to visit the Big Easy, and his great-grandmother, Ava, had finally given him the opportunity, much to his parents' disapproval. His mother, especially, had been against his leaving Savaria, but Ava had insisted she would go along and keep an eye on him. His task was to find out all he could about the new leader of the Knights of the Dark Wood and what the Brotherhood's intentions were, without revealing his parentage.

Dominic couldn't help wondering why the sudden interest in the Knights. His parents had left the States soon after he and his sister, Ava Liliana, were born twenty-five years ago. His great-grandmother had followed them to the homeland a year later. It was only in the last month that he'd learned that his parents had left the States because they feared for his safety, and that of his sister.

Dominic frowned. Perhaps his parents' interest was

due to the fact that there was still a small number of Hungarian vampires residing in the States who might be at risk from the appointment of a new, more radical Elder Knight.

Whatever the reason, being here on his own gave him a sense of freedom he'd never known before. Not that he didn't love his parents. They were two of the finest people he had ever known. His twin sister was his best friend. But ever since his vampire nature had kicked in, he had yearned to go out on his own, to test his powers and his abilities.

And Great-Grandma Ava had given him the chance. He wondered now if she had somehow divined his longing to be on his own all along, perhaps even fabricated her need to know about the new Elder Knight to give him a chance to get out of the country.

He had a hell of a family, he mused with a wry grin. His father was a powerful vampire, his mother and great-grandmother were witches, as was his twin sister.

Dominic came to an abrupt stop as he caught the scent of vampire. Not one of his kind, but the bloodthirsty, Transylvanian breed, as different from his people as night from day.

He felt a rush of excitement at the thought of finally meeting one of the others. And then he paused. Transylvanian vampires were notorious for taking his people prisoner in order to feed on their blood. Once they tasted it, they became addicted. Occasionally, one of them drank too much and went completely mad, but that risk didn't deter the rest.

But all such thoughts fled his mind when he saw her. She was incredibly beautiful, with clear, tawny skin and eyes so dark they were almost black. A riot of red hair fell over her shoulders like a silken waterfall.

She slowed, then stopped when they came face-to-face. Nostrils flared, she ran her gaze over him. "Vampire," she hissed. "What are you doing in my territory?"

"Just visiting," he drawled. "Do you mind?"

The words were barely out of his mouth when, in a blur of movement, she was on him, her fangs sinking deep into his throat. One taste and she reared back, her eyes wide with disbelief. "Who are you?"

Dominic covered the bite with his hand. "What the hell do you think you're doing?"

"I asked you a question."

Eyes narrowed, he grabbed a handful of her hair, pulled her body against his, and buried his fangs in her neck. He took a good, long drink before he pushed her away. Damn. His father had warned him about Transylvanian vampires. Why hadn't he listened? Muttering, "Now we're even," he vanished from her sight.

Claret licked her lips, reveling in the taste of the last drops of blood lingering on her tongue. Could it be? She inhaled sharply, drawing in his scent. And then she smiled. It had to be, she thought. Quill Falconer's son had come to Louisiana. She had known many men—human and vampire alike. But she had never forgotten Quill, or the exquisite taste of his blood.

And now his son was here, like the long-awaited answer to a prayer.

Dominic materialized in a residential neighborhood several miles away from New Orleans. Damn! He had never been bitten by a vampire before and he wasn't sure how he felt about it. Not that it had been unpleasant. Quite the opposite. Under ordinary circumstances, the vampire would have been able to find him again, but he had powerful witches in his family. His mother had woven a protection spell around him, one that thwarted Transylvanian vampires from tracking him. He wondered suddenly if his mother had had this particular vampire in mind at the time. He grinned inwardly. Although the vampire who had bitten him couldn't track him, he could track her, if need be.

Hands shoved into his pockets, he strolled down the quiet street. It was late and most of the houses were dark. It was a lovely neighborhood, with well-kept, two-story homes fronted by lush green lawns and well-tended flower beds. Stately trees grew here and there, providing welcome shade.

Rounding the corner, he found himself thinking about the vampire again. She wasn't his kind, that was for sure, which made her technically his enemy. She had looked surprised when she bit him, which was odd. She would have known what he was, so why had she been so taken aback?

Transylvanian vampires were vicious killers, whereas his people never killed their prey, or anyone else, unless it was to save their own lives or protect their family. But the main difference between his kind and the Transylvanian vampires was that his people were born that way, and the others were made. Perhaps that was why they were angry all the time, he thought with a wry grin. After all, few were given any choice in the matter.

He paused when he reached the end of the block,

wondering which way to go. He had no sooner decided to retrace his steps when he heard a faint cry coming from inside the house across the street.

Frowning, he opened his preternatural senses, but the cry didn't come again. Instead, he caught the tantalizing scent of fresh blood.

Maddy Bainbridge opened her mouth to scream again, but her attacker pulled a dirty handkerchief from his pants' pocket and stuffed it into her mouth. He slapped her hard, twice, as he pushed her down on the floor, then straddled her hips.

Maddy bucked beneath him, hoping to dislodge him, but he outweighed her by a good forty pounds. She beat her fists against his chest, his back, his head, but to no avail. Face split in an evil grin, he tossed her nightgown over her head and trapped both of her hands in one of his. When she continued to struggle, he clipped her on the jaw. Momentarily stunned and unable to move, she could only stare at him, fear and horror like ice in her veins as he unzipped his jeans. Helpless and terrified, she closed her eyes and prayed for help she knew would never come in time. As she felt the man's hands on her breasts, she let out a last, desperate scream for help.

And then, suddenly, there was the slap of flesh striking flesh, the sound of a heavy weight hitting the wall, and she was free.

Hardly daring to look, afraid of what she might see, Maddy opened her eyes.

A dark-haired man dressed in black stood over the thug

who had broken into her house and attacked her. A shiver ran through her when the newcomer turned to look at her.

"Are you all right?" he asked. His voice was soft, melodious, almost hypnotic.

Too frightened to speak, Maddy nodded as she jerked her nightgown down over her knees.

The man's gaze ran over her from head to foot, missing nothing.

She stared up at him, wondering if he had come to help or to take the other man's place. He was tall, over six feet, with broad shoulders, inky black hair, and dark gray eyes that seemed to see right through her. His nose was a blade, his lips full and well-shaped, his jaw strong and square.

Her eyes widened when he offered her his hand. She hesitated a moment before letting him pull her to her feet.

"Did he hurt you?"

"If you mean did he rape me, no." Trembling all over, she wrapped her arms around her waist. "I don't know how you realized I was in trouble, but you got here just in time. Thank you."

He shrugged off her thanks. "I heard your cry for help. Maybe you'd better call the police before he wakes up."

"What?" She stared at him blankly for a moment. "Oh. The police. Yes, of course." She reached for her cell phone, but her hands were shaking so badly, she dropped it.

"I'll take care of it." He wiped a bit of blood from the corner of her mouth with his fingers. "Your forehead's bleeding. Why don't you go get cleaned up while I call the cops?"

Maddy hesitated. Then, with a nod, she edged into the bathroom, closed and locked the door. Still feeling shaky, she sat on the edge of the bathtub, a washcloth pressed to her forehead. She wondered if she should have left him alone in the other room. What if he robbed the place?

Dominic took a deep breath, then licked her blood from his fingers. Pulling his phone from his pocket, he called 9-1-1. After ending the call, he grabbed a silk scarf from the top of her dresser and tied her attacker's hands behind his back.

There must have been a cop car in the area, because one pulled up in front of the house a few minutes later. Not wanting to explain his presence, or get involved with the police and have to respond to a lot of questions he'd rather not answer, Dominic transported himself out of the house.

"I want to thank you for helping me," Maddy said as she opened the bathroom door. "If there's ever anything I can do for . . ." Her voice trailed off. The man who had attacked her lay on his stomach, his hands tied behind his back.

There was no sign of the tall, dark-haired man.

Dominic strolled down the dark streets until he came to a seedy bar that was still open. He paused inside the door and opened his vampire senses. Detecting no hint of danger, no hunters lurking in the shadows, he stepped inside.

He ordered a glass of red wine and carried it to an

empty booth in the back. His first night in New Orleans had been interesting, to say the least. He thought of the two women he had met—an incredibly beautiful and dangerous vampire and the loveliest mortal woman he had ever seen. Like sunlight and moonlight, he thought with a grin, and wondered what his chances were of getting to know the pretty blond female better.

Thinking over what had happened, he was surprised he'd been able to enter her house. His kind usually required an invitation to cross a mortal threshold. And then he shrugged. Perhaps her desperate cry for help had been invitation enough.

Dominic tensed when he felt a shift in the atmosphere. The next thing he knew, his great-grandmother, Ava, was sitting in the booth beside him. He grinned at her. She looked nothing like a great-grandmother. She was another beautiful woman, with golden-blond hair and bright blue eyes. He knew she was over a hundred years old, but she appeared to be in her early thirties, an easy spell for a witch. Why look your age when you didn't have to?

"What brings you here at this time of night?" he asked.

"What do you think? You were sent here to learn what's happening with the Knights, not to provide nourishment for a Transylvanian vampire, or rescue a mortal woman from danger."

"Would you rather I'd let her be raped? Perhaps killed?"

"Of course not!"

"What have *you* found out about the new Elder Knight?"

"Not a thing. All I know is that the Brotherhood has moved to a new location. They left nothing behind, not so much as a footprint. Every spell I tried failed, which can only mean one thing—they've found a new witch."

"So, what do we do now?"

"Wait for them to find you."

"And then?"

"We'll track them to their new headquarters and speak to the Elder Knight. Perhaps we can reason with this one, although I doubt it."

"And if he refuses?"

"One thing at a time. Three of our people have been killed in this city in the last few months, which leads me to believe that the odds of making peace with the Knights are slim at best."

"Those deaths are the real reason we're here, isn't it?"

Ava nodded, her expression grim.

"Wouldn't it be easier for my great-grandfather to call all of our people home?" His great-grandfather, Andras, was the undisputed leader of the Hungarian vampires. His word was law.

"It would, indeed. But those who live here have homes and businesses. Some were born here. Some have never been to the Homeland. Andras feels it would be unfair to demand that they leave behind everything they have worked for."

Dominic grunted softly.

"Sooner or later, a member of the Brotherhood will make a mistake. Until that time, you be careful. I promised your mother I'd keep you safe. She'll never forgive me if anything happens to you."

"I'm always careful."

Ava laughed at that. "I'll see you at home."

Dominic grinned. He had rented a house when he'd first arrived, and she had decided he needed a roommate.

"A chaperone, you mean," he had said with a scowl. But she'd just laughed and moved into one of the bedrooms.

Dominic blew out a sigh as she sashayed out the door. He was about to call it a night when the vampire he had met earlier slid into the booth across from him.

Eyes narrowed, she asked, "Who are you?"

"Who are you?"

"I'm Claret, mistress of the New Orleans coven. No one stays in my territory without my permission. What are you doing here?"

Dominic shrugged. "Sightseeing." He tensed as her power rolled over him. She was strong, but he was stronger. He knew a moment of triumph as he easily blocked her efforts to probe his mind.

"You're Quill's son, aren't you?"

Dominic's eyes widened in surprise. "You know my father?"

"Indeed. You look just like him. I should have realized who you were right away." Her eyes glinted red as she licked her lips. "Not only do you look like him, but you taste like him, too."

Dominic stared at her. Who the hell was she? And how had she known his father? Surely they hadn't been lovers. He was just as certain that his father hadn't willingly given a Transylvanian vampire his blood. Had they been enemies, then? "What do you want?"

"The same thing I wanted from your father."

"And what was that?"

Her gaze darted to his throat.

It was all the answer he needed. "What's so special about my father's blood?"

"It was powerful. The most powerful I've ever tasted. I've craved it ever since."

"Well, forget it. I'm not sharing."

"We shall see." She smiled, revealing her fangs. "We shall see," she said again and vanished from his sight.

Chapter 2

Dominic had a lot to think about on his way home. The Knights of the Dark Wood were killing his people. A Transylvanian vampire who had not only known his father but had also tasted his blood was now hungry for his.

But it was the woman he had rescued who preyed on his mind. Who was she? Was she single? Engaged? Married? How could he arrange to see her again? It had to look like a chance meeting, he thought as he unlocked the door to the rented house he shared with his great-grandmother. He didn't want her to think he was some depraved character who was stalking her.

In the bedroom, he undressed and slid under the covers. When he closed his eyes, her image rose in his mind—she had a wealth of wavy, dark blond hair, beautiful deep brown eyes, and a mouth he yearned to kiss.

One way or another, he had to see her again, he thought. And then he frowned. How was he going to explain his abrupt disappearance from her house? Dammit, he should have stayed and introduced himself. Instead, he had vanished without a word. No doubt she thought he had something to hide from the police, and that was why he'd taken off before they arrived.

Dominic swore under his breath. He had something to hide all right, he mused as he sank into the dark sleep of his kind. An ancient secret he was duty bound to keep.

Maddy woke late after a restless night. In the clear light of day, she felt foolish for leaving every light in the house on when she'd gone to bed, but the attack had shaken her badly. She no longer felt safe in her own home, even with all the doors and windows closed and locked. If the police released her attacker from jail, would he come after her?

Wondering if she would ever feel safe again, she went from room to room, turning off the lights, double-checking to make sure all the doors and windows were locked, even though she knew they were. She switched off the porch light and then headed for the kitchen in search of coffee.

Sitting at the table, she found herself thinking about the man who had come to her rescue. Who was he? How had he known she was in trouble? Had he heard her screams? Why had he left without a word? He had been an incredibly handsome man. Even now, she could see him clearly—tall and broad-shouldered, with thick, black hair and dark gray eyes. Like the Lone Ranger, he had come to her rescue and left without telling her his name.

With a sigh, Maddy refilled her cup. She hadn't had any interest in men since she had ended her relationship with her last boyfriend nine months before. But her rescuer . . . there had been something about him. Or maybe she had just imagined it. After all, she had only seen him for a few brief moments.

Just her luck that she would likely never see him again.

Dominic rose with the setting of the sun, his first thought for the pretty woman with the deep brown eyes. He knew where she lived. Would she think it strange or suspicious if he stopped by her house? He could say he just wanted to make sure she was all right.

He thought about it while he showered, and the more he thought about it, the more reasonable it sounded. Stepping out of the shower, he pulled on a pair of jeans and a black T-shirt, stepped into his boots, and went out into the night.

She lived in a two-story white house with yellow shutters on a quiet street that smelled of jasmine and magnolias. Standing on the sidewalk, Dominic took a deep breath, then bounded up the stairs and knocked on the door before he lost his nerve.

A long moment passed before he heard the sound of footsteps, a shaky voice asking, “Who’s there?”

Her voice. He would recognize it anywhere.

“It’s Dominic. I’m the one who came to your aid last night.”

“What are you doing here?”

“I just wanted to stop by to make sure you were all right.” He heard the sound of a dead bolt sliding back, and then the door opened just enough for her to peer out.

Brow furrowed, she looked him up and down. He saw the uncertainty in her eyes as she decided whether or not to let him in.

"I don't blame you for being cautious," he said. "I won't bother you again. Good day."

"Wait!" She unfastened the chain and opened the door. "Please, come in."

Dominic felt a familiar shimmer of power as he crossed the threshold. Some mortals were sensitive to supernatural power. She was one of them, whether she recognized it for what it was or not.

He followed her into a spacious living room decorated in shades of blue and white with yellow accents.

"Please, sit down."

He sat on the love seat she indicated.

"Can I get you anything? A glass of tea, perhaps?" she asked as she perched on the edge of the sofa across from him, keeping the glass-topped coffee table between them.

"No, thank you." She was leery of him, he thought. Not that he could blame her after what she'd been through the night before. Listening to the rapid beat of her heart, sensing the uncertainty she was trying to hide, he was surprised she had let him in.

"I don't want to keep you," he said quietly. "I just wanted to see for myself that you were okay."

"To tell you the truth, I'm not okay." She laughed self-consciously. "Last night I slept with all the lights on."

"It's understandable."

"You don't think it's cowardly?"

"Not at all. If it will make you feel better, I'll come by later tonight and keep an eye on the place."

"I can't ask you to do that."

"You didn't." He paused as a little white lie formed in the back of his mind. "I'm a bodyguard. It's what I do." It was true, in a way. He protected mortals from Transylvanian vampires.

"I'm not sure I can afford to pay you. I'm between jobs at the moment."

"No charge."

"But . . ."

He held up his hand to still her objections. "After last night, I feel sort of responsible for you."

When his gaze met hers, something indefinable passed between them, a connection unlike anything she had ever experienced before. It sent a shiver of awareness skittering down her spine. With his gaze holding hers, she knew in some way she couldn't explain or understand that he would never hurt her.

Dominic felt it, too, like an invisible thread connecting the two of them. It penetrated his very soul. "I never got your name."

"It's Madison. But everybody calls me Maddy."

"It suits you."

"I was about to make dinner," she said, somewhat shyly. "Would you like to stay?"

"I'd be glad to take you out. Anywhere you'd like to go."

She bit down on her lower lip. "I don't know."

"We could meet somewhere if you'd rather."

Why was she so reluctant to go out with him? Maddy wondered. If she trusted him to be in her home, why not in a car? "That won't be necessary." A strange warmth spread through her, and she was again struck by the feeling that he would never hurt her, that she could trust him with her life.

"Great. I hope you don't mind driving. I don't have a car."

She stared at him in astonishment. "Really?"

"Really."

"No problem. Just let me grab my keys."

He followed her out of the house, waited on the sidewalk while she backed a light blue Chevy Malibu out of the garage. "Nice car," he said as he settled into the seat.

"It belongs to my parents. I left mine at home. Where did you want to go?"

He shrugged. "Why don't you decide? I've only been in town a couple of days."

"Do you like seafood?"

"Sure."

She thought a moment, then turned left out of the driveway onto the road and headed for the Bourbon Street Restaurant.

Inside, the hostess led them to a booth.

"Nice place," Dominic remarked. Large picture windows gave a clear view of the street.

Maddy nodded. "I come here as often as I can. I love their shrimp. And the lobster," she added with a grin. "Although I can rarely afford that."

"Order whatever you like," Dominic said, smiling.

"Are you sure?"

"Yes," he said with a wink. "I'm sure."

When the waitress arrived, they ordered two lobster dinners and a bottle of the house wine.

"So," Dominic said, "tell me about yourself."

"There's not much to tell. My parents are on a worldwide cruise. I'm staying in their house while they're gone. I was recently laid off from my job due to some cutbacks. They said it was a layoff, but I don't think they'll hire me back. Last one hired, first one to go."

"Where did you work?"

"I was a teller at a bank in Baton Rouge."

"Have you heard anything from the police about the man who broke into your house?"

"Only that he's being held without bail. Apparently, he has a long record, including burglary and assault. There's also a warrant out for him for rape and a double murder."

Dominic grunted softly, sorry now that he hadn't killed the man and saved the courts a lot of time and trouble. He smiled at the waitress as she delivered their meal. Unlike Transylvanian vampires, his people could consume mortal food if they wished. Doing without for long periods of time increased the desire for blood.

"What about you?" Maddy asked.

"I'm here on vacation." It wasn't exactly a lie, nor was it the whole truth. "I've always wanted to see New Orleans."

"It's a lovely city, although it has a dark side."

"I've heard about that. I've also heard a lot about witches and voodoo, zombies and vampires. And your famous St. Louis Cemetery Number 1."

"You've got to see it while you're here," Maddy said. "It's amazing. It's called the City of the Dead because many of the tombs look like small houses or churches." She grinned at him. "I read somewhere that it costs forty thousand dollars to be buried there."

"Forty grand?" Dominic shook his head. "I find that hard to believe."

"I also read that Nicolas Cage wants to be buried there. He bought a nine-foot pyramid. Marie Laveau, the famous voodoo priestess, is buried there. A lot of her followers are convinced she still works her magic for those who believe." Maddy took a bite of her lobster.

"How is it?" he asked.

"Wonderful. Practically melts in your mouth. You don't believe in that kind of thing, do you?"

"Magic from beyond the grave? I don't think so." But he believed in witches and magic. "Do you?"

"Of course not. Everyone knows there's no such thing as vampires or zombies."

"And witches?"

"Well, everyone knows there are witches, or at least people who believe they're witches. I went to high school with a girl who thought she was a witch. She had the weirdest yellow eyes, but I never saw her do any magic," Maddy said. And then she laughed. "She did make one of my boyfriends disappear, though."

Dominic lifted one brow.

"She stole him from me."

He smiled at her over his wineglass, thinking how lovely she was.

They ate in silence for several moments before she asked, "Where are you from?"

"I was born in the States, but my parents left shortly thereafter for Hungary."

"Wow, I've never known anyone from there."

"My mother is American." Dominic paused, wondering if he should tell her that witchcraft ran in his family, but decided against it. At least until he knew her better. And he very much wanted to know her better.

Maddy folded her napkin and placed it on the table. "I'm stuffed."

"No dessert?"

"Not for me. How about you?"

"I'm good." Dominic paid the check when it came,

left a generous tip for the waitress, and followed Maddy outside.

"Would you like to go for a walk?" he asked.

She glanced up and down the dark street. "I don't know."

"Just a block or two," he said with a wink. "I need to walk off that dinner."

"Good idea."

They turned left and strolled down the sidewalk. Music drifted out of a nightclub across the way. Outside, several young men stood around, talking and laughing. Moving on, they passed a voodoo shop and a gift shop, a cigar store and a place that sold T-shirts.

They were near the end of the block when Dominic sensed vampire. A moment later, Claret stepped out of the shadows. She wore a vivid green dress that outlined her voluptuous figure and displayed a generous amount of cleavage.

Dominic moved closer to Maddy and took hold of her arm.

"Dominic," Claret crooned. "How nice to see you again." Her narrow-eyed gaze ran over Maddy from head to foot. "Who's your friend?"

"What do you want?" he asked brusquely.

"I was hoping we could get together."

"I don't think that's a good idea."

"Aren't you going to introduce me to your friend?"

"No. Good night."

Anger flared in the depths of the vampire's eyes as she looked at Maddy. "I'm sure we'll meet again," she growled, and then turned on her heel and disappeared back into the shadows.

"Who was that?" Maddy asked.

"No one you want to know."

"She's lovely." But a little scary, Maddy thought.

Dominic grunted. "Maybe on the outside. Come on," he said, "let's get you home."

Dominic was quiet on the drive back to her house. Maddy slid several sidelong glances his way, wondering about his relationship with the redheaded woman. An old girlfriend? A jilted lover? She shrugged off her curiosity. It was none of her business. She had just met the man, she reminded herself. His personal life was his own.

At home, she pulled into the driveway and turned off the engine.

Dominic got out of the car and came around to open her door for her, then walked her up the stairs to the veranda. "Thanks for going to dinner with me."

"Thanks for asking me. I had a wonderful time."

"Me too."

Silence stretched between them. Maddy waited, wondering if he would kiss her, wondering if she should let him. It was their first date. For all she knew, she might never see him again.

"I'll be around later tonight to keep an eye on things," he reminded her.

"It's probably not necessary. I mean, my attacker is in jail."

Dominic nodded slowly, thinking that Claret was a lot more dangerous than the man who had attacked her.

"Thanks again for dinner," she said as she unlocked the door.

"Maddy?"

She gazed up at him, felt her heart skip a beat at the look in his eyes.

He lowered his head toward hers, giving her all the time in the world to back away.

But she didn't. Her eyelids fluttered down as his lips brushed hers, ever so lightly, yet she felt the heat of it all the way down to her toes.

She was breathless when he lifted his head.

"Good night, Maddy."

"Good night."

Whistling softly, he turned and strode down the walkway to the street, then disappeared into the darkness beyond.

Maddy stared after him, her lips still tingling from the heat of his kiss.

Chapter 3

Filled with a jealous rage unlike anything she had ever known, Claret stormed through the night. She had waited years to taste Quill's blood again, had almost given up hope until, like a miracle, his son appeared in New Orleans. She had bitten him and savored the taste of blood so like his father's—warm and rich and filled with preternatural power. She could feel the strength of it flowing through her, even though it was already growing weaker. She wanted more.

Much more.

She had intended to seduce Dominic tonight, to mesmerize him so that he would never leave her side, giving her an endless supply of his blood.

And seduce him, she would. Confident of her ability, she discounted the puny mortal female. She wasn't woman enough to satisfy a man like Dominic Falconer. He needed someone his equal, someone strong and powerful who could be his mate forever.

She smiled, confident that he would soon tire of the mortal woman. And if he didn't . . . Claret grinned into the darkness. She could easily make the woman disappear without a trace.

Chapter 4

After leaving Maddy's house, Dominic went in search of prey. The lobster had been filling in its own way, but it didn't satisfy his hunger. Only blood could do that. He headed for the dark underbelly of the city. Melding into the night, he stalked the streets looking for prey. And there was plenty to choose from. It seemed every alley and byway was inhabited with drug dealers, addicts, and prostitutes. Disgusted by the smell, he willed himself to the next town, where he found a middle-aged couple strolling down an otherwise deserted street.

He mesmerized them both, then took the woman in his arms. He spoke to her mind, quietly assuring her that he meant her no harm, before he lowered his head to her neck. Relief flowed through him as he drank. He took only what he needed to assuage his thirst before he released her and her companion from his thrall and disappeared from their sight.

As he made his way back to Maddy's house, he wondered what her blood would taste like. Some was sweeter than others, some more potent, some more satisfying.

When he reached her place, he made his way around

the perimeter, all his senses alert. But there was no sign of an intruder.

There was, however, a predator of a far more dangerous kind, he thought, as Claret materialized out of the shadows.

"What the hell are you doing here?" he hissed as all his protective instincts sprang to life.

"Looking for you, of course."

Shit. "Why is that?"

She moved closer to him, her hand sliding up and down his arm. "Why do you think?"

"I have no idea," he said, removing her hand. "You tell me."

"So we can get to know each other better, of course."

"I don't think that's a good idea."

She glanced toward the porch. "Because of that woman?"

"No. Let's just say we have nothing in common."

"Of course we do. We're both hunters, both powerful." She grinned wolfishly as she jerked her chin toward the house. "Why don't we go inside and have a drink?"

"I'm only going to tell you this once," Dominic said. "If you lay a hand—or a fang—on her, I'll rip your heart out. Are we clear?"

To his amazement, she burst out laughing. "My oh, my. You're more like your father than I thought."

"I'll take that as a compliment."

"Oh, you should, believe me." She wrapped her hand about his biceps and gave it a tug. "Come, have a drink with me." Seeing the refusal rising in his eyes, she said, "I meant in a bar. So we can get to know each other better."

Dominic considered it for a long moment. He was

nowhere near as old as Claret. Still, with a witch and a vampire as parents, he had considerable power at his command. And Ava at his back. Tempted as he was to refuse, he was anxious to get Claret away from Maddy, and yes, curious to hear what the vampire had to say.

His decision made, he followed her into the city.

Claret took him to a tavern on Beale Street. It was dark inside, so dark that mere mortals would have been nearly blind. A jazz band played in one corner. A long bar ran the length of the back wall. The air smelled of beer and wine and blood.

All the patrons were Transylvanian vampires.

She led him to a booth in the back of the room. A moment later, a waitress brought them a bottle of wine and a pair of crystal goblets.

"The house special," Claret said as she splashed wine into his glass and then hers.

Dominic swirled the dark red liquid in his glass, unleashing a rich bouquet and the underlying scent of fresh blood.

Claret lifted her goblet. "To new friends," she purred.

He touched his glass to hers, acutely aware that he was surrounded by her kind and playing with fire. He wondered how long she had been a vampire. She was old in the life, of that he was certain. He was intrigued by the fact that she had known his father and wondered again what their relationship had been.

As though reading his thoughts, she said, "How is Quill?"

"Same as always," he said with an easy smile. "In love with my mother."

Something that might have been jealousy smoldered

in the depths of the vampire's eyes and was quickly gone.

"Just how well did you know my father?"

"Intimately."

Dominic lifted one brow. "You were friends?"

"Not exactly. He destroyed my coven and tried to kill me," she said with a dismissive wave of her hand. "But it was a long time ago."

"I hope you're not looking for revenge."

"Not right now. Why have you come to New Orleans?"

"That's my business, and it has nothing to do with you." He stilled as there was a shift in the atmosphere of the room, a sense of movement in the dark, of malevolence. "Thanks for the wine," he said and willed himself out of the bar and back to Maddy's house.

Dominic strolled around the grounds, then settled down on the front porch swing. He wondered why Claret had followed Maddy's scent home. Did the vampire mean her harm? Or had she assumed she would find him there?

Closing his eyes, he listened to the soft, steady sound of Maddy's breathing as he inhaled her sleep-warmed scent and imagined her in his arms. In his bed.

Damn, he thought with a wry grin. He felt like a horny teenager with his first crush.

Hopefully, this affair would last longer and have a happier ending.

At dawn, Dominic returned to the rented house he shared with his great-grandmother. He was surprised to find her awake and sitting on the sofa, an ancient grimoire open on her lap.

"You're up early," he remarked, dropping down beside her.

"So are you." She put the heavy book aside. "Where have you been?"

"I spent the night with Maddy."

Her brows shot up. "You just met the girl and you're already spending the night?"

"It's not what you're thinking," he said with a laugh. "I slept on the front porch."

"What on earth for?"

"Do you know a Transylvanian vampire named Claret?"

Ava stared at him. "In a manner of speaking. Don't tell me you met her?"

"She bit me."

"Stars above! She's a vicious creature. She captured your parents years ago. Kept your father in a cage and fed off of him. She threatened to give your mother to her coven."

"How did they get away?"

She fluffed her hair with one hand. "How do you think?"

"Ava to the rescue?"

"Indeed. I freed your father and then turned the warlock who had been helping Claret into a rather large, ugly vulture." She smiled at the memory. "Unfortunately, someone has released Jasper from my spell."

"How is that possible?"

"I'm not sure, but it would take a powerful wizard to undo another witch's spell."

"So, where's this Jasper now?"

"I have no idea, but he's a nasty piece of work. I suspect he's under the thumb of whoever freed him. Be careful, Dom. Jasper is stupid but dangerous."

"I can take care of myself."

"I know." She patted his thigh. "You should get some rest."

"Yeah." Leaning over, he kissed her on the cheek. "You be careful, too."

Ava smiled as he rose and left the room. She loved the boy dearly. Heaven help anyone who caused him pain.

Chapter 5

Jasper paced the floor, wringing his hands as he waited for the Elder Knight. What did Gregory want now? He came to an abrupt halt when the Elder Knight entered the room.

"I have a task for you," Gregory said.

"You have only to ask."

"There are Hungarian vampires living in New Orleans. I am looking for one in particular. His name is Dominic. When you find him, I want you to learn everything you can about him: who he is and why he is there. And if he's alone."

"Yes, my lord. Shall I dispose of him for you?"

"No. I want that pleasure for myself. Leon 48 is also searching for this particular vampire."

"Yes, my lord." *Vampires*, Jasper thought. He hated the lot of them. "Why are you seeking this vampire out of all the others?"

The Elder Knight glared at him. "My reasons are my own. Do not fail me." Pivoting on his heel, the Elder Knight strode out of the room.

Jasper stared after him. He owed the man a great debt

for releasing him from the witch's dreadful spell, but he hated being indebted to anyone. It gnawed at his vitals to be in subjection to another man. Any man.

In his own quarters, he packed a leather satchel with the implements of his trade—a wand made of hickory, a silver-bladed dagger, a scrying mirror, a pentacle, a chalice, and a shaker filled with salt. He added a change of clothes, as well as an ancient spell book, and closed the valise with a snap.

New Orleans, he thought. Not his favorite city.

The Elder Knight paced his quarters. He had known the witch called Ava when she worked with the Knights of the Dark Wood. Once considered an ally, she was now viewed as a traitor. He knew she was incredibly powerful, as was her granddaughter, who had not only produced a male child, but a female as well, something unheard of among Hungarian vampires, who sired only sons.

And he wanted the son.

Chapter 6

Maddy sat at the kitchen table, her breakfast dishes pushed to one side as she checked for available jobs in the area on her cell phone. Sadly, she didn't qualify for most of them, and she was not yet desperate enough to work at a fast-food chain. Of course, at the moment, she didn't really need to work at all.

Pushing away from the table, she rinsed her dishes and loaded them into the dishwasher, then went to read her email, which was mostly spam. Sitting back in her chair, she put her slippered feet up on the desk and let herself daydream about Dominic—her knight in shining armor. If someone had asked her to paint a picture of the perfect man, he would have been the ideal model. Tall, black hair, broad shoulders, muscular arms . . . she'd always had a weakness for men with nice arms. And his eyes . . . a dark gray that reminded her of storm clouds on a winter day.

She enjoyed his company, his laughter, his protective instincts. Sure, she was supposed to be a liberated woman. She even had a T-shirt emblazoned with the words *A woman without a man is like a fish without a bicycle*. But she still liked it when her dates held the door for her or insisted on buying her dinner. She preferred hunks like Chris Hemsworth, she thought. Give me an Alpha male every time.

And she preferred Dominic to any of the men she had ever dated. He had offered to spend last night guarding her house to keep her safe. She had assured him it wasn't necessary. Maybe that had been a mistake. Maybe he would think she didn't want to see him again.

With that depressing thought in mind, she went for a walk, hoping a morning stroll through the park at the end of the block would brighten her mood.

Maddy had been walking about ten minutes when she passed an elderly woman sitting on a bench. When the woman smiled at her, Maddy automatically smiled back. She was very pretty, Maddy thought. There were a few streaks of silver in her hair, which had probably once been golden-blond but was faded now. But her blue eyes were still bright. No doubt she had once turned men's heads wherever she went.

"Lovely day, isn't it?" the woman remarked.

"Yes, very."

"I don't suppose you'd sit a spell and keep a lonely old lady company?"

Maddy hesitated only a moment before sitting beside her.

The woman smiled again. "I'm Ava."

"Maddy."

"Nice to meet you, dear."

"You too. I'm sorry you're lonely."

Ava shrugged one shoulder. "At my age, it's to be expected, I suppose. Children grow up and move away. After a certain age, visiting Grandma isn't as exciting as it once was. They'd rather be on their phones with their friends."

Maddy felt a twinge of guilt. She hadn't seen her grandparents in several months. Of course, they lived clear across the country, so it wasn't as if she could just drop in and say hello. But there was no excuse for not calling. Or shooting off a quick text.

"You must have plenty of company," Ava said. "Especially young men."

"Not really."

"No? A pretty girl like you? I don't believe it."

Maddy sat back, completely at ease in the woman's company. "I was dating a guy about nine months ago, but it didn't work out. There was just no spark between us, and he didn't really want a wife. Just someone to clean his house and do his laundry."

"You're better off without that one," Ava said solemnly.

"I agree."

"I'm sure you'll meet someone."

"Actually, I did. Just the other day."

"Oh? Do tell."

"He's gorgeous and polite and seems really nice. We went out to dinner together."

"Are you going to see him again?"

"I don't know. I hope so."

"Give me your hand."

"What?"

"I'm going to tell your fortune."

"I don't believe in that sort of thing."

"No matter." Ava reached for her hand and turned it palm up. She studied it for several minutes. "Your young man will call on you again. You will learn things about him that you may find hard to understand, perhaps even a little frightening, but he will never hurt you. He will protect you from harm."

A chill ran down Maddy's spine. "He . . . he already did that. A man broke into my house a couple of nights ago and he rescued me."

Ava nodded. "He will always do so." She paused a moment, then said, "You will have a very long life. And one day, you will have a son. Perhaps more than one. Happiness will be yours," Ava said. "If you are brave enough to reach for it."

Maddy stared at her. There was no way Ava could see her future, and yet she spoke with such certainty, it was hard to dismiss her predictions.

Ava patted Maddy's knee. "It's been nice chatting with you, dear. I hope to see you again," she said, easing to her feet.

Maddy also stood. "Have a wonderful rest of the day."

"I will. Goodbye, dear."

Maddy watched Ava walk briskly down the path that led to the street. Ava must be in good health, she thought, because she moved like a much younger woman.

"You did what?" Dominic stared at his great-grandmother.

"Oh, for goodness' sake, calm down. I just wanted to meet her."

"I'm a big boy now, in case you haven't noticed. I don't

need you to check out my dates. I don't even know if I'm going to see her again."

"Oh, you will," Ava said with an airy wave of her hand. "You will."

"You sound awfully certain."

Ava laughed as she kissed his cheek. "She'd like to see you again, too. Why don't you call her and take her to the movies or something?"

"Are you matchmaking?"

"Who, me? I'll see you later, Dom. I have a date."

Dominic stared at her as she changed her appearance from a seventy-something grandmother in a flowered housedress to her favorite guise, a thirty-year-old woman in a formfitting black sheath. Her hair lost its gray and her body took on a shape Miss America would envy.

Before he could ask who she was going out with, she was gone.

Witches, he thought, with a rueful shake of his head. And then he grinned. Ava had been right about one thing. He should call Maddy.

Maddy found herself thinking about Ava long after she returned home, and the more she thought about her, the more she realized there had been something truly strange about the woman. She appeared to be in her seventies, but she didn't really act like a senior citizen, at least not like her grandparents, who were roughly the same age. Watching Ava walk away, she would have sworn she was looking at a woman in her late twenties or early thirties.

She was being silly. Lots of older women were in great shape these days. She had seen a few on TV who were in better shape than she was! These days, senior citizens were out running marathons and climbing mountains. She really needed to start going to the gym again, Maddy thought, even though she knew she wouldn't.

But it was Ava's predictions that troubled her most, because she found herself believing them. And that scared her a little. What could she possibly learn about Dominic that would be hard to understand or, worse yet, frightening? Maddy shook her head. She was just being fanciful. No one could foretell someone else's future, and she was silly for letting Ava's predictions bother her. She'd never believed in fortune-telling or tarot cards or Ouija boards and she wasn't going to start now.

She was wondering what to thaw out for dinner when someone knocked at the door. To her surprise, it was Dominic.

"Hi," he said. "I was going to call until I realized I don't have your number."

"Not to worry. Come on in."

He followed her into the living room, took the seat she indicated.

After sitting beside him, she asked, "What can I do for you?"

"I was wondering if you might like to take in a movie or go for a walk or bowling, or . . ." He shrugged. "Whatever you're in the mood for. If you feel like going out, that is."

"I don't know."

Dominic frowned. "Is something wrong?" Her heart

was beating too fast. He caught the faint scent of fear on her skin.

"I met a lady in the park today."

"Oh?"

"She assured me that I would see you again."

"Really? So, you've been discussing me with perfect strangers?"

"Not exactly. I simply said I'd met a young man."

"Go on."

"She read my palm."

Oh, crap. "Did she promise you the usual? A long life and a happily ever after?"

"Not exactly."

"What, exactly?"

"It doesn't matter. She was just very good at it. So good, I almost believed her."

"I'd really like to know what she said."

"Well, she told me you'd call. And that . . . never mind. This is all so silly."

Forcing a little power into his voice, Dominic said, "Go on."

"She said I'd learn things about you that might scare me, but that you'd never hurt me. It was almost as if she knew you."

"Sure sounds like it. So, what does that mean for us, exactly?"

"Is there an 'us'?"

"I was hoping there would be."

Maddy felt her insides melting as their gazes met. His voice was warm and caring, his eyes filled with tenderness and concern. He had saved her life. What was she afraid of? Trying to lighten the mood, she said, "You're not an alien or anything, are you?"

"No, nothing like that."

"You're not like Superman, hiding your real identity?"

"No, I'm definitely not Superman. Or Batman. Or Thor."

"Too bad," she said with a wry grin. "I love superheroes."

"Then I'll try to be one."

"Is your invitation still open?"

"Yes, ma'am."

"Then I'd love to go out with you."

"Pick you up in an hour?"

"Sure. Wait. I thought you didn't have a car."

He grinned at her. "I do now."

He did, indeed, have a car, Maddy thought when he called for her—a brand-new Camaro, yellow with black racing stripes and black leather upholstery.

"Nice," she murmured as he held the door for her.

"Only has eleven miles on it," he said as he slid behind the wheel. "And I put eight of them on there."

When he started the engine, it purred like a well-fed tiger.

He took her to a nightclub in the Quarter that played a mix of rock, pop, and country music. They ordered pizza, hot wings, salad, and beer. It was Friday night, and the joint was jumping. They were lucky to find a table for two, Maddy thought as they navigated their way along the edge of the dance floor while couples swayed to an old Billy Ray Cyrus song.

"Do you line dance?" Maddy asked after they'd been seated.

"'Fraid not."

"I could teach you."

Dominic glanced at the dancers. He had to admit, it looked like fun. A little complicated, but fun. "Maybe after I've had a drink or two."

She grinned at him. "You're on."

She was as good as her word. After dinner, she took him by the hand and dragged him out on the floor and taught him the moves to the Electric Slide. Once he got the hang of it, he enjoyed it. But he liked slow dancing with Maddy in his arms better.

It was after midnight when Maddy suggested they call it a night, at least as far as dancing went, although Dominic didn't seem tired at all. She really had to get back into her exercise program!

At home, gentleman that he was, he opened the car door for her, then escorted her to the porch.

"Thanks for tonight," she said as she turned the key in the lock. "I had a great time."

"So did I. Maybe we can do it again one of these nights."

"I'd like that." She felt her heart skip a beat as he moved a step closer.

"If you give me your number, I could give you a call."

"Good idea." They quickly exchanged cell phone numbers. "Is it still okay if I just drop by without calling first?"

She felt a shiver of anticipation as he took another step toward her.

"Okay if I kiss you good night?"

"I thought you'd never ask," she murmured and closed

her eyes as he kissed her, gently at first and then a little more deeply, a little more intensely. Her heart was pounding like a drum, her knees weak, when he lifted his head.

"Good night, Maddy," he said, his voice gruff.

"Good night, Dominic," she whispered. And realized, in that moment, she was in danger of falling head over heels for a man she hardly knew.

Chapter 7

Ava loved New Orleans. She hadn't been there in decades, but it hadn't changed much. The same antebellum homes and mansions. Magnificent St. Louis Cathedral still stood on Pere Antoine Alley as it had since 1794. Dedicated to King Louis IX, it was the oldest cathedral in continuous use in what had become the United States.

As she walked along Bourbon Street, Ava sensed the tide of supernatural power that ebbed and flowed just below the surface of human awareness. But she felt it clearly. It danced over her skin—the magic of a voodoo priestess practicing her religion, the signature of a black witch conjuring a spell, all happening while mortal men and women went about their daily lives, completely unaware of the dark undercurrent of witchcraft and black magic.

And the unmistakable presence of bloodthirsty vampires lingering in the shadows when the sun went down.

But now the sun was up and everything appeared calm and peaceful. She walked through the city, searching for the signature of one warlock in particular.

She found it in a small, dimly lit café on a narrow, dark side street.

The man she was looking for sat hunched at a table in the back. Dressed all in black, he reminded her of the vulture he had once been.

He stiffened as she approached his table.

Ava laid a hand on his shoulder, a whispered incantation preventing him from spiriting himself away.

Jasper looked resigned as she slid into the booth across from him.

"You," he hissed. "What are you doing here? Haven't you caused me enough trouble?"

"I'm about to cause a whole lot more if you don't tell me what's going on."

"No way in hell!"

"Who's pulling your chain, Jasper? I can smell your fear."

"I'm not afraid of you. Not anymore."

"You're afraid of someone. Who is it?"

"I can't tell you."

"Did you like being a bird? How would you like being a worm instead?"

The warlock cringed at the threat.

"A worm on a hook," she said with an evil grin. "I haven't fished in years."

"The new Elder Knight sent me here."

"Why?" When he didn't answer, she unleashed a little more of her power.

"He's looking for a Hungarian vampire."

"Anyone in particular?"

"Quill's son," he confided with obvious reluctance.

"Why?"

"I don't know. He didn't tell me."

"What are you supposed to do if you find him?"

"Take him to the Elder Knight."

"Gregory." Her brow furrowed thoughtfully. Why would the Elder Knight be looking for a vampire? And not just any vampire, but her great-grandson?

Ava smiled a predatory smile. She hadn't been able to find the Brotherhood's new stronghold, but Jasper obviously knew where it was. Still, she couldn't force the location out of him, at least not here.

"I don't know what the Elder Knight has in mind," she said. "But as you're well aware, some of my family members are vampires. I am warning you, here and now, that you will not like what happens to you if you harm so much as a hair on their heads." She raised her hand when he started to speak. "I know you're afraid of Gregory, but his magic is no match for mine. If you're smart," she said, releasing him from her spell, "you will leave the States today and never come back."

Jasper stared at her for a long moment, his whole body still quivering uncontrollably from the residual force of her magic. Gathering as much dignity as he could muster, he stood and strode out of the bar, his head held high.

Jasper had every intention of following the witch's advice and getting the hell out of town just as fast as he could. He was planning his escape when he felt a rush of power, and the Elder Knight stood beside him. Jasper blinked at him in astonishment. He had never seen Gregory in anything but the robes of the Elder Knight. Now he wore an expensive, dark-brown suit, a pristine white shirt, and an intricately striped tie.

He looked even scarier than usual.

"Heading for the airport, were you?" the Knight asked, his voice filled with quiet menace.

"Y . . . yes. Of course. To bring you news."

The Elder Knight lifted a brow. "Indeed? Have your powers deserted you, along with your courage?"

Jasper swallowed hard. "I was coming to let you know that the witch, Ava, is here, and . . . and I didn't want her to know where I was going. I didn't think she'd be able to follow me if I left by plane."

"I see. And have you found the vampire?"

"Not yet, but her warning assured me that he's nearby." Jasper blurted out the words, his gaze darting from side to side as if he might find an unsuspected ally lurking nearby.

"And what do you intend to do now?"

Jasper forced the words through a throat as dry as the Sahara. "Find the vampire and bring him to you, as per your instructions."

"See that you do. Because there's no place on earth where you can hide if you fail me. And no one who can protect you."

Too frightened to speak, Jasper nodded.

A wave of his hand and the Elder Knight was gone as if he had never been there.

Jasper uttered every epithet he'd ever heard. Talk about being caught between a rock and a hard place, he thought bitterly, because he was in deep shit no matter what he did.

Chapter 8

Maddy spent Saturday morning cleaning house, not that there was a lot to do because she lived alone, but her mother had drilled it into her at an early age that Saturday mornings were for dusting and vacuuming and changing the sheets on the bed. And, like it or not, it was a hard habit to break.

She had just dumped the sheets into the washer when the doorbell rang. Blowing her bangs away from her forehead, she opened the door a crack and peered outside.

"Madison?"

"Yes."

"These are for you."

She opened the door wider as the deliveryman thrust a long gold box toward her. Flowers, she thought. Who would be sending her flowers? It wasn't her birthday. She thanked the man and locked the door—something she had been a lot more vigilant about since being attacked—and carried the box into the kitchen. Lifting the lid, she blinked in amazement when she found two dozen of the most beautiful long-stemmed red roses she had ever seen.

She plucked the envelope from the box and removed the card. It read, "*To Maddy. Just because. Dominic.*"

That sweet man, she thought as she searched for a suitable vase. That sweet, sweet man. No one had ever sent her flowers, let alone two dozen roses with petals that felt like velvet.

She found a crystal vase, filled it with water, and spent the next twenty minutes arranging the flowers. She placed the roses on the mantel in the living room, then picked up her phone, intending to text her thanks. And then she paused and punched his number, thinking she would rather hear his voice. Only he didn't answer.

Wondering where he was, she sent the text. Blew out a sigh. And went back to cleaning the house, thinking her mother would be proud of her.

Dominic woke with the setting of the sun. Sitting up, he checked his phone, and smiled when he saw Maddy's text. Thank you so much for the roses. They're beautiful. Hope to thank you soon in person.

Count on it, he thought as he called her.

She answered on the second ring. "Hi."

"Hi."

"I love the flowers. Thank you so much. No one's ever sent me roses before."

"I'll make it a habit."

"Are you coming over?"

"Of course. I have an in-person thank-you coming my way. What time's good for you?"

"Any time."

"Half an hour?"

"Perfect."

"See you then."

Maddy found herself grinning from ear to ear as she dropped her phone on her freshly made bed and hurried into the bathroom to shower.

Dominic arrived half an hour later, as promised. Dressed in a pair of black slacks and a long-sleeved, dark gray shirt over a white tee, he looked like he had just stepped out of the pages of a men's fashion magazine.

He whistled when he saw her. "Damn, girl, you look good enough to eat." She wore a pair of jeans and a sweater that outlined every delectable curve.

She flushed under his admiring gaze.

"What shall we do tonight?" he asked.

"The latest Bond flick is playing at that new drive-in theater." She frowned. "What are you laughing at?"

"My great-grandmother used to call them passion pits. But I'm game if you are."

"Dominic!"

"Hey, she said it, not me."

"I just want to see the movie," she said primly. "That's all. No passion or pits involved."

"Yes, ma'am. I'll keep both hands in my pockets and my eyes on the screen."

"Maybe not both hands," she said, stifling a grin. "Is it okay if we pick up something to eat on the way to the drive-in? I haven't had dinner."

They stopped at a fast-food place on the way to the theater. As they stepped in line to order, it occurred to Dominic that he'd eaten more mortal food in the last few days than he had in the last few months. Not that he was complaining; not when he had Maddy to keep him company.

She asked for a cheeseburger, fries, and a strawberry shake. He ordered a steak sandwich, rare, and a cup of coffee.

They found a table by a window.

"So, what kind of movies do you like?" she asked as they waited for their order.

"Pretty much anything, except for slasher flicks."

"What's the matter?" she teased. "Are you squeamish? Don't you like all that blood?"

He was tempted to ask if she was offering, but he doubted she would see the humor in it. "Do you?"

"Not really. I saw one *Halloween* movie and that pretty much put me off the genre for life. So, what do you like?"

"Comedies. Adventure. Superheroes. You know, the usual."

"Favorite comedy?"

"You can't beat *Galaxy Quest* or *Young Frankenstein* for laughs. Yours?"

"Mine's an old one, too. I really love *The Devil Wears Prada.* I watch it every time it's on cable. That and *The Holiday*. I watch that one a lot, too. Have you seen it?"

"Sure. Cameron Diaz," he said with a wink. "She's hot."

They fell silent for a moment when their dinner arrived.

Maddy grimaced when she saw his sandwich. "Are you sure that steak is cooked?"

"Just the way I like it."

"I thought you didn't like blood."

"Well, there are exceptions." When she looked away,

his gaze moved to her throat. Just one taste, he thought, to see if she was as sweet as he suspected.

It was the perfect night for a movie under the stars, Maddy thought as they pulled into the theater. The sky was clear, the air was warm. They arrived just as the trailers started.

Dominic found a parking place, killed the ignition, and rolled down the windows. "Do you want popcorn or anything?" he asked.

"Not right now. I'm still full. The new *Jurassic World* movie looks good. I can't wait to see it." She glanced at Dominic. "Chris Pratt," she said, feigning a swoon. "He's hot."

Dominic laughed. He liked her more every time he saw her. And more than any other woman he had ever known. He thought of what Ava had said about drive-ins and grinned. Had he known Maddy better, or longer, he might have suggested they crawl into the back seat and make out like horny teenagers. Because that wasn't an option, he reached for her hand and held it until the movie was over.

"Can I see you tomorrow night?" Dominic asked when they reached her front door.

"It's getting to be a habit," she said, her eyes twinkling.

Drawing her gently into his arms, he murmured, "One that I don't want to break."

"Me either."

"Seven o'clock good for you?"

"Six would be better."

"Anxious, huh?"

She laughed softly. "Should I play hard to get?"

"No." He pulled her closer, his gaze caressing her before he kissed her, long and slow, as if they had all the time in the world.

She was breathless when he lifted his head, her heart beating double time.

"Maybe five o'clock," he muttered as he released her. "I don't think I can wait until six. Good night, Maddy."

"'Night." She watched him descend the porch steps and slide behind the wheel of the Camaro. She smiled and waved when he blew her a kiss.

Lordy, but she had it bad, she thought as she went inside and closed the door. How was she going to wait until tomorrow night to see him again?

Chapter 9

Jasper ghosted through the streets of New Orleans and the surrounding towns, looking everywhere he could think for the Hungarian vampire the Elder Knight was seeking. He found a few Transylvanian bloodsuckers, but he had no interest in them, although he destroyed a couple of the younger, weaker ones.

And then his luck changed, and he found a Hungarian vampire bending over a young woman. Hoping it was the right one, he donned his invisibility cloak and sprang at the vampire. A moment later, the creature was his prisoner, his wrists bound by silver manacles, a noose coated with silver around his neck.

Jasper paused a moment, trying to decide who he was more afraid of—the Elder Knight or the witch. In the end, his fear of Gregory's retribution won.

Murmuring the words of his favorite transportation spell, Jasper transported himself and the vampire to the stronghold of the Knights of the Dark Wood.

* * *

"You idiot!" the Elder Knight exclaimed. "This is the wrong one."

"How was I to know? You gave me no description."

"You were supposed to question him, discover who he is and why he's in New Orleans. I would expect part of that interrogation to include his name."

"I . . . I'm sorry. In the heat of the moment, I forgot."

The Elder Knight glared at him, rage and frustration in his eyes as he stalked toward the prisoner. "What is your name?"

"Go to hell."

The Elder Knight struck him a vicious blow. It split the vampire's lip. "You will tell me what I wish to know."

"I don't think so."

"Is there another of your kind in New Orleans?"

"Not that I know of."

"You'd tell me if there was?"

"No."

The Elder Knight struck him again, and when that failed to elicit a response, he called a silver-bladed knife to his hand and raked the blade down the vampire's cheek. Blood sprayed from the wound and splashed across the Elder Knight's face.

Enraged, Gregory drove the blade through the vampire's heart.

The vampire gasped once and went limp.

"Cut off his head," the Elder Knight said. "Burn the body. Then return to New Orleans. And don't bother coming back until you have the vampire I want."

Chapter 10

Maddy rose bright and early Sunday morning. Besides being taught to clean her house on Saturday, her mother had taught her the importance of going to church on the Sabbath day. Maddy didn't make it every week, the way her mother did, but she tried. This morning, she felt she had a lot to be grateful for as she stepped into her heels, grabbed her keys, and left the house.

As it turned out, the first hymn was "Count Your Many Blessings" and the sermon was on gratitude. Sitting quietly in her favorite pew, Maddy listed her many blessings—she was healthy, she lived in a free country, she had food enough and money enough, and goodly parents. And she was certain the Good Lord had heard her desperate cry for help and sent Dominic to save her life.

As they sang the closing song, she murmured a quiet prayer of gratitude in her heart for all that she had, for parents who had taught her right from wrong by example, and for the power of love and forgiveness.

At home, she changed out of her Sunday best and into a pair of well-worn jeans and a baggy sweater, then went into the kitchen to see about lunch.

Later, she decided it was too nice a day to sit inside. She was about to go out and do a little weeding in the garden when she felt a sudden, unexplainable urge to go jogging in the park. Deciding that would burn up more calories than yard work, she pulled on her running shoes and headed for the park at the end of the block.

Ava sat on the same bench she had occupied before as she waited for Maddy. The girl was very susceptible to suggestion—not always a good thing, but handy just now. She knew Dominic would be angry if he learned she was seeing Maddy again, but Ava was curious to know how their relationship was progressing—although judging from the way Dominic had been behaving the last few days, he was obviously crazy about the girl. Did Maddy feel the same about him?

Ava felt a sense of anticipation as Maddy jogged into view. She really was a lovely girl. No doubt she would give Dominic handsome sons.

She waved as Maddy drew closer.

Maddy slowed to a walk when she saw Ava. "Hi."

"Hello, dear. I was hoping I'd see you again."

"Oh?"

"I so enjoyed chatting with you the other day. Do you have time to sit a spell?"

"I guess so."

"How are you and your young man getting along?" Ava asked as Maddy settled onto the bench.

"He's not 'my' young man."

"No? Don't tell me you didn't see him again?"

"Well, yes, I did."

"Did you have a good time?"

"Yes. It was wonderful. He's wonderful."

"I'm so glad. I knew he was the right one for you."

"Well, it's a little early to tell. We've only dated a couple of times."

"But you like him?"

"Oh, yes," Maddy said, smiling. "I'm seeing him again tonight."

Ava nodded. She was happy for Dominic, glad he had found a woman to love. At the same time, his interest in Maddy was keeping him from doing what they had come to New Orleans for in the first place. But no matter. The Knights of the Dark Wood weren't going anywhere. "What's your young man's name?"

"Dominic," Maddy said, and frowned when she realized she didn't even know his last name. But then, she had never given him hers either.

"A strong, masculine name," Ava said. "I predict the two of you will have a long and happy life together."

"How can you know that without reading my palm?" Maddy asked, even as she told herself again she didn't believe in fortune-telling or tarot or anything like it.

Oh, crap, Ava thought. *I forgot about that*. Smiling brightly, she said, "Just an old woman's intuition, dear."

"Well," Maddy said, "I don't know him well enough to know if I want to spend the rest of my life with him. But I like what I do know."

"That's enough for now," Ava said, patting her hand. "Have a wonderful day."

Gaining her feet, Maddy said, "You too."

Ava sighed with satisfaction as she watched the girl

jog down the path. Maddy was perfect for Dominic, and he was perfect for her.

Maddy was dressed and ready by four thirty. She spent the next half hour thinking about her conversation with Ava. She was an odd duck, with her predictions of the future for two people she didn't even know.

Her heart skipped a beat when the doorbell rang. It was Dominic, of course, looking as tall, dark, and handsome as always.

"Hey, gorgeous," he said, taking her into his arms. "How was your day?"

"Quiet." Taking his hand, she led him toward the sofa and pulled him down beside her. "I went to church and then I had this sudden urge to go jogging. You'll never guess who I met in the park."

Dominic groaned inwardly. He knew exactly who she'd met. "Who?"

"Ava. She's the old woman I told you about, remember?"

"The one who said you'd see me again."

"Right. Today she told me we'd have a long and happy life together. She's quite the romantic."

"You have no idea," he muttered.

"What?"

"Nothing." He kissed her lightly. "I hope she's right."

"Do you? We hardly know each other."

Slipping his arm around her shoulders, he said, "I know a way to remedy that."

"I'll bet you do," she said dryly.

He traced her lower lip with his fingertips. "We start

here," he said and kissed her, his mouth moving seductively over hers, his tongue slipping inside. His fingers delved into the silky hair at her nape as he deepened the kiss.

Warmth flooded her being as she leaned into him. She was melting from the inside out, she thought, as she slid her hand up his arm. Her fingers curled around his biceps. The muscle bunched and flexed at her touch, sending a shiver of delight coursing through her.

He pulled her down until they were lying side by side on the sofa. For a moment, she lost herself in the warmth of his arms, the magic of his kisses, but as his kisses grew deeper and more intense, alarm bells went off in Maddy's mind. Gasping for breath, she pushed against his chest.

He sat up immediately. "Sorry. Guess I got a little carried away."

"A little?" She blew out a sigh.

"Guess I wanted to get to know all of you at once," he said with an apologetic smile. "Maybe we should go for a walk and cool off."

"Good idea."

Maddy grabbed a sweater and her keys. They definitely had to slow down, she thought, because his kisses were hotter than dynamite.

She locked the door and they walked hand in hand down the front steps toward the sidewalk.

Sunday evening and the streets were quiet. They passed a few people sitting on their porches, and a couple of boys playing catch in the street.

Maddy looked up at Dominic. "Do you believe in fortune-telling?"

He shrugged. "Depends on who's doing it."

"Really? Have you ever had anyone read your palm?"

"I'm going to tell you a secret. One you might not believe."

"What?"

"My mother's a witch."

"Dominic, be serious."

"I am. It runs in the family."

Maddy stared at him, wide-eyed. "Are you telling me that *you're* a witch?"

"No. It only applies to the women in my family." Seeing the skepticism in her eyes, he said, "You don't believe me, do you?"

"No. But tell me about your family. Is it big?"

"Not really. Just my grandparents, my mom and dad, me and my twin sister. And my great-grandmother."

"Is your sister a witch, too?"

"Yes. So are my mother and my great-grandma."

"Do they live here, in Louisiana?"

"Just my great-grandmother. The others are in Savaria."

"Oh. Guess I won't get to meet them."

"You've already met my great-grandmother."

"Really?" Maddy shook her head. "I'm sure I would have remembered that."

"I'm serious. Her name is Ava."

"What?" Maddy came to an abrupt halt.

"I just thought you should know. She has a tendency to poke her nose in places where it doesn't belong. Like my love life."

"I don't believe this."

"Well, it's true." He gave her hand a squeeze. "She likes you."

Brow furrowed, Maddy started walking again. "Do you believe all that stuff she told me? About us?"

"She's usually right."

"What if I don't want to marry you?"

"Well," Dominic said, laughing. "When I ask you, just say no."

"This isn't the least bit funny."

"Hey," he said, taking her in his arms. "Calm down, sweetheart. Fortunes aren't cast in stone. Nothing's changed. I just didn't think it was fair for her to be talking to you when you didn't even know who she was. She thinks she had a hand in bringing my parents together, and now she's decided to try her luck with me."

They walked in silence for a moment.

Brow furrowed, Maddy asked, "Does Ava cast spells and things?"

"Yeah, from time to time."

"How do I know she won't cast some kind of magic spell on me that will make me love you?"

Dominic grinned inwardly. He didn't need Ava's brand of magic for that, not when he had his own. But he wasn't ready to share that with Maddy yet. If ever.

"I can assure you that she won't. If I can't win you on my own . . ." He shrugged.

"Have you ever seen her do magic?"

"Sure. When my sister and I were young, Ava was always casting spells. Innocent things, like turning water into hot chocolate or making our toys float through the air. By the time my sister was ten or eleven, she could do those things, too."

"Did you feel left out?"

"Yeah, in a way, especially when they tried their magic on me. One day, my sister turned my hair pink on our way to school. I didn't find out about it until we got there and the other kids started teasing me."

Maddy laughed. "I have a sister, but I always wanted an older brother, someone who would protect me from the bullies at school."

"Lily and I had some good times," he said, smiling.

"You must miss her."

"Yeah, but if you ever meet Lily, don't tell her I said so."

"No worries."

"So, do you and your sister get along?"

"Yeah. Fran is three years older than I am. Married with a little girl, Melanie, who's two. They live in New Jersey."

"Why don't you come home with me?" Dominic suggested. "I'll introduce you to Ava. I have to warn you, though, she might look different than you remember."

Maddy didn't know what to expect as they pulled up in front of a lovely, two-story home on a quiet street just outside the city. A number of wind chimes made gentle music as they walked up the long, flower-lined path to the double front door.

Maddy frowned, thinking there were flowers growing along the walkway she had never seen in Louisiana before, beautiful blooms that filled the air with an exotic fragrance.

Dominic called, "Ava, we have a guest," as he opened the door.

His great-grandmother—in her younger guise—glanced up from the sofa, eyes wide with surprise. She glanced at Maddy, who was staring at her in open-mouthed astonishment.

Ava huffed a sigh. "Hello, dear."

Dominic slid his arm around Maddy's waist. "It's just a bit of witch magic," he explained. "She doesn't like looking her age, which, by the way, no one knows."

Maddy knew it was rude to stare, but she couldn't help it. How could this possibly be the same woman she had met in the park? She tried to reconcile the Ava she'd met the other day with the one she saw now as Dominic led her to the flowered love seat across from the sofa and tugged her down beside him.

"Well, what a nice surprise," Ava said, glancing at Dominic. "I guess Dom has told you about our family."

"I thought she ought to know who you really are."

"Did you?" There was a hint of accusation in Ava's tone. "What else did you tell her?"

"Nothing. It just didn't seem fair for you to know who she is when Maddy didn't know who you were."

"I suppose," Ava agreed somewhat grudgingly. "Can I get you anything, Maddy, dear? A cup of tea? Smelling salts? You look a bit faint."

"I . . . I'd love a cup of tea. Thank you," Maddy stammered, even as she wondered if it was safe for her to drink something brewed by a witch.

A smile danced over Ava's lips as an engraved silver tray laden with a flowered teapot, matching sugar bowl, cream pitcher, and three cups appeared on the coffee table between them.

"Oh my," Maddy exclaimed. "You really *are* a witch."

"Runs in the family for generations," Ava said as she filled the cups. "Do you take cream or sugar?"

"Just sugar, please."

Ava added a generous helping and handed the cup to Maddy, who took it with a hand that trembled.

"So, now that the cat's out of the bag, do you have any questions?" Ava asked.

Stalling for time, Maddy sipped her tea. Questions? She had about a million.

Ava filled a cup for Dominic and one for herself, then sat back.

In the silence, Dominic met Ava's gaze. *I didn't tell her about my father or why we're in New Orleans. And I don't want you mentioning it either.*

I can't believe you told her about me. You could have at least warned me.

It was unfair for you to know who she is without telling her the truth about yourself.

I didn't think she'd believe me.

Well, she does now.

Finding her voice, Maddy said, "What kind of witch are you?"

"Do you mean am I more like Glinda the Good Witch or the Wicked Witch of the West?"

"Something like that. The only thing I know about witches is what I've read. For instance, all the books say there are white witches and black witches." Maddy shrugged. "I guess that's like Glinda and the Wicked Witch."

"That pretty much sums it up," Ava said. "Of course, there are shades of gray in between."

"So, are witches born that way?"

"The powerful ones are. There are mortals who claim

to be witches, and some have a small degree of magic. But I believe true witches are born. The gift is passed from woman to woman. In my family, it usually skipped a generation. The fact that my granddaughter and great-granddaughter both have it is some sort of anomaly, I guess."

Interesting, Maddy thought. She had known there were men and women who claimed to be witches or warlocks, but she had never believed there was real magic, like what she had seen tonight. She wondered what else Ava could do. Did she cast spells on people? Make love potions? Heal broken hearts? Find lost objects? Was she like the Sorcerer's Apprentice, capable of bringing inanimate objects to life? Did she have a broom? Did it sweep the floor for her?

Feeling suddenly overwhelmed, Maddy put her teacup aside and tugged on Dominic's hand. "I think we've taken up enough of Ava's time."

He winked at her, then put his cup on the coffee table. "I guess we'll be going." Rising, he took Maddy's hand and lifted her to her feet. "Thanks for the tea, Grams."

Ava also stood. "You're welcome. Maddy, dear, now that you know where we live, feel free to drop by anytime."

"Thank you."

"I'll see you later," Dominic said, kissing Ava on the cheek. "Don't wait up."

She nodded, understanding in her eyes.

Maddy's head was spinning when Dominic walked her to her door.

"Are you gonna be all right?" he asked.

"I guess so. It was just a bit of a surprise. After all, I've never met a real witch before."

"Not many people have." Some lived to regret it, he thought, which was why he was in New Orleans in the first place. "See you tomorrow?"

"Until then."

"Until then." Taking her in his arms, he kissed her tenderly, hoping he hadn't made a mistake in telling her about Ava.

And wondering what her reaction would be if she ever learned the truth about him.

Chapter 11

After leaving Maddy's house, Dominic drove his car home, parked it in the driveway. and then set out in search of prey. But instead of finding a meal, he found a body lying in the alley behind a small strip mall, fresh blood oozing around the stake in its heart.

He swore a vile oath as he knelt beside the body. He didn't know the man, but it was one of his kind. And he had been destroyed by one of the Knights of the Dark Wood. The scent of the hunter was unmistakable. His mother had taught him how to identify the Brotherhood by the faint signature of dark magic that clung to the medallions they wore—medallions Ava had conjured for them centuries ago. He'd thought them all destroyed years ago.

Heaving the body onto his shoulder, Dominic transported himself home.

Ava was waiting at the door. "Is he . . . ?"

"Yes."

"Take him into the back room. Let's see if he's carrying any ID."

Ava spread a sheet on the quilt that covered the bed

and Dominic laid the body on it. He stood back while Ava conjured the wallet from the dead man's pocket and checked the contents. A Louisiana driver's license identified him as Roger St. James, thirty-six years old. A business card in the same name listed a phone number.

"You need to notify the family," she said quietly.

"Why me?"

"It's what your father would do if he were here. Now it's up to you."

Muttering under his breath, Dominic plucked the driver's license from her hand and left the house.

Roger St. James had resided in a small, two-story house on a quiet street. Toys in the yard suggested he'd been the father of a couple of kids. Dammit. Dominic had no idea what to say to the widow.

As it turned out, no words were necessary. A tall woman with strawberry-blond hair and brown eyes opened the door. She took one look at his face and dissolved into tears.

Dominic followed her inside and closed the door behind him. The inside of the house was clean and neat. A baby snuggled in a blanket slept on the sofa. A little boy, perhaps four years old, sat on the floor playing with a fire truck.

"He's dead, isn't he?" Mrs. St. James asked through her tears.

"I'm afraid so. I'm sorry."

"How?"

"One of the Knights."

She sniffed loudly. "Where is he? Where's Roger?"

"I took him to my place."

"Who are you?"

"Dominic. Andras Falconer is my grandfather."

Her eyes widened. His grandfather was the next best thing to royalty among the Hungarian vampires.

"Do you need help with anything?" Dominic asked.

She sank down on the sofa, her hand resting lightly on the baby's back. "I don't even know where to start."

"Our people will take care of you. I'll reach out to my grandfather. He'll make the necessary arrangements. Do you have any other family in the city?"

"No. There's just us."

"My grandfather will be in touch with you."

"Can I see my husband?"

"Of course." Dominic gave her his address. "Why don't you come by tomorrow morning?"

She nodded. "Thank you for letting me know."

"I'm sorry for your loss, Mrs. St. James."

She nodded again.

Like all mortals married to vampires, Dominic thought as he left the house, she had known the risks and been willing to take them, but there was no way to actually be prepared when it happened.

Dominic fed quickly on the first mortal female he saw before returning home. He told Ava to expect a visit from the grieving widow in the morning while he was at rest. And then he retired to his lair in the basement. There was nothing more he could do for Mrs. St. James. His father and grandfather would take care of arranging for the funeral and would make sure the widow had the necessary funds to support her family.

His only responsibility was to find the Knight who had killed one of their own.

The smell of freshly spilled blood led Claret to a dark alley. There was no sign of a body, only a telltale stain on the ground. Dominic's scent was also there, along with another scent she didn't recognize. She frowned into the darkness. It was unlikely Dominic had killed one of his own. Had a new hunter come to town? Was that the scent she didn't recognize? She followed it until it suddenly disappeared.

How was that possible? She drew in a deep breath, and then she knew. Mingled with the hunter's scent was the faint signature of witchcraft.

She backtracked to the alley, hoping to follow the blood scent. But after a foot or so it, too, disappeared. So, who had taken the body? Dominic? Or the hunter? And where had they gone?

Dominic. Just thinking about him filled her with the desire to taste him again. To lock him up as she had done his father, to be able to drink his blood and his power whenever she wished. She didn't really care about dead vampires—Transylvanian or Hungarian. She didn't care about hunters. But Quill's son? He dominated her every waking moment.

She wanted him.

And one way or another, she intended to have him.

Chapter 12

Maddy dreamed about witches. Dark witches who rode on the wings of the night sowing evil. In one instance, she was Dorothy fleeing the Wicked Witch of the West. In another, she was Snow White hiding from the Evil Queen, and in still another sequence, she was herself, running from an unseen terror that snapped at her heels. And always, lurking in the shadows, dressed all in black, was Dominic, appearing in the nick of time to save her from certain destruction.

She woke in a cold sweat, relieved to find it was morning and she was safe in her own bed. "If I had to dream about witches, why couldn't they have been good ones?" she muttered as she tossed the blankets aside and headed for the bathroom.

She felt 100 percent better after a shower and a cup of coffee. Scrambled eggs and toast served as breakfast. With nothing better to do, she grabbed a book and sauntered outside to sit by the pool and soak up some sun.

But, instead of reading, she thought about her future. Sooner or later, she needed to find a job. And eventually a new apartment to replace the one she had given up to stay here. She had to admit, her parents' home was a lot nicer than her old apartment. The house had everything anyone could possibly imagine. It wasn't going to be easy, living in a one-bedroom apartment again, having to take her clothes to the laundromat, without a pool, probably without a dishwasher, and no Jacuzzi jets in the bathtub.

She shook off her dreary thoughts. Her folks wouldn't be home for months. Until then, she was in the lap of luxury—no bills to pay, no worries about rent.

Maddy closed her eyes and Dominic immediately sprang to mind. She had never known anyone like him. Or his great-grandmother, the witch. Maybe Ava could give her an amulet to turn away nightmares. Or concoct a love potion to make Dominic fall in love with her . . .

What was she thinking? Annoyed by the turn of her thoughts, she picked up her book and tried to concentrate on the story. But it was no use.

Closing the book, she padded into the kitchen, grabbed a soda from the fridge, and booted up her computer. In the search bar, she typed "what is a witch" and got over six million hits.

According to Wikipedia, witchcraft was the practice of magical skills, abilities, and spells. According to *The Atlantic* magazine, witchcraft was on the rise due to increasing instability in the country and a growing mistrust of the government. There were links to articles on the occult and how to become a witch, and on Wicca and paganism, as well as numerous sites explaining what a witch was and how to spot one. Some of it was interesting. Some amusing. And some just utterly ridiculous.

She soon became bored with the search and clicked on

a random site called Supernatural Creatures and How to Find Them.

Maddy perused the "Table of Contents" and saw chapters devoted to "Fairies—Good and Evil," "Ghosts and Spirits," "Imps," "Ogres," "Trolls," "Werewolves," "Witches and Warlocks," "Vampires," and "Zombies."

Remembering her nightmare, she signed off. She didn't really need to fill her mind with more scary creatures, that was for sure.

Forcing everything else from her thoughts, Maddy went back outside and picked up her novel. After forcing herself to concentrate, she soon lost herself in the story.

Dominic rose with the setting sun, his first thought for Maddy. He told himself he had no business seeing her when he was supposed to be hunting for the Knights' new stronghold, but if Ava couldn't find them, what chance did he have? Besides, Maddy was much more interesting. And if Ava was to be believed, somewhere down the road Maddy might be his wife—a thoroughly pleasant prospect.

He showered and dressed, told Ava not to wait up, and left the house whistling. He couldn't remember ever being this eager to see any of the other women he had dated. And likely never would be again. He had never believed in love at first sight, or that certain men and women were destined to find each other. Until he met Maddy, Dominic had scoffed at that idea. But no more.

* * *

Claret prowled the city streets, her senses searching, always searching, for Quill's son. It frustrated her that she couldn't find him. She had taken his blood. She should have been able to locate him with no trouble at all.

And then she frowned. His mother was a witch. Had Callie Falconer woven some kind of protective spell around Dominic, one that hid his presence from her kind? It was a distinct possibility. Witches! Good or bad, she despised them all.

Scowling, Claret stormed through the night. She almost pitied the young man who crossed her path. In no mood to be gentle, she backed him against a wall, buried her fangs in his throat, and drank and drank, inwardly cursing all the while because his blood didn't give her the same sense of power and invincibility as Dominic's. But she would find him, she vowed. One day, she would find him again.

Maddy smiled as she opened the door. "Hi!"

"Hi yourself. Damn, you look beautiful tonight."

"Thank you. So do you."

"Hey, men aren't beautiful."

"You are." She pulled him inside and closed the door, then stepped into his arms, her face lifted for his kiss.

His mouth was firm and warm, his tongue like a flame of fire as it dueled with hers. It did funny things in the pit of her belly, made her think of cold nights beneath satin sheets, of sweat-sheened bodies intimately entwined. . . .

Maddy was breathless when Dominic lifted his head.

She felt herself flush when she looked at him, embarrassed by her thoughts and oh so glad he couldn't read her mind.

His voice was whiskey-rough when he asked, "What do you want to do tonight?"

She swallowed the words, *take you to bed,* and shrugged instead. "Anything you want to do is fine with me."

"Anything?" His gaze moved over her, his eyes dark with desire.

Heat climbed up the back of her neck. *Lordy, maybe he* could *read her mind*. Clearing her throat, she said, "Well, almost anything."

"I guess that rules out curling up on the sofa and making out like horny teenagers?"

Trying for a light tone, she said, "Well, at least until I know more about you."

"How about if we go out for drinks and dancing instead?"

"That sounds better." *Not really*, she thought with some regret.

But a whole lot safer.

Dominic took her to a nightclub where the lights were low and the music was soft and slow. Line dancing was fun, but he wanted Maddy in his arms, not dancing beside him.

She ordered a strawberry daiquiri; he ordered a glass of Cabernet Sauvignon.

"How are you, Maddy?"

"I'm okay, why?"

"I'm thinking I never should have told you about the women in my family."

She shrugged, as if it was a matter of no importance. "It was a bit of a shock, that's all. How old is your great-grandmother, really?"

"I'm not sure. Well over a hundred."

Maddy stared at him, eyes wide. "How long do witches live?"

"A couple hundred years, usually."

She sent a look of gratitude toward the waiter who arrived with her drink just then. Picking it up, she downed half.

"Hey, better slow down, girl. I don't want to have to carry you home." Although that might not be such a bad idea.

"Whew!" Maddy fanned herself with her hand as the drink hit her stomach. "I think you're right." She took a deep breath. "So, if witches are real, do you think other supernatural creatures are, too?"

Uh-oh. He might have opened a Pandora's box. "Like what?"

"I don't know. Zombies? They're popular on TV and in the movies right now. Ghosts? Werewolves?"

"I've never seen any."

"Me, neither. Of course, witches are really just people with supernatural powers. It's not like they change into monsters." With a shake of her head, she said, "Let's talk about something else."

"Let's dance."

"Good idea."

She fit into his arms as if she had been made to order, Dominic thought. Her warm, womanly fragrance enflamed him, the tantalizing scent of her blood teased his senses even as it awakened his hunger. He spoke to her mind and then bit her lightly, just enough to break the skin, just enough for a single taste. It sizzled through him, more potent than 100 proof whiskey, more desirable than anything he had ever tasted. Though sorely tempted to take more, he sealed the tiny puncture, then lifted his head and quickly wiped the memory from her mind.

When she smiled up at him, he knew he was lost.

It was after midnight when Dominic took her home. He kissed her deeply before saying good night, acutely aware of her gaze on his back as he walked to his car.

He was in more danger than he had ever been in his life, Dominic mused as he turned to wave at Maddy.

And so was she.

Maddy felt giddy as a schoolgirl as she closed the door and floated up the stairs to her room. She hadn't lived at home for five or six years, but her mother hadn't changed anything. Posters of her favorite rock stars still hung on the wall over her double bed. A stuffed teddy bear her father had given her for her fifth birthday sat on her pillow. Her high school yearbooks remained on the bookshelf, along with novels and textbooks she had left behind, and a couple of old Barbie dolls.

Maddy kicked off her shoes and fell back on the mattress. Like it or not, she was falling head over heels for Dominic, and she wasn't sure how she felt about that. What if things got really serious? Did she want to marry into a family of witches? What would her sister think? What would her parents think? But the real question was, what did *she* think? And the answer was—it might be fun to have a sister-in-law who was a witch.

And then she frowned. Maybe not so much fun to have a mother-in-law who was a witch, though.

It was her last thought before sleep carried her away.

Dominic released the woman in his arms from his thrall and sent her on her way, thinking as he did so that drinking from her was not nearly as satisfying as the small sip he'd had of Maddy's blood. Maddy. Since the night he'd met her, she had been constantly in his thoughts.

He was near home when Claret suddenly appeared beside him.

"I knew I'd run into you again sooner or later," she purred as she linked her arm with his.

"Is that right?"

"You've been avoiding me," she accused.

"I haven't been thinking of you at all."

She glared at him. "That's not a very nice thing to say."

"Maybe I'm not very nice." Dominic tensed when her hungry gaze moved to his throat. It wasn't his company she wanted, but his blood. His preternatural senses kicked into overdrive as four vampires and a lone human suddenly surrounded him.

With lightning speed, they rushed him, driving him to the ground, while the human grabbed his arm and locked a silver manacle in place, thwarting Dominic's ability to transport himself to safety. Kneeling beside Dominic, the man locked the other shackle around his own wrist.

Claret dropped to her knees beside him, her eyes blood red as she sank her fangs into his throat.

Dominic clenched his jaw as she drank. He had expected her to take a few sips and let him go. But she continued to drink. He struggled as he felt his strength leaving him, and still she drank. And drank.

At last, she lifted her head and licked his blood from her lips.

"Our turn now," one of the vampires said, his eyes hot as he moved closer.

"He's mine!" she snapped. "And I'm not sharing." Her gaze settled on each one as they began to murmur among themselves. "Do any of you have a problem with that?"

"Damn right!" another hissed. "Who do you think . . . ?"

With the speed of a striking snake, she plunged her hand into his chest and ripped out his heart before he finished his sentence. "Anyone else have a problem?"

Shaking their heads, the other three backed away and vanished into the darkness.

Gathering what little strength he had left, Dominic sent Ava an urgent cry for help.

"Get him on his feet," Claret said to the human male. "I'm taking him home."

"You aren't taking him anywhere."

Claret whirled around as Ava appeared behind her. "Who the hell are you?"

Ava smiled. "I believe the usual answer is, your worst nightmare."

Claret snorted. "Somehow, I doubt that."

When the vampire reached for her, Ava began to chant. Only a few words, but it stopped the vampire in her tracks and held her frozen in place.

"Witch!" Claret hissed.

"Indeed." A wave of Ava's hand and the manacles that shackled Dominic to the other man turned to dust.

The man glanced from woman to woman and took off running down the street.

"Do not mess with me or my kin again," Ava warned as she helped Dominic to his feet. "You won't like the consequences."

At home, Ava offered Dominic one of the bags of blood she kept on hand for just such an emergency. He grimaced as he took it. Old blood. It was disgusting, but it was better than nothing, and he drank it all. "Thanks."

"You're getting careless," she scolded as he sank down on the sofa. "What were you thinking, roaming around the city with your guard down?" Seeing the sheepish expression on his face, she muttered, "Don't answer. I think I know."

"I can't think of anything else," he admitted.

"She's going to get you killed if you keep wandering around with your head in the clouds."

"I know." He rubbed his fingers over the bite marks on his neck, which hadn't healed. The last time Claret had bitten him, it had been pleasurable. But not this time. It had hurt like hell, and it still did.

"I think we should leave New Orleans," Ava said.

"Leave? We haven't found the Knight who destroyed St. James."

She lifted one brow. "I wonder why."

"Okay, so I've been a little distracted."

"A little?" she scoffed.

"All right, a lot. Can you blame me?"

"I guess not." Going to the desk in the corner, Ava

picked up a small white envelope and handed it to him. "Mrs. St. James sent you a note of thanks for your help."

"I didn't do anything. Andras and my father took care of all the details." Dominic opened the envelope and quickly read the note. "It says they took the body home to Georgia for the funeral, which is tomorrow. Dammit! That's too many of our people the Knights have killed here. Can't you figure out a spell that will lead me to the Knight or Knights responsible?"

Ava sat at the other end of the sofa. "It won't be easy. Jasper's soul may be as black as ten feet down, but he's a powerful warlock, although he tends to be a coward at heart." She tapped her fingers on the arm of the couch, her brow furrowed in concentration as she summoned her grimoire to her hand. "Go get some rest, Dom. I have work to do."

Chapter 13

The Knights of the Dark Wood assembled beneath a full moon, each trying not to show his unease. But it was the Knight from New Orleans who had the most to fear. He was the reason they had been called home. He knelt in the center of the circle, his head bowed.

A sense of dread fell over the Brotherhood as the Elder Knight strode into the center of the circle. "Leon 48, like my servant Jasper, you were charged to go to New Orleans in search of Hungarian vampires. You were not to destroy any that you found, but to bring them here, to me. You failed in your duty. Have you anything to say before I pronounce sentence?"

"No, my lord."

"The penalty for disobedience is death, to be carried out immediately."

A shudder ran through Leon 48 as the Elder Knight drew a sword from within the folds of his robe.

A gasp ran through the other Knights as the sword fell across Leon's neck, neatly separating his head from his body.

"Justice has been done. Philip 51, you are now assigned

to New Orleans. I will interview one of our Knights in training to replace Leon 48. Philip, I wish to speak to you privately. The rest of you are dismissed to return to your assignments."

Two of the Knights carried the remains away. There would be no formal funeral for Leon 48. He had died in disgrace and would be buried without ceremony in an unmarked grave.

The Elder Knight waited until he and Philip 51 were alone before asking, "Do you understand your charge?"

"Yes, my lord. I am to locate any Hungarian vampires in New Orleans and bring them to you. And to destroy any Transylvanian vampires I may find."

"Correct."

"My lord?"

"Yes?"

"How do you know the vampire who was killed was not the one you seek?"

"I know."

"Might I be so bold as to ask which vampire you seek? It might be helpful if I knew his name."

"Of course." The Elder Knight's eyes narrowed ominously for a moment. "More than twenty years ago, the Brotherhood stood on the brink of extinction because of one family of vampires."

"Falconer."

The Elder Knight's eyes widened in surprise. "You know of them?"

"I have studied our history."

"Falconer did not work alone. He was aided by a witch, a very powerful witch."

Philip nodded. "Ava."

"You have studied well indeed. It is the witch I want. But she is more powerful than any member of the Brotherhood. The only way to find her is to capture Quill Falconer's son, Dominic. I have reason to believe he is now in New Orleans. Once I have Quill's son in my power, the witch will come to me. Now go. Jasper is also in New Orleans, should you need help." The Elder Knight's gaze trapped Philip's in a merciless stare. "Do not fail me."

Philip 51 glanced at the ground where the blood of his comrade was drying. "I will not fail you, my lord. I swear it."

Chapter 14

Maddy sighed as Dominic took her in his arms. They had been together every night for the last three weeks. She loved being with him, whether they were holding hands at the movies, getting to know each other better over dinner, strolling through the park, or dancing the night away. And with each passing day, her affection for him grew stronger, deeper. Inevitably, they ended up in each other's arms on her sofa at the end of every date.

Not that she was complaining. Far from it, she thought as he claimed her lips in a long, slow kiss that left her wanting so much more. There was no place she would rather be than in Dominic's arms. She loved everything about him—the way he looked at her, as if she were the most wonderful woman in the world, the sound of his voice, the joy of his laughter, the way he cared for his great-grandmother.

She sighed as the clock above the mantel struck midnight. He left every night about this time.

"Something wrong?" he asked.

"No. I just hate to see the evening end."

"Me too."

"Sometimes I think you're Mr. Cinderella."

"What?"

"You always leave at midnight. Will you turn into a pumpkin if you stay longer?"

"I don't think so," he said, chuckling.

"Stay a little longer."

Dominic settled back on the sofa. He always left at midnight because it was the perfect time to hunt. But if Maddy wanted him to stay, he was more than happy to oblige her. He didn't have to feed every night, and when he did, he never took much. But he was a vampire. And he craved the taste. His gaze moved to the sweet curve of Maddy's throat. He'd been wanting another taste ever since the first one.

"I've been wondering," Maddy said. "What do you do for a living? You've never said."

"I'm a partner in my grandfather's business back in Hungary."

"Oh? What does he do?"

"He runs a large family organization that provides health care." *Another lie*, he thought. And yet, in a way, it was true. Andras cared for the needs of his people—not so much their material needs, but protecting them from hunters and making sure the mortal families of any who were killed by hunters were taken care of. Like St. James's widow and child, who would never want for anything as long as they lived.

"Sounds important."

"Lives depend on it."

"How long will you be here, in New Orleans?"

His gaze caressed her. "I may never leave," he murmured, and kissed her again, kissed her until she was mindless, breathless. Unable to resist any longer, he spoke to her mind, and then he bit her ever so gently. Only a sip of her life's blood—warm, sweet, like nectar on his tongue.

Wishing he dared take more, he sealed the tiny wounds in her throat and kissed her again.

"Things seem to be getting serious between you and Maddy," Ava remarked when he returned home that night.

"You could say that."

"You're supposed to be looking for Knights," she reminded him.

"I know. And you're supposed to be concocting a spell to help me find them."

"Perhaps it would be faster if I removed the protective spell that shields your presence and let them find you."

"Is that your way of saying you can't locate the Knights?"

"Not at all. But if we let them find you, you can decide when and where to be found."

Dominic grunted softly. "Maybe you're right."

"Let's think about it for a day or two. It'll take me that long to perfect the spell I'm working on, and then we can decide which way is best."

"I'm in love with Maddy."

"Tell me something I don't know."

"It complicates things, doesn't it?"

"It does, indeed."

"What should I do?"

"That's up to you, Dom."

"I can't let her go."

Ava leaned forward and laid her hand on his arm, her

bright blue eyes filled with understanding. "Then I guess that's your answer."

Philip 51 arrived in New Orleans at three a.m. His task weighed heavily on his mind. Not surprising, he supposed, because he had seen what happened to those who failed. He had never really wanted to be a Knight—he had joined the Brotherhood on a dare. It had seemed exciting in the beginning, learning how to track vampires, having a mystical invisibility cloak, a shiny medallion that told him when vampires were near, carrying weapons. The whole sworn-to-secrecy thing reminded him of a club he had joined as a child. But there was nothing childish about these guys. They played rough and they played for keeps. Until tonight, he had managed to stay under the Elder Knight's radar.

But he was in the thick of it now, tasked with finding a vampire from a powerful family. Destroying the vamp didn't worry him. But taking him alive? That was something else entirely. The Brotherhood kept detailed records of their history and he had studied them all. Quill Falconer and his witch-wife had been a formidable combination. They had already killed an Elder Knight and brought the Brotherhood to its knees.

Philip swallowed hard as he ran his fingers around the inside of his shirt collar.

His own neck was on the line now.

Claret glanced at the half-dozen vampires seated at the large booth in the back of her favorite vampire nightclub, the Crimson Rose. The place was shielded from mortal eyes by a bit of vampire magic.

All the vampires in the city resided here on her say-so. All had sworn their allegiance to the Queen of New Orleans.

"I'm looking for a Hungarian vampire," she said. "His name is Dominic. And I want him alive."

Chapter 15

Covered by his invisibility cloak, Philip 51 made his way along the crowded sidewalks of New Orleans. Up and down, dodging between tourists and citizens alike, one hand resting lightly on the medallion that would alert him to the presence of any vampire in the city, and hopefully to the one he was seeking.

He was about to call it a night when the medallion began to hum.

Philip turned and saw his quarry. A tall, dark-haired Hungarian vampire walking beside a woman. He drew closer as they turned the corner at the end of the block. The sidewalk ahead was deserted.

Philip cursed softly. It was forbidden to attack in the presence of humans, but if the vampire suddenly willed himself elsewhere, he might never find him again. He checked his pockets, his fingers brushing a noose coated with silver and a pair of silver manacles, both of which would drain the vampire's powers until Philip could render him unconscious and call for help, if needed.

He had not yet decided what to do when the vampire came to an abrupt halt and whirled around.

Overcome by a sudden, irrational panic, Philip yanked a stake from his pocket, lunged forward, and drove it into the vampire's chest, then bolted down the street.

Maddy let out a shriek as Dominic suddenly dropped to his knees, his fingers folding around the stake protruding from the center of his chest. Eyes wide, she glanced around, then fell to her knees beside him, only to watch in horror as he jerked the stake free and tossed it aside.

Dark red blood leaked from the hideous wound and stained his shirtfront.

She swallowed the bile rising in her throat. "Dominic . . ."

"I'll be all right. It's not as bad as it looks."

"You need a doctor."

He shook his head. "No." He stood and offered her his hand. "Let's go."

Maddy hesitated a moment before taking it. Trying to make sense of what she had just seen, she walked beside him to where they had left his car. "I think I'd better drive."

He started to protest, then thought better of it. How could he tell her that he didn't need a doctor, that his wounds would heal on their own?

Maddy waited until he was seated before going around to the driver's side and sliding behind the wheel. She drove slowly, her mind replaying what had just happened. They had been on their way to the parking lot when suddenly, out of nowhere, a wooden stake had appeared in Dominic's chest. Then, as if it was nothing at all, he had pulled it out and tossed it aside. Had she imagined the whole thing? But no, the proof was in the blood drying on his shirtfront.

Dominic checked behind them constantly, all his senses alert, but he detected no one following them.

"If you won't go to the hospital, at least let me drive you home," she said, casting a worried glance in his direction.

"Head for your place. It's closer than mine." He would need to get away from her before she noticed his wounds healing. He feared if he let her take him to the hospital, she would insist on staying with him. "I can make it home from there."

"Stubborn man," she muttered under her breath. "If you won't go to a doctor, at least let me wash and bandage the wound before you leave."

"Maddy . . ."

She didn't answer. After pulling into the driveway, she insisted on helping him out of the car. She put her arm around his waist as they walked toward the door. Inside, she tugged him toward the bathroom, where she filled the sink with hot water.

Dominic swore softly. Should he wipe the memory of what had happened that night from her mind? Or just tell her the truth?

She was unbuttoning his shirt, pushing it down over his shoulders, when her face paled and she swayed on her feet.

He grasped her shoulders to steady her.

"How . . ." She looked up at him in confusion. "There's no wound. How is that possible? And where did the stake come from? I didn't see anyone."

Shit!

He guided her toward the toilet, lowered the lid, and urged her to sit and put her head down. "I can explain."

Maddy took several slow, deep breaths. Maybe she was imagining things, refusing to see what was right before her eyes because it was so ghastly. But when she looked up again, there was no sign of injury save for a little blood. How was that possible?

Dominic knelt before her and took her hands in his. "I don't know how to tell you this except to just say it. I'm a vampire."

She blinked at him, her expression blank.

"It's true."

She glanced at his chest again, pulled one hand free and touched him with her fingertips. "I don't believe you," she said. But what other explanation was there? She had never believed in vampires, but she had seen countless movies about Dracula and the undead. She knew about wooden stakes and garlic and silver and mirrors. But she'd never heard of a stake materializing out of thin air. Clutching at straws, she said, "This is just some kind of morbid joke, right?"

"I'm afraid not."

"I don't know what to say." How could it be true? She had spent time with him, kissed him, laughed with him, and never suspected. But why would she? Sure, some of the people in the city believed in all that stuff—vampires and zombies, witches and curses and magic . . . Oh, Lord, his great-grandmother was a witch! Why hadn't Ava warned her? But why would she? Dominic was family.

"Maddy . . ."

She tugged her hand from his and clenched her fist. "I think you should leave."

"All right, if that's what you want. If it'll make you feel

better, I can wipe the memory of what happened from your mind."

He knew immediately he shouldn't have said that. She looked at him in horror, and he could almost hear her wondering if he had done other things and erased them from her memory.

Gaining his feet, he brushed a kiss across the top of her head and left the house.

Feeling the sting of tears in her eyes, Maddy stared after him. How could a relationship that had seemed so promising have ended in such an unbelievably bizarre way?

Vampire. How could it be true? Yet how could she deny what she had seen with her own eyes?

Lurching to her feet, she hurried from room to room, making sure all the doors and windows were locked, thinking she might never again go outside after dark.

Ava stared at the dried blood on Dominic's shirtfront. "What on earth happened to you?"

"I ran into a Knight. Or rather, he ran into me. With a stake."

"Oh, dear."

"Yeah. Maddy was with me at the time."

"Oh. I trust you wiped the incident from her mind."

"No."

"Why not?"

"I don't know. I guess I was tired of living a lie. I'm falling in love with her. Sooner or later, she'll have to know the truth. It's probably better this way." Assuming she was willing to see him again. Which he doubted.

"Perhaps. Did you kill the Knight?"

"No. He was wearing his cloak. I never even saw him. I'm sure he didn't follow me to Maddy's house. He couldn't have trailed me that far on foot. And there were no cars behind me on the drive to her house," he said, stripping off his ruined shirt. "I warded her place against intruders before I left, just in case."

"I guess now we can concentrate on the reason we came here."

"Yeah."

"I'm sorry, Dom," she murmured, touching his cheek. "I know how much you care for her."

He lifted his shoulder in a negligent shrug. "One good thing came out of it. The hunter left his scent on the stake. I'll know him if I see him again."

Philip 51 didn't remove his cloak until he was in his rented house, behind a locked and bolted door. Flinging it aside, he dropped into a chair and clasped his hands to still their trembling. He had hunted with his brethren, but never alone. And he'd panicked like a novice when he met the vampire face-to-face and felt the power radiating from him. Driven by fear and a deep-seated instinct for survival, he had driven his stake into Falconer's chest—and missed his heart by inches. Thank the Lord. Had he killed the vampire, his own blood would be drying on the ground beside that of Leon 48.

Stumbling to his feet, he paced the floor. How was he going to report his botched attempt to the Elder Knight? It was well-known that their leader had little patience or sympathy for those who failed, no matter the reason.

A cold chill ran down his spine when a thick mist appeared in front of him and solidified into the Elder Knight's warlock. "Jasper."

"The Elder Knight is not happy with you," the warlock said, his tone mild.

"I . . . I . . ." He swallowed hard. "It wasn't my fault."

"No?"

"I . . . I grabbed him, but he slipped out of my grasp and disappeared."

"Do not bother lying to me." Jasper settled onto the sofa. "You lack the courage to be a Knight of the Dark Wood."

"That's not true!"

"Indeed, it is. I am here to strip you of your cloak and your weapons," Jasper said, picking up the cloak from the floor. "I'll take your medallion and your weapons now."

With a growing sense of dread, Philip surrendered them to the warlock, one by one. "Is . . . is that all the Elder Knight requires of me?"

"Sadly, no," Jasper said, and with a wave of his hand, he sucked the life from the disgraced Knight, until all that remained was a small pile of gray dust.

Whistling softly, the warlock vanished from the house.

Claret materialized inside the house after Jasper disappeared. She had seen the incident between Dominic and the Knight and had followed the hunter home. She had been about to go inside to question the man when she sensed the warlock's presence. Still invisible, she had peered in the window and listened to their conversation and witnessed what had followed.

Interesting, she thought, that the wizard, who had once

been in her employ—until a witch turned him into a great black vulture— now worked for the Knights of the Dark Wood.

Claret smiled as she returned to her lair. With a little thought, she might find a way to turn things to her advantage and thereby gain power over Dominic. There were many options. She could exert her power over Jasper and force him to help her capture the vampire. She could kidnap the witch and obtain the same results, although the thought of facing Ava was daunting. With any other man, she would merely seduce him and then ensnare him, but Dominic seemed to be immune to her, may his soul rot in hell. Jasper seemed the safest way. He was powerful in his own right, though not as powerful as was she. As for the Elder Knight, he was a warlock to be reckoned with, something she hoped to avoid.

She was nothing if not persistent, Claret mused as the darkness faded from the sky. Where there was a will, there was a way. And one way or another, Dominic would be hers.

She licked her lips as she imagined having access to the Hungarian vampire's blood whenever she wished, feeling the power of it flow through her, savoring the sweet taste of it as she drank and drank. . . .

She smiled with anticipation as the dark sleep carried her away.

Chapter 16

With no reason to rise early, Dominic rested until well after the sun had gone down. And because he didn't want to endure Ava's sympathy, he showered, dressed, dissolved into mist, and left the house.

In the backyard, he resumed his own shape and then stood there, resisting the temptation to go see Maddy.

Willing himself to the city, he returned to the place where the Knight had attacked him. It took only moments to find the stake the man had used. He followed the Knight's scent to his house and knocked on the door. When there was no answer, he stepped inside. A small pile of dust gave evidence of the Knight's fate. The lingering signature of dark magic hovered in the air, attesting to the fact that a warlock had killed the Knight, because no vampire he knew was capable of turning humans to dust.

Still, it was Claret's scent that worried him the most. What was her involvement in what had happened here only hours before? Was she in league with the warlock? If so, that was bad news, indeed. The Brotherhood wanted him dead. Claret wanted his blood. But what was the warlock's interest?

Troubled, he went in search of prey to replace the blood he had lost the night before.

Spying a young couple up ahead, he spoke to their minds, willing them to stop and follow him around the corner to a quiet spot behind a tavern.

"I saw them first."

Dominic glanced over his shoulder to find Claret standing behind him. She wore a long dress the color of autumn leaves that outlined every slender curve. Love her or hate her, she was an incredibly beautiful woman. "Is that so?" he asked with a grin. "Then why are they here, with me?"

She glared at him, refusing to admit his powers were stronger than hers. "It doesn't matter. I saw them first. And this is my city. You have no right to hunt here without my permission."

"Yeah?" His gaze bored into hers. "How are you going to stop me?"

She growled low in her throat, and then smiled. "You don't need them both. Give me the man."

"Only if you promise not to kill him."

She sulked a moment, and then nodded. "Fine."

Dominic rested his hand on the woman's arm, his attention on the vampire to make sure she kept her word.

Claret drank long and deep before she released her prey.

"All right," Dominic said. "You've fed. Now go away and let me dine in peace."

A wave of her hand and she was gone.

Dominic took what he needed and no more. Lifting his head, he spoke to the man's mind, telling him to be sure to drink plenty of liquids before he went home, and then he released the two of them from his thrall and walked away.

He hadn't gone far when Claret materialized beside him. "Do you never kill your prey?"

"Never."

She studied him through narrowed eyes still faintly tinged with red. "And yet you are remarkably powerful for one so young."

"Good breeding, I imagine."

"Yes, there's no doubt about that." Her gaze moved to his neck. "I'll give you a thousand dollars for a taste of your blood."

"Sorry. I'm not for sale at any price."

"As you wish. Just remember, I always get what I want, sooner or later." And with that, she vanished from his sight.

With a shake of his head, Dominic moved out from behind the building and strolled down the sidewalk. It was Saturday night in the middle of summer and Bourbon Street was crowded. Music blared from dance clubs and bars; people sang and danced in the streets.

He made his way through the crowds and, after a time, found himself in the residential section, heading for Maddy's house.

He stopped in the middle of the block. What the hell was he doing? She'd as much as thrown him out the night before. He told himself it was for the best. Sure, his parents had worked things out, but a witch and a vampire had a lot in common. They both possessed magic of one sort or another. They both tended to live longer than most of humanity. But a vampire and a mortal? He just didn't see how it could work. With his kind, desire and hunger were closely entwined. He didn't see how he could make love to Maddy and resist the temptation to drink from her every time he took her to bed. He'd had a difficult enough time subduing his thirst in the short time they had been together, and all they had shared were kisses and a few caresses.

Despite his inner conflict, a quarter of an hour later he found himself standing in front of Maddy's house. After several moments of arguing with himself, he rang the bell.

He heard the sound of muffled footsteps, then her voice. "Who is it?"

"Dominic."

She opened the door as far as the safety chain would allow. "What are you doing here?"

"I miss you."

"I'm sorry. Good night."

"Maddy, wait."

"Dominic, please don't make this any harder than it has to be."

"I never meant to deceive you, but you must understand why I didn't tell you."

"I guess so. But it doesn't matter. I don't want to date a vampire. Tell Ava I'm sorry her predictions about us won't come true."

"Maddy, please . . ."

But he was talking to a closed door. Hands shoved deep in his pockets, he descended the stairs. Dammit, maybe he should have told her the truth from the start. And maybe he would have lost her that much sooner, he thought glumly. And wished he'd wiped the whole incident from her mind.

Perhaps it wasn't too late.

Lost in thought, Dominic paid little attention to his

surroundings. There had to be a way to get her back. She cared for him, of that he was certain. If he could just make her see that he wasn't a monster and that his people weren't like Claret and her ilk. Hungarian vampires didn't go around bleeding people dry or keep humans as pets. If not for his need for blood, he was pretty much like any other man on the planet.

He stopped at the end of the block and looked back at her house. He would go back tomorrow night and beg her to listen to him. And if that didn't work . . .

Dominic let out a startled cry as four vampires materialized from the darkness, attacking him with claws and fangs, driving him to the ground, their fangs tearing at his flesh. One of them carried a silver-bladed knife that he drove into Dominic's stomach and chest, careful to avoid his heart. Despite the racking pain, a small part of Dominic's mind told him they didn't want him dead.

Which gave him a bit of an edge. Summoning every ounce of supernatural power he possessed, he fought his way free, dissolved into mist, and used his remaining strength to transport himself into the middle of Maddy's living room.

Maddy was sitting on the sofa, staring into the cold fireplace, when a strange gray mist suddenly materialized in front of her. Muttering, "What the hell?" she scrambled to her feet and backed away from the couch as the mist solidified and Dominic lay sprawled on his back on the floor.

She stared at him in horror. His clothes were shredded.

He was bleeding from multiple cuts on his arms, legs, face, stomach, and chest. How was he even alive?

He groaned deep in his throat as he sat up.

Maddy's stomach clenched when he looked up at her through eyes tinged with red.

Her fear was palpable. Not wanting to frighten her further, he didn't move. "I'm not going to hurt you, Maddy. Trust me."

She took another step back, sat down hard when she hit the edge of the overstuffed chair in the corner. "What . . . what happened to you?"

"I was attacked by vampires."

"But why?" She frowned at him. "You're one of them."

"Not exactly."

"I don't understand."

"There are Transylvanian vampires and Hungarian vampires. The ones from Transylvania are the type described in the Dracula legend. My people are not like them. We don't kill people."

"I'd like to believe that," she muttered.

"Believe it. It's true."

"Do your people drink blood?"

"Yes. But we don't kill those we drink from. Except for that, we're pretty much like humans."

"I've never seen a human emerge from a . . . a cloud."

"We have a lot of supernatural powers."

"Why did you come here?"

"I've lost too much blood." His gaze moved to the pulse throbbing in her throat. He needed blood and he needed it badly. "I didn't have enough strength to make it to Ava's."

When she saw the direction of his gaze, her eyes widened and she lifted a hand to her neck.

"Please, Maddy? I only need a little."

"Are you crazy? I'm not letting you bite me! I don't want to be a vampire."

"You won't be. Just a little, Maddy, and I'll be strong enough to leave."

Before she could make up her mind, Ava appeared at Dominic's side. Rolling up her sleeve, she held out her arm. "Drink, Dom."

He didn't argue. Grasping her wrist, he bent his head and drank.

Maddy wanted to look away, but she couldn't. Watching him feed on Ava called to something primal within her, something that should have repulsed her but didn't. What would it be like, to let him bite her like that? Would it hurt? Ava didn't seem to be in any pain. Maddy watched for what seemed an eternity but was only a minute or two.

She stared in amazement as Dominic's cuts healed and disappeared, saw him grow stronger before her eyes. Was it witch magic? Or the effect of Ava's blood? Or both?

When he lifted his head, he licked the twin punctures in Ava's wrist, and they, too, disappeared.

Murmuring his thanks, Dominic rose fluidly to his feet and helped Ava up. "I'm sorry I bothered you, Maddy."

Ava looked at her but said nothing.

Before Maddy could frame a reply, they were both gone.

Maddy slumped back in the chair, unable to believe what had happened, but there was no denying the proof of her own eyes.

Dominic really was a vampire.

And she had let him down. He had come to her for help, and she had refused. She told herself there was no reason to feel guilty. Who in their right mind would willingly let a vampire drink from them? And how was she to know if he was even telling the truth about not killing people?

But try as she might, she couldn't ease her guilt, no matter how many excuses she made.

"What the hell happened?" Ava asked when they reached home.

"Four of Claret's coven attacked me. She wants my blood and seems determined to get it, one way or another."

Ava stared at him. "You never told me that!" she exclaimed. And then she frowned. "I should have known. All those of her ilk crave Hungarian blood. Is there anyone in this city who *isn't* after you?" she asked with a rueful grin.

"Maddy isn't."

Ava waved her hand in dismissal. "She doesn't deserve you."

Dominic removed his bloody shirt and tossed it into the fireplace. "Why? Because she wouldn't let a vampire feed on her?"

"Exactly! You saved her life. She could have returned the favor."

"It wasn't a matter of life and death."

"It could have been."

"But it wasn't. Anyway, it doesn't matter now. She's made her feelings for me perfectly clear."

"I had an email from your father, wanting to know if we've learned anything about the intentions of the Brotherhood."

"Have we?" Suddenly restless, he paced the floor in front of the hearth.

"To the best of my knowledge, their main goal is the same as it's always been—to destroy your people, as well as any others they consider unfit to live."

Dominic grunted. "So, we're pretty much wasting our time here."

Ava sank down on the sofa. "Are you saying we should go home?"

He shrugged. Jasper had killed the last Knight who'd tried to capture him, though he was sure others would come to take his place. And that was okay with him. He was in the mood for a good fight.

"Maybe we *should* go home," Ava mused. "We're not accomplishing anything here."

Dominic paused in midstride. If they left now, he would never see Maddy again. True, he didn't have much hope of that anyway, but there was always a chance she would change her mind. "You go, if you want."

"It's her, isn't it?"

"Yeah. I can't get her out of my mind."

"Or your heart?"

Dominic nodded slowly. "I can't leave Maddy until I'm sure there's no hope for us."

Chapter 17

The Elder Knight shifted his cell phone from one ear to the other as he listened with growing frustration to Jasper's rambling report. Damn Falconer! Was there no way to overpower the monster? Some of the Knights were beginning to question the feasibility of going after the Hungarian vampires, claiming there were but few of them left in the country, whereas there were hundreds of the Transylvanian vampires, who were far more of a threat to human life.

The Elder Knight refused to consider the possibility that they were right. He had a personal grudge against Falconer and his kind, and he meant to avenge the death of his father, no matter how many Knights died along the way.

"Continue as you have been. I want that vampire! Another Knight is on his way." Ending the call, the Elder Knight tossed his phone on the bed. Incompetent fools! Was he going to have to confront the vampire himself?

Chapter 18

Maddy woke bleary-eyed after a long and restless night. Every time she closed her eyes, she saw Dominic lying on the floor, bleeding from numerous cuts, while her refusal to help him played over and over again in her mind. He had saved her life and she had failed him.

She owed him an apology, she thought as she tossed the covers aside and headed for the shower. Admitting her guilt was the only way she was ever going to get a decent night's sleep.

Dominic was propped up in bed, trying to figure out the best way to get in touch with Maddy when his cell phone rang. Surprised, he picked it up. "Hey, Maddy. Is something wrong?"

"Yes. I want to apologize for last night."

"Apologize? For what?"

"You needed my help, and I wouldn't give it to you."

"It's all right."

"No, it isn't. Can you forgive me?"

"Sure, honey. Don't give it another thought."

Honey. He had never called her that before. Why now? she wondered.

"I don't suppose there's any chance we could get together?" he asked quietly. "Maybe just as friends?"

"Friends?"

"Well, you made it pretty clear you weren't interested in anything else."

Silence stretched between them.

"I'm not doing anything tonight if you want to come over."

Dominic smiled as hope unfurled within him. "What time?"

"Whenever," she said, and wondered if she was making a mistake. Maybe it would be better to end it now. Still, she did owe him an apology. And she'd already invited him.

"I could bring a pizza and a bottle of wine."

"Sounds good. I'll make a salad."

Resisting the urge to shout his happiness, he said, "See you around six."

He had no sooner ended the call than Ava poked her head into the room. "I guess I won't be able to convince you to go home now," she said, her voice sour. And then she winked at him. "Good luck."

He grinned as she closed the door. There was just no keeping secrets from his family.

Dominic stood in front of his closet. He tended to wear black most of the time because it made it easier to blend into the shadows, but he didn't want to look like a vampire tonight. He chose a pair of khaki pants and a tan shirt, stepped into a pair of brown loafers, grabbed his keys, and left the house.

He picked up the pizza he had ordered before he left, stopped for a bottle of Merlot, and again at a florist for a bouquet of pink roses.

When he pulled up in front of Maddy's, he switched off the engine, then took a deep breath, praying he wouldn't do or say anything to spook her.

She answered the door before he rang the bell. "Hi."

"Hi." He handed her the flowers, accepted her thanks, and followed her into the kitchen.

"Please, sit."

He set the pizza box on the counter, then pulled out a chair and made himself comfortable while Maddy found a vase for the roses. She handed him a corkscrew before placing a bowl of green salad in the middle of the table and dishing up the pizza. Glasses, napkins, and silverware were already on the cloth-covered table.

"Thank you again for the flowers," she said, taking the chair across from his. "They're lovely."

"So are you." He filled their glasses with wine, then lifted his. "To new beginnings?"

Smiling, she murmured, "To new beginnings."

They ate in silence for a time. Dominic was searching for a safe topic of conversation when she said, "How long have you been a vampire?"

He'd known the subject was bound to come up sooner or later. "Since I was thirteen."

Her brows shot up. "Someone turned you into a vampire when you were still a teenager?"

"No," he said, chuckling. "My kind are human for the first few years. The change takes place gradually once we reach puberty. As we grow older, our need for food grows less and our need for blood grows stronger. By the time I was eighteen or nineteen, the change was complete. When we turn thirty, we stop aging physically."

"Wow, that must be nice." No gray hair, she thought. No wrinkles or age spots. No menopause.

"I'll let you know when it happens."

So he wasn't yet thirty. "How old are you?"

"Twenty-five."

"Is your sister a vampire, too?"

"No. Just a witch."

Just a witch. He said it so casually, as if everyone had witches or vampires in their family. "So, are your parents vampires or witches? Or both?" She had never heard of vampires having babies.

"Mom's a witch. Dad's a vampire."

Maddy ate in silence for a moment, then pushed her plate away, her expression serious. "Have you ever killed anyone?"

"A hunter, a few years ago." He shrugged at the disapproval in her eyes. "It was me or him."

She considered that for a moment as she sipped her wine.

"Anything else?"

"When you . . . you take people's blood, does it hurt them?"

"No. I'm told it's quite pleasant."

"Pleasant! Who told you that?"

"Who do you think?"

Maddy frowned. Certainly the people he preyed on didn't fill out questionnaires. *Did you enjoy being bitten? Yes or No? Check the appropriate box.*

"Want to give it a try?"

"I don't think so!" she exclaimed, although she had to admit she was suddenly curious. And then she had another thought. What did vampire blood taste like?

"Some people find it addictive," he said, watching the conflicting emotions play over her face. "Want a taste?"

"Will it hurt me?"

"No."

She worried her lower lip between her teeth. Surely one taste wouldn't hurt. "All right."

Dominic bit into his wrist and held out his arm.

Maddy stared at it and then, before she could change her mind, leaned forward and licked his wrist. Warmth and a feeling of sensual pleasure washed through her. Startled, she looked up at him.

"I told you it was pleasant," he said.

Pleasant was an understatement, she thought. "You should sell it on the Internet," she said. "You'd make a fortune." And then she frowned. She had tasted his blood. Had he ever tasted hers? "You said you could make me forget that we met. Have you ever made me forget anything that happened between us?"

Damn. He hadn't seen *that* coming. Should he admit the truth? Or tell her a lie? In the end, the truth won. "I drank from you a couple of times. No more than a small taste," he added quickly. "I swear."

She lifted a hand to her throat. "You bit me?"

"Yeah. I don't think I can make you understand how it is, what it's like. I felt there was a connection between us the night we met, and the temptation to taste you . . ." He made a vague gesture with his hand. "I just couldn't resist it."

She'd felt that connection, too, she thought. "That might explain the first time it happened," she allowed somewhat grudgingly. "But not the second time."

Dominic grinned at her. "The second was because the first was so exquisite."

Maddy stared at him, unable to believe she was having this conversation. Needing something to occupy her hands, she stacked their plates and set them aside. "I guess that's a compliment."

"The best there is," he said with a wink.

Unable to think of a reply, she said, "Why don't you go make yourself comfortable in the living room while I clear the table and put things away?"

"I'll help." When she lifted one brow, he shrugged. "My mother made me do the same chores as my sister. And vice versa."

"Smart woman."

It didn't take long to put the kitchen to rights. Dominic followed Maddy into the living room, and after a moment's hesitation, he sank down beside her on the sofa. Close, but not too close.

Maddy bit down on her lower lip, all too aware of the man beside her—the man who wasn't a man at all. She had tossed and turned all night, her mind in turmoil, as she tried to convince herself to end their relationship. She ticked off all the reasons why she shouldn't see him again, but now that he was here, none of those reasons seemed to matter. Sure, the blood thing was a little off-putting, but she enjoyed being with him. He was kind and funny. He treated her like a queen. She loved the sound of his laughter, the way his smile did funny things in the pit of her stomach. She loved being in his arms and she desperately wanted to be held again, to feel the strength of his arms around her, the sheer ecstasy of his kisses. Right or wrong, he was here now and she wanted him to stay.

Dominic blew out a shaky breath. "I can read your mind, remember?"

Embarrassment warmed her cheeks. "Then you know what I want," she said, her voice little more than a whisper.

"Maddy! Honey, are you sure?"

"I know it's crazy," she said in a rush. "Maybe *I'm* crazy. We just met. You're a vampire. But I can't help the way I feel. I don't care what you are. I want to be with you."

"No more than I want to be with you." He drew her gently into his arms, his gaze searching hers. "I think I fell in love with you the first night we met."

"Dominic . . ." She buried her fingers in the hair at his nape and tugged his head down to hers. "Shut up and kiss me."

"Don't ask me twice," he muttered and claimed her lips with his in a long, searing kiss that turned her bones to liquid and her blood to fire.

She sighed as his hand slid under her sweater to skate up and down her spine, then crept around to cup her breast. Desperate to be closer, she climbed onto his lap, her arms going around his neck, her tongue darting out to meet his.

They fell back on the sofa, her body sprawled on top of his, their mouths fused together.

Dominic groaned as she writhed against him. "Maddy . . ."

"What?"

He ran his tongue the length of her neck, felt his fangs extend. "Maddy, we've got to stop."

"No." She rained kisses on his brow, his cheeks, before returning to his mouth.

Dominic fought for control, but he feared it was a losing battle. He had never wanted another woman the way he wanted—needed—this one. His body was on fire for her, his hunger clawing at him.

Calling on every ounce of self-control he possessed, he lifted her up and set her on her feet, then jackknifed into a sitting position, his head cradled in his hands.

Maddy stared at him, her whole body aching for his touch, her lips bruised from his kisses.

"Dominic? Dominic, what's wrong?"

When he looked up, his eyes were tinged with red.

"Dominic?" She took a hesitant step toward him. "Are you all right?"

"Don't come any closer." He took several deep breaths. "Just give me a minute."

Suddenly wary, she backed away from him, hands clenched at her sides. "Is there anything I can do?"

With a shake of his head, he closed his eyes. Damn! He had never come this close to losing control. It scared the hell out of him. He usually fed late at night, but from now on, he'd make it a point to satisfy his thirst before he came to see her.

For both their sakes.

Ava was waiting up for him when he got home. "So, you've kissed and made up," she said, a twinkle in her eyes. "I knew you would."

"Yeah, right. You know everything, don't you?"

"What's wrong now? I thought you'd be happy."

"I am. It's just . . ." He tossed his keys on the end table. "You have no idea what it's like. I want her so damn bad, but mixed up in my feelings for her is the constant desire for her blood. I don't know how long I can keep my lust separated from my hunger. Dammit, one mistake and I could kill her!"

Pushing out of her chair, Ava crossed the floor and put her arms around him. "Here, now. It can't be as bad as all that."

"How the hell would you know?"

"Watch your language, boy. I went through this same thing with your parents, and they both survived. So will you."

"I don't know what I'd do if I hurt her."

"Have some faith in yourself, Dom. Your father is a powerful vampire and he's passed that strength on to you. And even though you're not a witch, your mother's power also resides in you."

Dominic kissed the top of Ava's head. "Thanks, Grams."

"You'll be all right. But be careful. There's another Knight in town, Dom. Watch out for this one. He's been in the Brotherhood a very long time."

Chapter 19

Maddy slept like a baby and woke with a smile on her face and a song in her heart. Last night had been wonderful. So, Dominic was a vampire. It would only be a problem if she made it one. He wasn't like the ones from Transylvania. He didn't kill people, he could be up during the day, he ate regular food. The blood he needed was like vitamins, she thought, something he had to have on a regular basis. She could live with that.

She showered and dressed, skipped down the stairs and into the kitchen, where she made a big breakfast—bacon, eggs, a bran muffin, and a cup of coffee. Filled with energy, she ate quickly, washed the dishes, mopped the floor, and threw a load of clothes in the washer.

She was looking around for something else to do when her phone rang. She grabbed it, thinking it was Dominic. Instead, it was her mother. "Mom! Hi."

"Maddy, how's everything?"

"Couldn't be better."

"You sound awfully cheerful. Did you win the lottery?"

"Better! Mom, I met a guy."

"Well, it's about time! What's his name? What does he do for a living?"

"His name is Dominic and he's in business with his father. I don't know what they do exactly. We just met a few days ago. Wait until you see him! He's tall, dark, and gorgeous and I'm crazy about him."

"I'm happy for you, dear. But take it slow, okay? Remember what happened to your sister."

"Don't worry, Mom. That's not going to happen to me." Her older sister, Fran, had fallen head over heels for a guy three years ago, gotten carried away one night, and wound up pregnant. As soon as Jeffrey discovered he was about to be a father, he skipped town. Seven months later, Melanie was born. Fortunately for Frances, she had met a wonderful guy and they were now living happily ever after in New Jersey.

"You're my daughter," her mother said, a smile in her voice. "It's my job to worry. Listen, sweetie, I've got to go. Our table is ready. Call you when I can. Love you."

"Love you, too, Mom. Give Dad a hug for me."

"Will do."

Maddy grinned as she dropped her phone on the sofa. And then she sobered. What if things got serious between her and Dominic? How would she ever find the words to tell Fran and her parents that Dominic came from a family of witches and vampires?

At midday, Dominic rose and dressed before heading out in search of the Knight who had been sent to hunt him down. He scoured all New Orleans—every street, every hotel, every dive—with no results. Of course, the Knights had those blasted invisibility cloaks, which made the task darn near impossible.

By dusk, he was ready to give up the search. Maybe the guy wasn't staying in the city. Of course, the hunter wasn't his only problem. There was also the matter of the warlock, Jasper.

And then there was Claret. Of the three, she troubled him the most. If the Knight or the warlock captured him, they would deliver him to the Elder Knight, who wanted him alive. If Claret caught him unawares . . . it was something he didn't want to think about. She could do far worse than kill him. She would imprison him and feed on him at her leisure. She had done it to his father, for a short time. Quill had spared his son the gory details, but Dominic could easily imagine the horror of losing his freedom, being held in a cage charged with magic, being fed on at Claret's whim for decades, perhaps centuries. It was a fate worse than death.

When a clock chimed in the distance, he put all thoughts of hunters out of his mind. He would worry about them later.

For now, he wanted to see Maddy.

Raoul 29 followed the vampire through the city to the residential area. He smiled as the bloodsucker hurried up a red-brick walkway to the door of a lovely old home. He knocked once and the door was opened by a beautiful young woman.

A shudder of distaste rippled through Raoul as he imagined the vampire leaning over the woman's neck, drinking her blood, defiling her with his very presence.

Under the protection of his cloak, he ghosted up the stairs and turned the knob. The door opened on well-oiled hinges, but when he tried to enter, an invisible barrier prevented him.

Vampire magic, he thought irritably. Damn the man.

He circled the house, but he was repelled at every turn. He would have to wait and take the bloodsucker when he left.

With that in mind, he settled down on the grass beneath a live oak tree. He had all the patience of a lion stalking its prey. And, like the lion, he would emerge victorious.

"Dominic!" After closing the door, Maddy threw her arms around him. "I'm so glad to see you!"

He grinned as he pulled her closer. "How glad?"

"This glad," she exclaimed. Going up on her tiptoes, she kissed him.

He cupped the back of her head in his palm and deepened the kiss, his tongue sweeping across her lower lip, dipping inside.

Maddy clung to him as wave after wave of pleasure swept through her. Lord, but his kisses were like dynamite.

She was breathless, her knees shaky, when he lifted his head.

"I'm glad to see you, too," he said, grinning.

"I think I need a cold shower," she muttered, fanning her face with her hand.

"I'll wash your back."

"I don't think that would cool me off much," she said. "Probably set off the fire alarm."

Dominic laughed, thinking he'd never felt so happy, so free. Sure, trouble lurked in the city, but here, with Maddy, nothing else seemed to matter.

With his arm around her waist, they strolled into the living room and sank down on the sofa.

He coiled a lock of her hair around his finger. "Do you want to go out tonight?"

"Not really. I have everything I need right here."

"Damn, girl, of all the women I've known, you're the first to say what she really thinks."

"Am I? Just how many girls have you known?"

He leaned forward and kissed the tip of her nose. "Not that many."

"How many?"

"I don't know. Five or six, maybe. But I was never serious about any of them. We hung out. We went clubbing." He shrugged. "Like I said, nothing serious." His gaze met hers. "I hardly remember any of them. But you . . ." His knuckles caressed her cheek. "You, I'll never forget."

She melted against him. A little voice in the back of her mind said things were moving way too fast, while another part whispered they weren't moving fast enough. *Fran*, she thought. *Remember Fran*. Whenever she felt herself moving too far, too fast, Maddy always recalled what had happened to her sister, how she had come home one night, brokenhearted, pregnant, and alone. It usually worked like ice water. Tonight was no different.

With a toss of her head, she sat up. "I think maybe we should go out."

Dominic looked at her, one brow arched. "Did I miss something?"

"My sister."

"What about your sister?"

"Fran fell head over heels for a guy when she was nineteen. They dated for about eight months and she got pregnant. He wanted her to have an abortion, and when she refused, he left her flat. She never saw him again. So, whenever I think things are getting out of hand, I think about my sister."

"Better than birth control, huh?"

"My niece, Melanie, is six."

Dominic grunted softly.

"Fran's happily married now. Ryan treats Melanie like his own. And Fran's expecting again."

"I'm glad everything turned out all right."

"Me too."

"So, where do you want to go? Someplace crowded, I'm guessing."

"You're making fun of me."

"No. You're probably right. We need to take it slow." For a lot of reasons, he mused, thinking about those who were hunting him. And that, unlike Transylvanian vampires, he was perfectly capable of getting Maddy pregnant.

They decided on a movie. Dominic bought a big tub of popcorn and a king-size drink. Maddy watched the screen and he watched her, noting the way Maddy's hands clenched when the heroine was in danger, the way she smiled when the hero took the heroine in his arms and claimed his reward. It was a romance, and after the requisite breakup, the couple reunited. Dominic didn't miss the tears Maddy tried to wipe away so he wouldn't see them.

They went out for ice cream afterward. She ordered a hot fudge sundae with extra hot fudge and marshmallow. He opted for a vanilla malt.

"Just a sucker for romance, huh?" he said as they found a table and sat down.

"So, what if I am?"

"Nothing. I like a girl who's a romantic at heart."

"I admit it, I love a happy ending. It seems they're few and far between in real life."

"Aren't your parents happy?"

"Sure. It's just that most of the girls I went to college with are getting divorces or they're already on their second or third marriage."

He shrugged. "Too many people today don't want to put any effort into it. They want to marry and have everything their parents spent their lives working for. And when they can't have it all at once, they think there's something wrong with the marriage and they move on."

"Maybe. I don't know. I just know that when I marry, I want it to be forever."

"Me too," he murmured, thinking he could give her the forever she wanted. Leaning across the table, he licked a bit of hot fudge from the corner of her mouth. "Sweet," he murmured. "But not as sweet as you."

Raoul had followed the couple when they left the house but found no opportunity to take the vampire because there were always other people around. Now, he waited by the tree again, watching as the vampire kissed the woman good night, then turned away, whistling as he descended the porch steps.

With his sword in one hand and a rope dipped in silver in the other, Raoul raced across the lawn, threw off his cloak, and sprang at the vampire. He had intended to drive the blade into the vampire's shoulder, then capture him with the noose, knowing the silver blade and the noose would negate some of his powers, but the vampire moved faster than lightning. The blade meant for his shoulder sliced across his left arm, just above his elbow as he dodged the rope, and Raoul found himself staring into a pair of angry eyes as red as hellfire.

In one swift move, Raoul dropped the noose, donned his cloak, and vanished from sight, relieved that he would live to fight another day.

Dominic pressed his hand to the wound, cursing mightily as the hunter disappeared. Damn, it hurt. He glanced at the gash, which should have been healing. Instead, the flesh around the edges of the cut was turning black.

Pain lanced down the length of his arm, gradually turning to agony as it reached his hand.

Poison, he thought. The Knight had dipped the blade in poison.

Chapter 20

"The good news is, it won't kill you," Ava said as she examined the ugly wound. "The bad news is, it'll hurt like hell until I can concoct an antidote."

Dominic groaned low in his throat as he tried to get comfortable. The poison had spread up and down his arm and now burned beneath his skin on his whole left side. "How long will that take?"

"I'm not sure, perhaps a day or two. I've never seen anything like this before." She pulled the covers over him. "Try to get some rest."

With a faint nod, he closed his eyes and let the darkness carry him away.

Ava brushed a lock of hair from his brow. He looked just like his father—tall, handsome, rugged. But not yet as strong. Or as wise. It grieved her to see him in pain. She knew she should call Callie and let her know what was going on, just as she knew Dominic would resent it if she did.

Bending down, she kissed his forehead. He was burning up. Turning off the light, she tiptoed out of the room and quietly closed the door behind her.

Gliding into the den, she turned on the light. She had made this room her own. A long table held a black cauldron, a silver-bladed knife with a gold handle, a pentagram, her wand, and an ancient grimoire. The book was old and heavy, and she lifted it with care, then settled into the easy chair in the corner. As she'd told Dom, she had never encountered a poison spell like the one that was burning through him, but if there was a cure to be found, it would be in this ancient tome.

Blowing out a sigh, she ran her hand over the cover. Eyes closed, she murmured a prayer before she opened the book. A whisper of power flooded the room as she carefully turned the pages. The answer must be in here, she thought. It simply must.

Because there was nowhere else to look.

Claret strolled along Bourbon Street, eyes and ears attuned to every sight, every sound, yet try as she might, she could find no sign of Dominic Falconer. Had he left the city?

She turned the corner at the end of the street and caught the scent of a hunter. Shielding her presence, she followed it to a small nightclub frequented by those who did not wish to be found.

He sat alone at a small, round table for two in the back of the room, head bowed, shoulders hunched.

Dropping her shield, she slipped into the chair across from his.

He looked up sharply, his eyes narrowing. "Who are you?"

"I am Claret. Who are you?"

"Raoul." His gaze moved over her, and then he hissed, "Vampire."

"Hunter." She smiled with a flash of fang. "I hope you're not hunting me."

"Not at the moment. I'm here for the one they call Falconer."

"Indeed? Have you found him?"

"I've found the next best thing."

She leaned forward. "What might that be?"

"That's for me to know, not you."

She sat back and then, faster than lightning, she lunged across the table, tore the medallion from his neck with one hand and dug her fingers into his throat with the other. "If you want to leave this place alive," she hissed, increasing the pressure around his neck, "you will tell me what I want to know."

"A . . . girl," he gasped.

"What girl?"

His fingers curled around hers as he tried to pry her hand from his neck. "I . . . don't . . . know her . . . name."

"Where does she live?" She shook him, wondering if it was another woman or the one she had seen Dominic with before. "Tell me!"

"Can't . . . breathe."

She loosened her hold slightly.

He sucked in several gulps of air, then gave her the address.

The same girl she had seen him with before, Claret mused with some satisfaction.

Claret flashed a smile, then dragged him across the table and buried her fangs in his throat, her eyelids fluttering down with pleasure as she drank and drank the sweet elixir of his life's blood. When nothing remained, she transported him to the outskirts of town and left him in a ditch filled with rainwater.

Ava stood by Dominic's bed, her brow furrowed. Even without touching him, she could feel the fever burning through him. She laid a hand on his shoulder, but he didn't stir. Vampires were strong, virtually immortal. But that didn't mean they couldn't be killed. Nothing he ingested would destroy him, but this poison was different from most. It had been conjured with dark magic. Thus far, she had not found a spell to counter it.

She replaced the covers he had thrown aside and left the room.

Hurrying into the den, she found her wand and began to chant softly.

Maddy had just finished an early dinner when she felt an overwhelming urge to drive to Ava's house. She tried to shake off the impulse even as she found herself grabbing her car keys and hurrying outside. Feeling as though she had no control over her movements, she got behind the wheel and headed across town. She hit no red lights on the way. The traffic ahead of her seemed to part as if by magic, and she arrived at the witch's house in record time.

She parked in the driveway, ran up the steps, and rang the bell. "Ava! It's me, Maddy. Let me in."

The door opened almost immediately. "Maddy. How good of you to answer my summons."

Maddy stared at her. "You . . . you magicked me here?"

"Indeed. Come in, child."

"Why am I here?" she asked as she followed Dominic's great-grandmother into the living room.

"I need you."

"You need me? Whatever for?"

"Dominic is in danger," Ava explained, turning to face her.

"From who? He's a vampire."

"He's being hunted by a ruthless group known as the Knights of the Dark Wood. Their sole purpose in life is to destroy his kind."

Feeling suddenly light-headed, Maddy sank down on the sofa. "But what has that to do with me?"

"One of the Knights poisoned him."

"I thought vampires were, you know, immortal." Until now, she had assumed that Dominic was in no serious danger, that whatever was wrong with him would pass.

"To a certain extent. Dom has considerable power, but even vampires are susceptible to some kinds of magic. The Knight who attacked him used an insidious poison. I haven't been able to find a cure. My great-grandson is in a lot of pain just now. I've tried several spells and incantations, numerous potions. None have been effective."

"So, what do you expect me to do? I'm not a witch or a doctor."

"I found a description of an ancient potion. The ingredients are very rare, but I've managed to find all but one."

A shiver of foreboding ran down Maddy's spine. "I'm afraid to ask—what is it?"

"The blood of the one he loves."

Maddy shook her head. "He doesn't love me. We hardly know each other."

"Time has nothing to do with love, my dear."

Maddy glanced nervously around the room, her mind whirling. This couldn't be happening. Maybe she was home in bed, caught up in some wild nightmare. "He loves you. Wouldn't your blood work better than mine? You're family, after all."

"In this case, witch blood will not help."

"How . . . how much do you need?"

"A cup of blood, freely given."

"A . . . a cup?" Maddy swallowed hard. "So much?"

"A cup of blood. And a lock of your hair. Is it too much to ask if it will save his life?"

"How do you know it will work?"

"Alas, I don't. But it's my last hope. Believe me, I would take what I need by force if I could." Unfortunately, doing so would render the blood powerless.

"That won't be necessary."

"Come along," Ava said, reaching for her hand. "The sooner we do this, the better."

Maddy followed the witch down a wide hall lined with pictures of Louisiana and into a room paneled in dark wood. Heavy drapes covered the windows. There was nothing in the room save an easy chair covered in a dark print, a long, narrow, oak table covered with strange implements, and a large black cauldron. A horrible smell rose from a thick, ebony-hued liquid simmering in a beaker over a low flame. Three large wooden trunks lined one wall.

"Have a seat," Ava said.

On shaky legs, Maddy crossed the room and sat down heavily.

Ava rummaged around in one of the trunks for a moment, then muttered, "Ah, here it is," and came out with a syringe, a narrow piece of rubber, and a length of clear tubing. She plucked a heavy brass cup inscribed with runes from the table before kneeling beside Maddy.

Maddy squeezed her eyes shut as Ava probed the inside of her arm for a vein, then tied the strip of rubber in place. She winced as the needle struck home. She had never liked the sight of blood. Especially her own.

After what seemed like forever, Ava withdrew the needle and slapped a bandage over her arm to stop the bleeding. Reaching forward, the witch plucked a strand of Maddy's hair.

"Let us pray this works," Ava said as she walked to the table and held the cup over the beaker.

Rising, Maddy followed her to the table. "How will we know?"

"You'll see. If the liquid stays black, we've failed."

Maddy held her breath as Ava dropped the hair into the beaker. A moment later, she slowly added the blood. It hissed and bubbled up, threatening to spill over the edge. A long, thin spiral of black smoke rose from the container.

Maddy clenched her hands to still their trembling. Was that a good sign? She watched, unblinking, as the liquid continued to bubble and then, ever so slowly, the bubbling stopped and the liquid turned white. Pressing a hand to her heart, Maddy blew out a sigh of relief. It had worked!

Ava poured the liquid in a large, clear glass. "Now, for the final test."

"What do you mean?"

"We have to give it to Dominic."

"But I thought you said if it changed color, it would cure him."

"It means the potion contains the right amount of all the ingredients. There's no guarantee it will work."

Maddy's shoulders slumped. "What if . . . what if it doesn't work?" Tears stung her eyes. "Will he . . . will he die?"

"I don't know. But if it works, he will be immune to the poison."

Maddy trailed Ava down the hall to another room, all the while sending a silent prayer to heaven—*please let it work, please let it work*. It had to work. She couldn't bear to think of how empty her life would be if anything happened to him.

She paused in the doorway. Dominic lay on his back on a big brass bed, a colorful quilt covering him from the waist down. His chest was bare, his skin and hair damp with sweat. She couldn't tell if he was breathing.

Ava tenderly lifted his head and held the glass to his lips. In a voice filled with power, she cried, "Dominic Falconer, I command you to drink!"

For a moment, nothing happened. And then, slowly, he obeyed her command. When the glass was empty, he lay quiet for a moment. Just when Maddy thought the poison was gone, he began to thrash on the bed, arms and legs jerking wildly as a harsh cry of pain rose in his throat.

Ava took a step back, her eyes wide with alarm.

Maddy pressed her hand to her mouth, her stomach

roiling as a thick black mist emerged from his throat. It hung suspended in the air over him like some evil wraith come to steal his very soul.

Throwing her head back, Ava screamed, "Be gone!" and dropped to her knees, her head cradled in her hands as her strength drained away.

Dominic suddenly went still.

As the ominous black cloud swirled around her, Maddy shuddered in horror, then let out a strangled cry of fear as she tumbled into oblivion.

He struggled through layers of darkness, searching for the light that was Maddy. As from far away, he heard her voice, thick with concern. Who was she worrying about? Ava drifted in and out of his consciousness, her hand cool on his heated flesh, yet each touch caused him pain. He could feel the Knight's poison coursing through his veins like venom, knew he was dying and didn't care, if only it would put an end to the excruciating agony. And then Ava was there again, her voice like thunder as she commanded him. At first, the revolting concoction she forced down his throat burned through him like the fires of hell, and then he tasted Maddy's blood, warm and sweet and alive. It smothered the fire in his veins and filled him with a sense of peace. . . .

Dominic woke abruptly. Had it all been nothing but a bad dream? But no, Ava sat on the floor, her head bowed. The signature of residual magic lingered in the air. He turned his head, let out a harsh cry of denial when he saw Maddy sprawled on the floor beside the bed, her face pale.

Sliding down beside her, he pulled her onto his lap. "Maddy?" He stroked her hair, her cheek. "Maddy, wake up."

She stirred in his arms, her eyelids fluttering as she looked up at him. Smiling faintly, she lifted a hand to his cheek as she murmured his name.

Relieved, he hugged her close. Thank the Lord, she was all right.

Later, after he had showered and dressed, Dominic sat on the sofa in the living room, with Maddy pressed close to his side, while Ava told him all that had happened.

"Like my father always said," he murmured with a faint grin, "it pays to have a witch in the family. Especially one as powerful as you, Grams."

Ava nodded, but she was watching Maddy. "How do you feel, child?" They had both been touched by the spell's aftereffects for a short time. Ava felt fully recovered, but she wasn't sure about Maddy.

Maddy started to say fine, then shook her head. "I don't know."

Concern flickered in Ava's eyes.

"What is it?" Dominic glanced from one woman to the other. "What's wrong?"

"Nothing," Maddy said quickly. "I just feel a little . . . strange." She shuddered as she recalled the ominous dark mist that had hovered over her.

"It's probably nothing more than the aftereffects of the magic I used," Ava said with a reassuring smile. "And the loss of the blood I took."

She was lying, Dominic thought. But why? "What kind of magic was it?" he asked sharply.

"We'll talk about it later. Why don't you take Maddy home so she can get some rest?"

"Yeah." It was obvious that whatever Ava had to say, she didn't want to share it with Maddy. "That's probably a good idea."

It was late when they reached Maddy's house. Dominic settled her on the sofa, covered her with a blanket, and insisted she drink a glass of wine.

"I'm fine," she said. "Really."

"I know. Just humor me."

She obediently drained the glass, frowned when he filled it again.

"You need to replace the blood you lost. The wine will help."

"I was so worried about you," she said. "You were in such pain, and I was so afraid Ava wouldn't be able to help you."

Sitting beside her, he slipped his arm around her shoulders. "I'll be all right. It's not easy, getting rid of one of my kind."

"It looked like a close call to me."

He grinned wryly. "I won't argue with that. Are you sure you're okay?"

"Yes. Stop worrying about me."

"I'll never stop," he said, cupping her cheek in his palm. "I owe you my life."

"More likely it was Ava's magic."

"It wouldn't have worked without your blood. I could

feel it running through me, easing the pain, destroying the poison."

"Really?"

"Really." He kissed the tip of her nose. "I need to go."

"Where are you go . . . oh."

"Yeah. That poison drained my strength. I need to . . . you know."

"Feed."

"I'll stay if you want."

"No. You should go and do what you have to. I'll be okay."

"I'll come by later to make sure you're all right. I'm curious about one thing, though. Did Ava tell you why she needed your blood in particular?"

Maddy nodded. "She said the spell required the blood of someone you love."

Dominic kissed her tenderly. "Then she went to the right place," he said, giving her hand a squeeze.

Maddy watched him go and then closed her eyes. She didn't feel like herself. She felt different inside, as if . . . as if . . . A chill ran through her. As if that dark mist had settled in her very soul.

But that was impossible. Wasn't it?

Dominic left Maddy's place, his hands shoved into his pockets. He had felt something when he kissed Maddy, and it wasn't the rush of pleasure he usually felt, but something dark and disturbing. He told himself he had imagined it, that it was just some leftover effect of the potion Ava had concocted. But it was more than that.

He fed on the first lone mortal he found, wiped the

memory from her mind, and sent her on her way. Still troubled, he headed for home.

Ava smiled when she saw him, but the smile quickly faded when she saw the look on his face. "What's wrong?"

"What kind of spell did you use?"

"Why? Is it no longer working? Are you in pain?"

"I'm fine. What did you do to Maddy?"

"Nothing."

"You're lying. I felt something when I kissed her. Something dark."

"It's nothing. Just a little residual magic. It should be gone in a day or two."

"You'd better hope so."

Ava's eyes grew wide. "Are you threatening me?"

"Sounds that way, doesn't it?" He didn't wait for an answer. With a wave of his hand, he transported himself back to Maddy's.

He found her asleep on the sofa, her face pale.

The signature of potent magic hung heavy in the air. She looked like a fairy-tale princess lying there, her hair spread across the sofa pillow, her lips slightly parted. Sitting on the couch beside her, he brushed a kiss across her lips.

And tasted the darkness within her.

"Maddy? Maddy! Wake up."

She stirred, her eyelids fluttering open. "Dominic." She smiled at him. "What are you doing here?" She glanced at the clock. "It's late. What are you doing here?" she asked again. "Is something wrong?"

"No." He brushed a lock of hair behind her ear. "I just came back to check on you. Make sure you were feeling all right after all you've been through tonight."

She frowned as she sat up. “Did something happen?”

“You don’t remember?”

“Remember what?”

He scrubbed a hand over his jaw. What the hell? Had that potion erased her memory? “You drank something that didn’t agree with you,” he lied. “That’s all. I came by to check up on you. Make sure there were no after-effects.”

“Oh. Well, I feel fine. Just kind of tired. I think I’ll go up to bed.”

“Okay if I stick around until you fall asleep?”

“Thank you, but I don’t think that’s necessary.”

“Are you sure?” Whether she liked it or not, he’d be back later to make sure she was all right.

“I’m a big girl. I’ll be fine.”

“If you need anything, call me.”

“I will, I promise. Will I see you tomorrow?”

“You bet.” He kissed her lightly. And tasted the same darkness he had tasted before.

It worried the hell out of him.

Chapter 21

Claret stalked the dark streets until she found Jasper sitting in a booth in one of the city's most disreputable nightclubs.

He glared at her when she slid in across from him. "What the hell do you want now?"

"I want you to leave the vampire alone. I intend to make him mine and I don't need any interference."

Jasper snorted. "I don't take orders from you."

Leaning toward him, her voice filled with menace, she said, "Maybe you should start."

He sat back as far as the booth allowed, unsettled by the faint tinge of red in her eyes. He considered himself a powerful warlock, but she was stronger and they both knew it. He had a quick memory of being turned into a vulture by the witch, Ava. What had made it worse was that he remembered who and what he was the whole time.

He cringed as Claret's preternatural power rolled over him, even as he told himself she wasn't a witch. She couldn't turn him into a bird or a beast. But that didn't mean she couldn't do something worse.

"I won't warn you again," the vampire growled and vanished from his sight.

Weak with relief, Jasper downed the remainder of his drink in a single swallow. He'd had enough of Knights and vampires and witches to last him the rest of his life.

However long that might be.

The Elder Knight paced the floor of his cell. He had tried repeatedly to connect with Raoul 29, but to no avail. Either the Knight was refusing to answer, which seemed highly unlikely, or he couldn't answer, in which case he was most likely dead.

Hands clenched, he forced his rage down to a manageable level. There was nothing to be gained by acting rashly. He had known Falconer wouldn't be easy to take. Perhaps he was wasting his resources by sending one Knight after another after the vampire. As for Jasper, the warlock didn't seem to be making any progress, nor did he seem to be trying very hard.

Perhaps the time had come to take matters into his own hands.

Chapter 22

Lost in thought, Dominic strolled along Royal Street, famous for its art galleries, antique shops, fine restaurants, and music. But it was Maddy and the darkness he sensed within her that held his attention. Had Ava's spell caused it? There seemed to be no other explanation. How long would it last? What if, instead of disappearing in a day or two, the darkness only grew stronger?

His worries about Maddy vanished when Claret sidled up beside him. As always, she wore a long gown that emphasized her abundant curves. This one was turquoise blue, with a plunging neckline and a slit on one side that exposed her leg from ankle to thigh.

"I was looking for you," she purred.

He grunted in reply.

"I thought you'd like to know that I killed one of the Knights hunting you."

"Yeah?"

"And I warned Jasper to leave you alone or face my wrath."

"You put him in a hell of a spot," Dominic remarked.

"Having to choose between you and the Elder Knight. Sort of a no-win situation."

She shrugged one bare shoulder. "I thought maybe you would give me a sip of your blood to show your gratitude."

"Did you?"

"Are you going to make me beg?"

Dangerous or not, it was hard to hate her. "One drink. If you try for more, I'll wring your neck."

She smiled up at him, her eyes shining with victory as he paused in a darkened doorway. Going up on her tiptoes, she bit him. And spat his blood from her mouth. "What the hell!"

"What's wrong?"

"Your blood! What have you done? It's vile!"

Dominic stared at her. She had tasted the dark magic lingering in Maddy, he thought. And if Claret could taste it, it must be even stronger than he feared.

Before she could question him, he transported himself home.

He found Ava in the den, bent over her grimoire, her brow furrowed.

"Other than Maddy's blood, I don't know what the hell was in that potion you gave me, but there's some sort of strange darkness lingering inside her. I want to know what it is, and why the hell she has only a hazy memory of what happened that night."

Ava looked up, her eyes dark with guilt. "I'm trying to find out."

"Yeah? Well, whatever the hell you concocted is affecting me, too."

"What do you mean?"

"I mean I gave Claret a taste of my blood, and she spat it out. Said it tasted vile."

"You gave that vampire your blood? Willingly? Are you mad?"

"That's not the problem."

Ava took a step back and dropped into the easy chair in the corner. "I must have done something wrong," she murmured. "But I don't know what it could have been. I followed the steps in the grimoire exactly. Even if the potion affected your blood, it shouldn't have affected Maddy the way it did. She never touched it or tasted it . . . but . . ."

Ava's face paled suddenly. "After you drank the potion, you expelled something that looked like a thick black mist, which I assumed was the poison leaving your system. For a moment, it . . . it hung over Maddy."

"What?"

"Only for a moment! But . . . I don't know. Perhaps it affected her memory, although that makes absolutely no sense. As for your blood being bitter, I think that's normal considering you drank poison. Maybe it's a good thing," she said. "Maybe Claret will leave you alone now."

"It was dark magic you used, wasn't it?"

Her gaze slid away from his as she nodded. "I looked in every book I have. It was the only spell that had the slightest chance of working. I thought it was worth the risk."

"Did you?" he asked, his voice tight with suppressed anger. "I wonder if Maddy would agree."

* * *

Maddy woke abruptly. Alarmed, she glanced around her room. She knew she was at home, in her bed, and yet it didn't feel familiar. Her head ached, her eyes hurt, and she felt vaguely disoriented and a little dizzy.

Was she sick? She lifted a hand to her brow. It didn't feel hot. Did she have a hangover? But that was impossible. She hadn't been drinking. Had she?

The last thing she remembered was going to Ava's house. Watching her work some kind of magic. A potion. She'd been making a potion for Dominic. Had it worked? It must have, she thought, because she had seen Dominic last night . . . had it been last night? Or the night before? Why couldn't she remember?

Throwing the covers aside, she padded into the bathroom and washed her face. Feet dragging, she made her way to the kitchen for a much-needed cup of coffee.

Sitting at the table a short time later, Maddy stared into the steam rising from the mug, her thoughts on Dominic. Always Dominic . . . he was at home, asleep in his bed. A dark blue sheet covered him. . . .

Her head snapped up. How on earth could she possibly know that?

Engulfed by a sudden chill, she ran into her room, pulled on a pair of jeans, a thick sweater, and a pair of boots, and ran out to her car.

Five minutes after that, she was pounding on Ava's front door.

If the witch was surprised to see her, it didn't show on her face. "Maddy, what brings you here so early?"

"I want to know what's going on. I can't remember anything that happened after you made that potion and took my blood. And this morning, I was wondering about Dominic, and the next thing I knew, I saw him lying in bed, covered by a blue sheet."

Ava stared at her, her expression one of pure astonishment. "How is that even possible?"

"That's what I want to know!"

"Come in, child."

Maddy hesitated a moment before crossing the threshold.

Ava shut the door behind her. "Have you had visions of Dom before?"

"No. At least, I don't think so. He's here, isn't he? In bed, asleep?"

"Yes." Ava waved her toward the sofa. "Have a seat. I was just brewing a pot of tea. Would you like a cup?"

"No."

"Afraid I'll add more than sugar?"

"Exactly."

With a shrug, Ava disappeared into the kitchen. She returned shortly carrying two large ceramic mugs. She set one on the coffee table in front of Maddy, then sank into the overstuffed chair across from her.

Maddy glanced at the cup, her eyes narrowed with suspicion.

"There's nothing in it but herb tea and a bit of honey," Ava said. "Dominic would never forgive me if I offered you anything else."

Somewhat reassured, Maddy lifted the cup and took a taste.

"I'm not sure how to explain this link between you . . ." Ava paused, and a look of comprehension flashed in her eyes. "Of course! He's tasted your blood before. And you've tasted his, haven't you? That's the only answer that makes sense. The potion somehow intensified the bond between you. Combined with the blood in the potion, it's formed some kind of odd connection."

"I don't understand."

"Neither do I, but it's the only explanation. As for your memory . . ." Ava made a dismissive motion with her hand. "I can't explain that either."

"So, from now on, I'll always know where he is and what he's doing? Is that what you're saying?"

"Not at all, although I suppose it's possible, unless he blocks you."

"Can he do that?"

"Easily."

Maddy nodded slowly, thinking that was the best news she'd heard all day. "Does he know this is happening to me?"

"I don't know. I would imagine so."

Maddy stared at Ava in horror. It was disconcerting, having images of Dominic pop into her mind. What if he'd been in the shower? Or changing clothes? Heat flushed her cheeks. How embarrassing would that have been! "How long will it last?"

Ava shrugged one shoulder. "I have no idea. I've never heard of anything like this happening before."

"Just my luck," Maddy muttered under her breath. "Can you make it stop?"

"Probably. But it would be easier to simply ask Dom to block you."

"But then he'll know!"

"He already knows," Dominic said as he stepped into the room.

Blushing furiously, Maddy pressed her hands to her cheeks, wishing she could crawl under the rug.

Dominic threw Ava a look. "Do you mind?"

"Hmm. I know when I'm not wanted." Rising, she flounced out of the room.

"Listen, Maddy," Dominic said, taking Ava's place in the chair, "there's nothing for you to be embarrassed about. I don't know how this happened . . ."

"How do you even know about it? You were asleep."

"I don't know, but I did. Like I was saying, don't let it upset you. I'll block my thoughts and it'll be as if it never happened."

Looking doubtful, she nodded.

Dominic sat back, suddenly troubled by a new thought. Maybe what was happening to Maddy had nothing to do with his blood and everything to do with the black mist Ava had seen.

Pleading a headache, Maddy left Ava's house. At home, she plopped down on the sofa and pulled a fuzzy throw over her lap, wishing she had a cup of hot chocolate to warm her insides.

She let out a startled gasp when a cup suddenly appeared on the coffee table in front of her. A cup filled with steaming hot chocolate.

She was dreaming, she thought, and pinched herself. It hurt. And the cup, when she reached for it, was all too real. How was that possible? Feeling suddenly cold all over, she pulled the blanket up to her chin.

What was happening to her?

And how could she stop it?

Chapter 23

First thing in the morning, after a sleepless night, Maddy drove to Ava's house.

The witch answered the door in a fluffy white robe and furry slippers. "Maddy, come on in. I've been expecting you."

Maddy frowned as she followed Ava into the living room. How had Ava known she was coming? She hadn't known it herself until she got into the car.

"Sit down, dear."

Maddy took a place on the sofa. Ava took the chair.

"So, Maddy, I take it you're here because of what happened last night."

She didn't bother to ask how Ava knew. "Yes. What's happening to me?"

"I'm not exactly sure why it's happening, but apparently some of my magic has been transferred to you."

Feeling suddenly cold all over, Maddy stared at Ava, open-mouthed.

"I know, dear. I'm a little surprised myself. And I have no idea how it's possible. The only thing I can think of is that it's blood-related. Dominic has tasted yours. He's also tasted mine. And you've tasted his."

"Does he tell you everything?"

"Not everything," Ava said. "The three-way exchange of blood is the only explanation I can think of."

"But . . . am I a witch now?"

"It certainly seems that way. Just how powerful you are remains to be seen."

Alarmed, Maddy asked, "Am I a vampire, too?"

"No, dear. If you were, you'd be lost in the dark sleep now."

"Like Dominic." As soon as the thought crossed her mind, an image of Dominic lying in bed covered by that blue sheet flashed across her mind once again. Rising on shaky legs, she said, "I need to go home."

"Are you sure?" Ava asked, her brow furrowed with worry. "Perhaps you should spend the day here."

"No." Maddy shook her head. "I want to be alone for a while." It was a lie, she thought as she left the house and opened the car door. What she needed was Dominic. When he'd called about coming over last night, she had said she didn't feel well enough for company. She regretted it now, but it would be hours before he woke.

At home, Maddy paced the living room floor. *I'm a witch.* How could that be possible?

She tried saying the words out loud. "I'm a witch." The word *witch* seemed to echo off the walls. *Witch. Witch. Witch*. It was impossible. Inconceivable. She bit down on her lower lip. Had summoning a cup of hot chocolate been an aberration? A fluke? A one-time thing? If she tried to summon something else, would it work? Or had her magical ability vanished like the morning dew?

Pausing in front of the fireplace, she closed her eyes and held out her hand. In her mind's eye, she pictured one of the apples sitting in a bowl in the center of the kitchen table. *Come to me.*

And it was there, in her palm, red and real and solid.

Startled, she dropped it on the floor, then sank down on the sofa. "I *am* a witch," she murmured.

Unless Ava was playing some kind of supernatural joke on her. But if she was, it wasn't the least bit funny.

Maddy's tumultuous thoughts penetrated the dark sleep. Sitting up in bed, Dominic opened the blood link between them. He muttered an oath as he read her tangled emotions. She was frightened and confused about being a witch. A witch! What the hell?

He dressed in record time and transported himself to her house. On the porch, he pounded on the door.

It opened immediately. "Dominic! What are you doing here?"

"What the hell is this about you being a witch?"

She stood back so he could cross the threshold, then led the way into the living room. "How do you know about that?" she asked.

"Your thoughts woke me."

"I'm sorry."

He frowned at her. "Tell me what's going on."

She dropped down on the sofa and leaned back, her arms folded across her chest. "I don't know. Last night, after I left your house, I was sitting here, wishing I had a cup of hot chocolate, and the next thing I knew, there was a cup on the coffee table. And this morning, I thought about an apple, and one appeared in my hand."

Dominic swore softly. That was how his sister's magic had started. Calling small things to her—an orange, a book, her hairbrush, a DVD. But Lily had been born a witch.

"I went to see Ava earlier," Maddy said. "She thinks this is happening because of the potion she gave you."

"Why would that have any effect on you?"

"She thinks it's because you've tasted her blood and mine and I tasted yours."

A hell of a trifecta, Dominic thought as he dropped down beside her, his hand seeking hers. "That's the damnedest thing I've ever heard."

"Maybe it will go away."

"Yeah, maybe," he agreed. But he didn't think so. Maddy's sudden magical ability wasn't what bothered him. It was the kind of magic she might possess, he thought, remembering the darkness he had tasted when he kissed her. Was it still there? Pulling her closer, he claimed her lips with his. And quietly cursed Ava as he tasted the darkness once again. "Other than discovering that you're a witch, how do you feel?"

Maddy shrugged. "The same as always," she said slowly. "But not. I don't know how to explain it."

Seeing her troubled expression, he said, "Why don't we go get something to eat? Maybe a change of scene will take your mind off things for a while."

"Maybe," she agreed, although she doubted it. Still,

getting out of the house, being around other people, sounded better than sitting here, worrying.

Because Dominic had transported to her house, they took Maddy's car and drove to the mall. In the food court, they ordered hamburgers, shakes, and fries, then found a table.

They made small talk while they ate—the weather was cool, it looked like rain. She had a postcard from her parents. They were in Paris.

And all the while, in the back of her mind, Maddy wrestled with the thought that she might be a witch. She couldn't decide how she felt about it. Blessed? Or cursed? Gradually, she ran out of things to say, and silence fell between them.

Dominic sensed her thoughts but couldn't think of anything to say that would ease her mind. All the advice in the world wouldn't help.

"Do you want to take a walk through the mall?" Dominic asked as they left the food court.

"Might as well. I don't have anything else to do."

Hand in hand, they strolled from store to store, stopping now and then to look in this window or that.

Maddy came to an abrupt halt in front of a store already selling Halloween costumes, her gaze focusing on a mannequin dressed as a witch—black dress, black cloak, pointy black hat, a broom at her side. "Are you a good witch or a bad witch?" she muttered under her breath.

Sensing her distress, Dominic drew her into his arms, heedless of the other people strolling past. "It'll be all right, darlin'. I'm here for you," he murmured. And then wondered if that was the right thing to say. If not for him, none of this would have happened.

Maddy was silent on the drive home.

Dominic sat beside her, trying not to read her mind. But her thoughts came through crystal clear. She was afraid. She was curious. In the morning, she planned to go online and read everything she could find about witches and magic, black and white.

At home, she parked in the driveway, exited the car without waiting for him to open her door.

Dominic followed her up the stairs, waited while she unlocked the door, but didn't follow her inside.

She turned when she realized he wasn't behind her. "Aren't you coming in?"

"I didn't think you'd want me to."

Reaching out, she took his hand and tugged him across the threshold.

"That odd shift in the air I feel every time you come in, that's because you're a vampire, isn't it?"

"Yes. Most people don't notice it."

"What does it mean?" she asked as she threw her coat over the back of the sofa and sat down, gesturing for him to join her.

"Thresholds have power."

"What do you mean?"

"Not all thresholds," he explained. "Not businesses or public buildings. Just homes. Vampires can't enter uninvited. And can't remain in a house if their invitation is rescinded. It's an ancient protection that has survived for centuries and doubtless saved a lot of mortal lives."

"Amazing," she murmured. "Do you like being a vampire?"

"I didn't really have a choice in the matter, but yes, I like it fine."

"Does your sister like being a witch?"

"Yeah. She thinks it's great fun."

"And your mother?"

Dominic grinned. "She didn't know she was a witch for a long time. From what I've heard, she was surprised at first. She's very powerful now, almost as powerful as Ava."

"Is your sister married?"

"No. My father is very protective of Lily. He's a powerful man. So far, he's managed to scare off every boyfriend she's had."

"That's terrible."

Dominic shrugged.

"I guess all fathers are the same," Maddy remarked.

"I'm afraid it's worse for my sister," he said. "You see, among my kind, twins are rare. And offspring are always male."

Maddy stared at him, wide-eyed. "What? How is that possible?"

"I don't know, but that's the way it is. The way it's always been. Until my sister was born. My parents suspect that Ava somehow managed to work a little magic when my mother was pregnant."

"But . . . that's impossible."

"Everybody thought so. But there's no other way to explain Lily. So you can see why everyone in the family is so protective of her."

Maddy's first thought was to feel sorry for the girl. No

doubt her family watched her like hawks. And then she grinned. Being so rare among his people, Lily was likely everyone's favorite and probably spoiled rotten.

"Are we okay?" Dominic asked.

"What do you mean?"

"I feel responsible for everything that's happened. I wouldn't blame you if you never wanted to see me again."

"I was upset at first, but it's not your fault, not really. It's going to take some getting used to, but . . ." Maddy shrugged. "What else could I have done?"

"You should have refused to be part of Ava's cure."

"And let you die?" She shook her head. "I don't think so. Anyway, Ava didn't know there would be repercussions."

"Well, she should have." *Dammit*. He knew how dangerous dark magic could be. And so did Ava. He didn't know what he would have done if the spell's results had been worse. Or fatal.

"What's done is done," Maddy said, wishing she felt as okay with it as she sounded.

"It's getting late," Dominic said, fighting the urge to take her in his arms. "I should go home."

"I wish you wouldn't."

He looked at her, one brow arched in question.

"I don't want to be alone tonight, Dominic. Please stay with me."

"Sure, honey. Why don't you go get ready for bed and I'll tuck you in."

"Thank you."

"No problem." He watched her leave the room, determined to always be there when she needed him. He knew a lot about witches, having grown up with three of them. Hopefully, he could help Maddy learn to live with her new powers.

Sitting there, he listened to her get ready for bed—the splash of water as she washed her face, the rustle of clothing as she changed into her nightgown, the faint creak of the mattress as she settled under the covers.

When she called, "I'm ready," he went to her side.

"Sweet dreams, darlin'," he murmured as he drew the blankets up to her chin. "I'll be on the sofa if you need me."

"Thank you, Dominic."

"I love you, Maddy," he whispered, and wished he had the right to crawl into bed beside her, take her in his arms, and make love to her all night long.

Bending down, he kissed her lightly and left the room before his good judgment surrendered to his desire.

Chapter 24

When Maddy rose in the morning, she found Dominic asleep on the sofa. For a moment she simply stood there, watching him. She had read somewhere that vampires looked like corpses when they slept, but he looked wonderful, his dark hair tousled, his eyelashes like dark fans on his cheeks, his lips firm and well-shaped. She was sorely tempted to bend down and kiss him. Would he wake if she did? How would she explain it if he woke up?

Shrugging off the impulse, she tiptoed into the kitchen and put the coffee on, then sat at the table. The words, *I'm a witch*, whispered through her mind. Concentrating, she stared at the cupboard and summoned her favorite mug.

The door opened and the mug floated toward her and landed on the table in front of her. Maybe being a witch wasn't so bad, she thought, as she directed the pot to fill her cup.

"I could get used to this," she muttered as a whispered word added sugar to her coffee.

She glanced at the bread box and silently summoned a blueberry muffin. Unable to help herself, she laughed with pleasure when it instantly came to her hand. "The Sorcerer's Apprentice has nothing on you, Maddy Bainbridge," she said with a grin. "Move over, Glinda. Out of the way, Samantha. Maddy is here."

She flushed when she heard laughter behind her. Glancing over her shoulder, she saw Dominic standing in the doorway, grinning at her.

"Feeling pretty good this morning, aren't we?" Sauntering into the room, he took the chair across from her.

"I was just, ah, practicing."

"And doing a fine job from what I could see."

"How long have you been standing there?" she asked, feeling her cheeks grow hotter.

"Not long. Think you could magic a muffin for me?"

"Sorry, this is the last one, but if you stop grinning at me, I'll give you half of mine."

Dominic laughed. "I'm just kidding. I don't usually eat breakfast."

"Why not?"

"The hunting is better at night."

She blinked at him, wondering how she could have forgotten, even for a moment, that he wasn't like other men.

"I should probably go home," he said. "Ava must be wondering where the devil I am." Or maybe not, he thought, because she always seemed to know where he was. And what he was doing. Not necessarily a good thing.

"Oh."

He paused at the note of disappointment in her voice. "I can stay if you want."

"I wish you would. I don't know why I'm so reluctant to be alone."

"Big change in your life. I can understand it." Rising, he kissed her on the forehead. "I need to rest a little longer. Okay if I use one of the bedrooms?"

"Sure," she said, wondering why he hadn't done so last night. "Take any one you like."

He kissed her again, then headed up the stairs.

She listened for his footsteps and frowned when she didn't hear anything. That was odd, she thought, because the fourth step always creaked. He must be incredibly light on his feet.

Leaning back in her chair, she sipped her coffee. A vampire upstairs. A witch in the kitchen. What a couple they made.

She smiled as she imagined asking Dominic to move in with her. Not here, in her parents' house, of course, but in a new apartment after her folks got home. Living with a vampire would be like living with a man who worked nights and slept days, she mused. He wasn't so different from other men, except for the blood thing. Oddly enough, it didn't bother her as much as it should have. Or as much as she thought it should.

Of course, he was only here on vacation. He'd told her he was in business with his father, which meant that, at some point, he would have to go back to Hungary. That might be a deal breaker, she thought, and then shook her head. What was she thinking? As crazy about him as she was, she still hardly knew him. Certainly not well enough to be thinking of sharing an apartment with him.

Rising, she tucked her cup in the dishwasher and made her way upstairs to dress. When she reached the guest room, she stopped. And backed up. Surrendering to her curiosity, she opened the door a crack and peeked inside. The curtains were closed, the room dim.

Dominic had removed his shirt, boots, and socks. He lay on his back on top of the covers, one arm draped across his hard, flat belly.

Maddy grinned, wondering why no one had ever written a story about a sleeping prince. Dominic would have been perfect for the part. Tall, dark, and handsome as sin. She bit back a grin as she fought the urge to kiss him for the second time that day. Would he awaken? How deeply did he sleep?

Throwing caution to the winds, she tiptoed across the room, bent down, and kissed him lightly.

The next thing she knew, she was flat on her back and he was leaning over her, his expression momentarily fierce. And then he frowned down at her. "What are you doing?"

"Nothing," she squeaked.

"Did you kiss me?"

She nodded weakly.

"Couldn't you wait until I was awake?" he asked, grinning broadly.

"It was an experiment," she retorted.

"Do you want to explain that?"

Sitting up, she felt her cheeks grow warm. "I was wondering whether it would wake you up if I kissed you. You know, like the sleeping princess in a fairy tale?"

"Do I look like a princess to you?"

Maddy glared at him. "Of course not! But you looked like a prince. I just wondered if it worked in reverse. I didn't expect you to attack me."

"I'm sorry about that. I may have overreacted a little.

But in my defense, it *is* daylight and I *am* in a strange bed." He shrugged. "I guess my instinct for self-preservation just kicked in."

"I guess so," she muttered.

"I'm sorry," he said again. "Maybe we could kiss and make up."

"Do you promise not to attack me again?"

"On my honor." Drawing her gently into his arms, he kissed her lightly, and then more deeply.

She moaned softly as he stretched out on the bed, aligning her body with his as his mouth claimed hers again, his tongue doing incredible things.

She ran her palms up and down his back, loving the cool feel of his bare skin, slipped her fingers into the silky hair at his nape. Heat flowed through her, as warm and sweet as honey.

Maddy quivered as his tongue laved the side of her neck. She was drowning in pleasure—until she felt the prick of fangs. Feeling as if someone had doused her with ice water, she bolted upright.

Dominic stared up at her, and then swore softly. "I'm sorry, Maddy. Dammit, I didn't mean for that to happen."

She pressed her hand to her throat, her eyes filled with accusation.

"I'm sorry," he said again as he sat up.

"I can't believe you did that," she said, and shook her head as she realized how stupid her words sounded. He was a vampire, for crying out loud. It was what they did.

Dominic huffed a sigh, then reached for her hand, relieved when she didn't pull away. "It's like this," he said. "My desire for you is closely interwoven with my hunger, and my hunger increases my desire. It's hard for me to separate one from the other when you're in my arms. Do you understand?"

"Not really."

"Well, I can't blame you. I don't really understand it myself. Forgive me?"

She looked at their entwined hands, his so big and strong, hers smaller, weaker. Different and yet the same. "I forgive you. Do you want to go back to sleep?"

"No." *It wasn't really sleep*, he thought.

"Do you want to go to the store with me?"

"Depends on what you're going to buy."

"I was thinking of having steak for dinner. If you want to stay, that is."

"What do you think?" Swinging his legs over the edge of the bed, he stood and reached for his shirt.

Dominic hadn't been inside a grocery store for a good long time. At home, the house and pretty much everything that went on there was his mother's realm. Sure, she had sent him to the market from time to time when he was a teenager, but that had been ten or twelve years ago, and then usually only for milk or bread and butter.

Trailing after Maddy was a whole new experience, one he thoroughly enjoyed, he thought, as he admired the provocative sway of her hips. She was a careful shopper, checking prices, looking for specials. She bought a lot of fruits and vegetables, as well as eggs, milk, and bread. At the meat counter, she selected a couple of thick rib eye steaks. She also picked up a quart of Neapolitan ice cream, a can of whipped cream, and a bag of candy. Sweets for the sweet.

Maddy was keenly aware of Dominic trailing behind her. She had never gone shopping with a man in tow before—especially a vampire—and she wondered what he was thinking.

She had no trouble knowing what the other women in the store were thinking, though. One and all, every woman over the age of puberty slowed to look at Dominic. She glared at a pretty young woman who smiled at him, felt a hot rush of jealousy when he smiled back.

She chided herself for feeling that way. He was a handsome man. It was only natural that other women would check him out. There was no harm in looking. Heck, she would have done the same.

He followed her to the checkout line, and she felt another sharp stab of jealousy when the female checker smiled and batted her big blue eyes at him.

Dominic grinned inwardly, pleased and amused by Maddy's reaction.

He insisted on paying the bill even though she assured him it wasn't necessary.

"Hey, you're doing the cooking. It's only fair that I pay for the meal."

Outside, he loaded the groceries into the Mustang's trunk. When he opened the driver's side door, she handed him the keys. "Why don't you drive?"

"Sure, if you want."

With a smile, she went around to the passenger side. "I'm curious about something," she said as he pulled out of the parking lot.

"Oh? What's that?"

"Everywhere we go, women stare at you. I know

you're a good-looking guy, but I can't help wondering if you're purposely exerting some kind of vampire voodoo on them."

"Vampire voodoo?" he said with a grin. "No way. I'm just sexy as hell. Haven't you noticed?"

"Conceited much?" she asked, her voice laced with sarcasm.

"Hey, I'm kidding. It's just part of what I am. It's a little hard to explain."

She frowned at him. "So, they have no choice?"

"Of course they do. Maybe not initially. Mortals have a natural attraction to vampires of the opposite sex. It makes it easier for us to . . ." His voice trailed off. He probably shouldn't be telling her any of this.

"Easier to what?"

"To entice them."

Her brows went up. "So, this is all about seduction," she said, and then frowned. "Does that mean my feelings for you aren't my own?"

"The initial attraction doesn't last longer than a few minutes. Believe me, whatever feelings you have for me now are yours. The initial attraction just makes it easier to . . ." He raked his fingers through his hair. "It helps to . . ." Damn, this was harder than he'd thought.

She stared at him a moment and then understood. "It makes it easier for you to . . . to prey on them."

He nodded curtly.

Looking thoughtful, Maddy settled back in her seat. She guessed it made sense. Lots of animal predators had an innate allure to their prey. Why not vampires?

But she was jealous just the same.

* * *

Later that night, after dinner, Maddy found herself thinking about Dominic's parents. The idea of married vampires pricked her curiosity.

She glanced at Dominic, who was sitting beside her, and wondered what it would be like to be married to a vampire. Except for the blood thing and sleeping a good part of the day, he didn't seem so different from other men. Well, she amended, there was the longevity thing.

"How long do vampires live?" she asked.

Dominic frowned, somewhat surprised by the question. "A long time."

"How long?"

Knowing it would make the differences between them seem more insurmountable, he was reluctant to tell her.

"Dominic?"

"Hundreds of years."

"Hundreds? Of years?" she repeated, her face suddenly pale. "Do the other kind of vampires live that long, too?"

"Pretty much."

Maddy slumped back against the sofa as she tried to fathom living that long. It was inconceivable. Most people were lucky to live to be a hundred. With luck, a good marriage might last seventy years. A vampire marriage might last for *seven hundred*.

A burst of hysterical laughter bubbled up inside her. How on earth could anyone keep the excitement in a relationship that lasted for centuries? Wouldn't boredom set in after the first century or so? Surely there wouldn't be any more surprises, nothing new to discover. What would they find to talk about? What would it be like to see your grandchildren and great-grandchildren and great-great-grandchildren grow up and have children of their own? Merciful heavens, a family Christmas could involve hundreds of people.

The laughter died abruptly. Dominic might live hundreds of years. But she wouldn't.

"Maddy?" He reached for her hand, alarmed by the look in her eyes.

She took a deep, shuddering breath. "I'm okay."

"Are you?"

"What happens when your people marry mortals?"

"What do you mean?"

"If you marry, your wife will pass away long before you do."

So that was what was bothering her.

"Wait a minute," she said. "You said your father's a vampire, but your mother isn't."

He knew where this was going. "My mother was born a witch. They also tend to live longer than most people."

Maddy sighed. Why was she worrying about this? He hadn't mentioned marriage, and she certainly wasn't ready to tie the knot.

"Among my people, there are ways to prolong human life."

"What ways?"

"I don't know, exactly. I just know it's been done."

He slipped his arm around Maddy's shoulders. "How did this conversation turn so serious?"

"I don't know. I was just curious, I guess."

"That's understandable, all things considered." He

cupped her cheek in his palm and kissed her lightly. "I need to go check in with Ava," he said. "Are you going to be okay here alone?"

"Sure."

"I'll call you later."

"All right."

Dominic sighed. He hated to leave her, but he needed to find out if Ava had learned anything new about the Knights. He kissed Maddy, long and deep, savoring the sweet taste of her lips. troubled by the faint darkness that lingered there.

"Don't forget to lock up after me."

Maddy nodded as she followed him to the door, her lips still tingling from his kiss.

Later that night, as she got ready for bed, she found herself thinking about marriage again, imagining Dominic as her husband, sharing her life with him, bearing his sons.

Sons who would grow up to be vampires and have sons of their own.

It was a long time before sleep came.

After checking in with Ava and learning she hadn't made any progress in locating the Knights' stronghold, Dominic left the house to go hunting in the city. He was aware of being watched, knew the eyes following him belonged to members of Claret's coven. He frowned into the darkness, wondering if they were trailing him at her orders, of if they had some mischief of their own in mind.

After easing his hunger, he walked along Bourbon Street, then ducked into a nightclub. A moment later, one of the vampires passed in front of the doorway.

Dominic was on him before the vampire knew what hit him. “Why are you following me?”

“I’m not.”

“Like hell. What do you want?”

“Nothing.” The vamp twisted and turned, trying to escape, but Dominic held him fast. “If you don’t tell me, I’ll break your fool neck.”

Knowing that wouldn’t kill him, the vampire snorted.

Leaning closer to the vampire’s ear, Dominic whispered, “And then I’ll rip out your heart and burn it.”

“I don’t mean no harm,” the vampire gasped. “I’ve just never seen a Hungarian vampire before.”

“You’re lying.” Dominic sank his fingers into the man’s chest.

“All right! All right! She asked me to follow you.”

“Why?”

“She don’t want no one else to have you. Just her.”

Muttering, “That I believe,” Dominic turned the vampire loose.

Rubbing his chest, the vampire vanished.

Dominic heaved a sigh. This was getting out of hand, he mused as he turned and headed for home. Something had to be done about Claret. The sooner, the better . . .

Chapter 25

Keeping well out of sight, Jasper followed Dominic and the woman at a distance, waiting for his chance. Time after time, he'd let one opportunity after another to catch the pair slip by. But it had to be tonight.

The Elder Knight's patience was rapidly running out. And so was Claret's. He swore as he followed Dominic and the girl out of the movie theater to the parking lot. How the hell had he gotten into this predicament? And if and when he managed to capture Dominic, how the hell was he going to decide who should get the vampire—the witch or the Knight? No matter in whose favor he decided, the other one was going to be mad as hell. He couldn't decide which was more dangerous, the Elder Knight or the Transylvanian vampire. Both were powerful. Both were ruthless.

Cursing the fate that had brought him to such a precarious decision, Jasper got in his car. Keeping a safe distance between them, he followed the pair to the woman's house and drove on past.

He parked his car three blocks away, concealed his presence, and walked back to the female's residence, hoping to take the vampire unaware after he told the woman good night.

Hunkered down in the shadows, he waited for the vampire.

Dominic sat on the sofa, his legs outstretched. Maddy slept beside him, her head pillowed in his lap. He had hoped going out for dinner and a movie might cheer her up a little. It hadn't. He knew she was worried about the sudden change in her life, frightened by what it might mean. Hell, he was worried, too. Which was why he planned to spend the night.

As far as he knew, Ava hadn't yet figured out a way to dispel the darkness he still felt inside Maddy. Was the darkness linked to her magic?

Lifting her into his arms, he carried her into her bedroom. She stirred when he removed her shoes and tucked her into bed, but didn't wake.

He stood beside her for a long moment before returning to the living room. He paced the floor for a few minutes, then stepped outside to reinforce the wards he had set on the house.

He had just turned to go back inside when pain exploded through the back of his skull, dropping him into a well of blackness.

Dominic woke slowly, his head throbbing. Groaning softly, one hand pressed against the back of his head, he sat up. Where the hell was he? The room was pitch-black.

Small. Empty. It took him a moment to realize he was inside a cage.

Frowning, he stood, wondering who the hell had whacked him as he reached for the door. Pain lanced through his hand. Silver, he thought dully. The bars were coated with silver.

Light filtered into the room as someone opened a door and stepped inside.

"Claret," he muttered. "I should have known."

Her smug laughter filled the air.

Dominic glared at her as a little voice in the back of his mind whispered that history was repeating itself, only this time it wasn't his father inside the cage.

The vampire sashayed toward him. As always, she wore a long gown. This one—bright yellow—revealed her slender figure and lots of cleavage.

Her eyes gleamed red, and her fangs flashed when she grinned at him. A pair of heavy gloves protected her hands. Beckoning with one finger, she said, "Come here."

"Go to hell."

"Now, Dominic," she purred, "you might want to re-think your attitude."

"Yeah? Why would I do that?"

"Possibly because your girlfriend's life depends on it."

Dominic stared at her, even as fear for Maddy's life congealed in the pit of his stomach. "Where is she? What have you done with her?"

"I've done nothing to her. Yet. But her future health depends entirely on you."

"Where is she?" he asked again.

"I have someone looking after her. She's quite safe. For now."

Shit! "Who the hell hit me?"

"Jasper. He's been following you for days, waiting to take you by surprise."

Dominic grunted. "Working both sides of the street, huh? He must have decided the Elder Knight was the lesser of two evils."

She glowered at him. And then she laughed. "I fear the consequences would be the same if he had picked the Knight."

"He's dead?"

"Not yet."

"Who's holding Maddy?"

"Some humans under my control," Claret replied with a negligent shrug. "She'll come to no harm, as long as you cooperate."

It could be worse, Dominic thought. Maddy was better off with some human watchdogs than with Claret's coven. At least the mortals wouldn't be tempted to feed on her.

"I know you're thinking of contacting Ava in hopes she will rescue your ladylove," Claret remarked. "At the moment, your friend is under a powerful sleeping spell. But at the first sign that someone is trying to rescue her, my men will kill her. The consequences for the woman will be the same if Ava tries to come to your rescue. Do you understand?"

"I understand. I'll block my connection to Ava. I won't contact her, and she won't be able to contact me. I won't try to escape. Just promise me you won't harm Maddy."

"I promise, if you'll give me your word in return."

Jaw clenched, Dominic nodded. Ava had warned him that Jasper was a powerful wizard. He had no cause to doubt it. Nor did he doubt that Claret's powers were even stronger. Or that she would kill Maddy without a qualm.

"Your arm," she said, a layer of steel underlying her tone.

"I thought you said my blood was vile?"

"I'm willing to try again." She smiled wolfishly. "Even though it tasted awful, the power was still there."

Jaw clenched, Dominic stood as close to the bars as he dared and thrust out his arm. He grimaced as she grasped his wrist and bit down, hard.

He was sorely tempted to make a grab for her, even though he knew it would be foolish. She would simply elude him by dissolving into mist. And she might make Maddy pay for it. With that thought in mind, he stood compliant while she fed.

After several minutes, the vampire lifted her head, her lips crimson with his blood, her smile one of pleasure and triumph. "Until tomorrow night," she murmured, and with a flick of her hand, she vanished from the room.

Dominic swore long and loud as he sank down on the cement floor. He could endure whatever he had to, he thought as he blocked his thoughts from his great-grandmother, as long as it meant Maddy's survival.

Chapter 26

She was lost in a hazy, dreamlike world. She could hear voices around her but couldn't open her eyes, couldn't speak, couldn't move. The air was cold, the bed beneath her—if it was a bed—hard and unyielding. Fear took hold of her, permeating every fiber of her being. Was she dying? Dead? Buried alive? Where was she? Where was Dominic?

Her mind screamed his name, over and over again.

But there was only emptiness.

And darkness.

Dominic roused to the sound of Maddy's silent screams. Bolting upright, he reached out to her. *Maddy, love, I'm here.*

Dominic? Dominic, help me!

Hush, darlin'. Don't be afraid. You're under a sleeping spell of some kind. Not a very powerful one, he thought, if they could still connect.

Where am I?

I don't know. But I'll come to you as soon as I can.

When?

It might be a while. But don't be afraid, he said again. *I'll find you, no matter how long it takes. I love you, Maddy. We'll see the better side of this yet, I promise.*

I love you, Dominic. I love you. . . .

Hands clenched, Dominic stared into the darkness that surrounded him as her voice faded away.

One way or another, he'd find a way out of this mess and rescue Maddy before it was too late. And Claret would pay dearly for her treachery.

Ava swore softly as one location spell after another failed to reveal Dominic's whereabouts. Frustration rose within her. Never before had her magic failed her so completely. She could only assume that Dominic did not wish to be found, that he was employing some kind of vampire magic to thwart her efforts. The question was, why?

Next, she tried to locate Maddy, but she saw only darkness. Confused, she picked up her phone and tried calling Dominic again. But there was no answer.

It was as if he had disappeared off the face of the earth.

Dominic stretched out on the floor of the cage. Leaning back against the silver bars was out of the question. His interior clock told him it was after midnight. The pain clawing at his vitals told him he needed to feed to replace the blood Claret had taken the night before.

And even as the thought crossed his mind, the door opened and she glided into the room, her long, white gown glowing in the dim light from beyond the doorway. Another room, perhaps?

"How are you this evening?" She dropped a leather satchel on the floor, then pulled on the gloves she had worn the night before to protect her flesh from the thin layer of silver that coated the bars.

"How do you think?"

She laughed softly. "Aren't you going to ask me how I am?"

Dominic snorted. "I really don't give a damn."

"I'd think a man in your position might be a little nicer."

"I'll treat you like Cleopatra or the Queen of Sheba, whichever you like, if you let me out of here."

"If only I could believe that." She looked wistful for a moment, then said, "Come to me."

Dominic longed to refuse, but there was no point in it. Not when Maddy's life was in the vampire's hands. Feeling like a whipped cur, he obediently closed the distance between them and thrust his arm through the bars.

Claret smiled triumphantly as she latched onto his wrist and drank. And drank.

Until he thought she would never stop. This wasn't a taste, or a sip, but a meal, he thought morbidly, and wondered what would happen if she drained him dry. Would it destroy him? Or leave him an empty husk, aware of his surroundings but unable to move or speak?

She purred like a contented cat when she lifted her head. "I can feel your power running through me like lightning," she murmured, a dreamy look in her dark eyes. "And because you've been so good to me, I've brought you something to drink." Reaching into the satchel, she withdrew a plastic bag and handed it to him. "Bon appétit," she said cheerfully and vanished from the room.

Dominic stared at the bag in his hand. Old, cold blood. But beggars couldn't be choosers; he desperately needed to replace what he'd lost before his body reacted and the pain went from a dull ache to excruciating. Eyes closed, he bit into the bag and pretended it was Maddy's blood spreading through him, easing his agony.

The Elder Knight stood in the middle of his chambers, his rage growing with every breath as he listened to Jasper make one poor excuse after another for his failure to produce Quill's son.

Reaching the edge of his patience, the Elder Knight muttered an incantation.

Jasper immediately stopped talking. Frozen in place, he could only stand there while the Elder Knight probed his mind. It felt like a knife slicing into him, uncovering every secret, exposing every lie.

"So," the Elder Knight drawled. "You delivered Quill's son to a female vampire by the name of Claret. I hope you have made your peace with whatever god you worship."

Terror congealed in the pit of Jasper's belly. He tried frantically to speak, but to no avail.

"If you have any last words, now is the time to say them."

Jasper swallowed hard. "My lord, I know I failed you, but I had no choice," he said, one word tripping over another in his haste. "She was there, threatening my life. I knew I would never be able to bring you the vampire if I was dead. But I know where she is holding him. I can take you to him."

The Elder Knight's eyes narrowed thoughtfully. If Jasper was telling the truth, if Quill's son was truly imprisoned in New Orleans, it would be wiser to go to where the vampire was being held rather than trust Jasper to bring the vampire back to the stronghold.

"Do not fail me again," the Elder Knight warned. "Or what Ava did to you years ago will be as nothing compared to what I have in mind."

Hands clenched at his sides to still their trembling, Jasper whispered, "I understand, my lord."

"We will leave in the morning," the Elder Knight said curtly.

The vampires would be at rest then, which would greatly reduce the risk of discovery and confrontation.

Chapter 27

Maddy felt as if she was being cocooned in cotton wool. She seemed to experience the world through a thick, white haze. Her arms and legs felt like lead and it was almost impossible to move. The room was dark, but she sensed it was daylight outside. She also sensed a presence in the room.

Gathering all the strength she could muster, she turned her head to the side, felt a chill run through her when she saw two men standing across the room, one on each side of the door. Unmoving. Unblinking. At first, she thought they were vampires, but that didn't seem right. If they were creatures of the night, wouldn't they be trapped in the dark sleep? They looked like . . . like zombies.

Dominic had said she was under some kind of spell. Could she break it? How did one break a spell anyway? She had never even cast one. So far, her abilities had been limited to summoning apples and hot chocolate, though she still didn't understand how one born without magic could suddenly possess it.

She had watched Ava cast a spell, Maddy thought

darkly. But she had no cauldron, no herbs or magical words. No magic wand.

Nothing but her will to be free.

Concentrate, Maddy.

She focused on one of the zombies.

Concentrate.

She stared into his eyes. *Look at me,* she commanded. *Look at me!*

Nothing.

She tried again, and when that failed, she took a deep, calming breath before focusing on the other zombie. *Look at me.*

Ever so slowly, he turned his head toward her, although she wasn't sure if he actually saw her. *Open the door.* Nothing. *You will open the door. Now!*

He blinked at her. Once. Twice.

Moving like a tin soldier, he did as bidden. Then stood beside the bed. Unmoving. Unblinking.

Now for the hard part, Maddy thought. She had to get up.

It seemed to take forever to sit up, to swing her legs over the side of the bed. Feeling as though she had just fought her way through an invisible wall, she sat there for several minutes. And then she glanced at the door. It seemed to be a million miles away. After what seemed like an eternity, she gathered the strength to stand.

It was an effort to put one foot in front of the other. As she neared the door, she glanced back at the zombie standing beside the bed, but he just stood there. Unblinking. Unmoving.

Her heart pounded as she reached for the doorknob. Would they let her leave?

But they simply stood there, as though waiting for someone to command them.

Her whole body was trembling by the time she made it out of the room and discovered she was in a dilapidated house that should have been dismantled decades ago. The door creaked like a soul in torment when she opened it.

She blinked against the sun and for a moment, she forgot why she had wanted to go outside.

A gust of wind made her shiver. It rattled the window frame and sent a handful of dead leaves scudding across the street.

Home, she thought. *I want to go home.*

With no idea where she was, and no idea how to find her way home, Maddy stumbled out of the ramshackle building. She shivered as she made her way through a yard thick with weeds and broken bottles, paused when she reached what was left of the sidewalk. Which way to go? Deciding it didn't matter, she turned left and staggered down the street.

Ava paced the living-room floor, her concern for Dominic growing with every passing minute. Where was he? And why couldn't she contact him? Had he blocked their bond? And if so, why now?

Determined to try one more time, she went into the den and picked up her scrying mirror. Peering into it, she chanted, "Powers of earth, wind, and fire, reveal to me what I desire. Show me my great-grandson."

Nothing but her own worried face staring back at her.

"Show me Maddy."

A ripple in the mirror's surface, the blackness swirling,

fading, until it revealed an image of Maddy moving like a sleepwalker down a rutted path in the middle of nowhere.

After jumping into her car, a location spell led Ava to an abandoned patch of land. She breathed a sigh of relief when she saw Maddy stumbling slowly along, her head down. Thank the good Lord, the girl was still alive.

Ava slowed and pulled up alongside the girl. "Maddy?" She frowned when Maddy kept walking. "Maddy!"

Worried now, Ava parked the car, jumped out, and darted around the front. Coming up behind Maddy, she laid a hand on her shoulder, bringing her to a stop. "Maddy!"

No response.

Ava frowned as she detected the faint, lingering signature of magic. Vampire magic. Maddy seemed to still be under the spell, but if that was true, how had she managed to escape?

Ava glanced around, her nerves suddenly on edge. Grabbing Maddy by the arm, she opened the passenger door and shoved her into the seat, then slammed the door and hurried around to the driver's side. Pulling the door closed, she stomped on the gas and didn't slow down until she reached civilization.

At home, she undressed Maddy, slipped a nightgown over her head, and tucked her into bed. After weaving a protective spell around her, Ava went into the den in search of answers.

Claret let out a string of epithets when she entered the dilapidated old house and found the girl gone. How had she escaped? And where had she gone?

Enraged, she sank her fangs into the first man and

quickly drained the life from him, then tossed him aside and buried her fangs in the other one.

Dominic felt Claret's rage before she entered the room.

She glared at him, her eyes red, her hands clenched, her mouth stained with fresh blood.

Dominic went cold all over. "You didn't . . . tell me that's not her blood."

"We had a deal," she said. "You broke it."

"What the hell are you talking about?"

"She's gone!"

"Gone?" Dominic stared at her. "I had nothing to do with it, I swear."

Claret regarded him through narrowed eyes for several moments. "If you didn't break your word, how do you explain the shadow of magic left behind? Was it left by your great-grandmother?"

Dominic frowned thoughtfully. "I don't believe it," he murmured. But it was the only explanation. "It wasn't Ava," he said with a grin. "It was Maddy."

Claret looked at him in disgust. "Do I look like a fool? How could that puny mortal undo my magic?"

"Ava cast a spell on me when I was hurt. The spell she used was dark magic, and one of the ingredients was Maddy's blood. The fact that I've consumed both Ava's blood and Maddy's must have altered the spell in some way. I don't know how it happened, but I think some of Ava's magic was transferred to Maddy."

"That's the most ridiculous thing I've ever heard."

Dominic shrugged. "It's the only answer that makes sense."

"Come here."

"No."

"Come here," she demanded.

"If you want it, come and get it."

Turning on her heel, she stalked toward the door. "Jonathan, Pierre, Tomás, I need you."

Dominic swore as three burly vampires sauntered into the room. Two of them carried sharp wooden stakes; the third held a silver-bladed dagger in one gloved hand and a pair of shackles in the other.

"Chain him to the bars." A wave of Claret's hand unlocked the door.

Smiling faintly, the vampires entered the cage, a challenge in their eyes as they dared him to resist.

Shit. In his weakened condition, denied fresh blood for a couple of days, he couldn't take on all three of them. Especially with Claret waiting in the wings. "Call them off," he muttered. "You win."

She motioned the vampires out of the cage and locked the door. "Your arm. Now."

He shuffled forward and held out his arm. "I could use a drink, too," he said with a faint smile.

She grasped his arm, her gaze on his face, her expression pensive.

"Come on," he coaxed. "If you're going to keep feeding on me, I'm going to need more nourishment than a bag of cold blood."

"I'll think about it," she growled, and sank her fangs

into his wrist. She took a long drink, looked up at him, and smiled before sinking her fangs into him again.

Dominic lay stretched out on his back, his hands folded behind his head. Apparently the taste of his blood was no longer vile. What the hell did that mean?

Maddy had escaped. He had no idea how she'd managed it. He had to believe she'd made it safely home. Any other outcome was unthinkable.

Closing his eyes, he opened the link between them. *Maddy? Maddy, are you there*? When there was no answer, he feared the worst, and then realized she was asleep. Deeply asleep. Needing to make sure she was unhurt, he opened the link between himself and his great-grandmother. *Ava?*

Dominic! Thank the Lord, you're alive. Where are you?

In a cage somewhere.

A cage? she questioned. And then she cursed. *Claret.*

Right the first time. Is Maddy with you?

Yes. She's fine, just recovering from some sort of vampire spell. She's remarkably strong, Dom. I don't know how, but she managed to escape the vampire's magic.

But she's all right?

She will be in a day or so. I gave her something to help her sleep. Why have you been blocking me?

I promised Claret I wouldn't have any contact with you or try to escape if she wouldn't hurt Maddy.

Ava grunted. *Keep our link open. I'm going to cast a location spell.*

Wait until morning, he said, *when Claret and her coven are at rest.*

Dominic closed his eyes, opened them again when he heard footsteps. A moment later the door opened and two of Claret's vampires entered the room. One held a wooden stake. The other a sword.

Dominic sat up when they unlocked the cage door.

"All we want is a taste," one of the vampires said.

"And then what?"

"I'll bring you some fresh blood. Make up your mind quick. It's almost dawn. What do you say?"

"I could use some fresh blood."

"We have a deal, then?"

"What will Claret say when she finds out about this?"

"She doesn't need to know."

"You're not shittin' me about the blood, are you?" Dominic asked, taking note that they hadn't locked the door behind them.

"Blood for blood," the guy with the sword said.

Dominic held out his arm.

The two vampires grinned at each other. The one with the stake handed it to his partner. The guy with the sword laid it across the back of Dominic's neck.

Dominic held still as the first vampire bit down on his wrist. He let the man drink until he was high, thinking that a few more sips and the guy wouldn't be good for anything for a day or two.

The second vampire watched avidly, licking his lips. Finally, he pulled the first away, grabbed hold of Dominic, and buried his fangs in his arm.

With an oath, Dominic grabbed the stake from the first vampire's hand, kicked him out of the way, then drove it into the feeding vampire's back and into his heart.

"Blood for blood," Dominic muttered as he dispatched the second vampire.

Scrambling to his feet, he darted out the door and willed himself home.

Ava threw her arms around him when he materialized in the living room. "Thank the good Lord," she murmured. "I was just about to come after you." Taking a step back, she looked him up and down. "Is that your blood?"

"No. I destroyed two of Claret's vampires."

"Good for you."

"How's Maddy?"

"She hasn't fully regained consciousness yet. I'm beginning to worry."

"Yeah, me too."

On his way to the guest room he took a detour into the bathroom. He hadn't showered in days. And he didn't want Maddy to see him in a bloodstained shirt. He was in and out of the shower and dressed in less than five minutes.

Barefooted, his hair still damp, he headed for the guest room. Maddy lay on her back, her hair spread across the pillow, her face almost as pale as the white sheet that covered her.

Sitting on the edge of the mattress, he took one of her hands in his. "Maddy, come back to me." His mind brushed hers. *Maddy?* He swore softly when there was no response. Parting her lips, he bit into his wrist and let several drops of his blood fall into her mouth.

She grimaced and let out a low groan.

"Maddy?"

Her eyelids fluttered open. For a moment, she stared

at him, her expression blank, and then she sat up and wrapped her arms around his neck. "Dominic! Oh, Dominic, I thought you'd never come."

"I got here as soon as I could," he replied, one arm holding her close while he stroked her back. "Are you all right? How do you feel?"

"I don't know. What happened?"

"It's a long story. Let's just say all's well that ended well."

"Tell me."

"As near as I can figure, Jasper managed to sneak up on me and knock me out. When I came to, you were gone and I was Claret's prisoner. She threatened to kill you if I tried to escape or tried to get in touch with Ava." He caressed her cheek with his knuckles. "How did you get away?"

"I don't know. I was just so afraid. Two men were watching me. They never spoke, just stood there, hardly blinking. I concentrated on the two of them, trying to make some sort of connection. I'm not sure how I did it, but I finally got through to one of them and convinced him to let me go. It was strange, but the other one didn't try to stop me. I don't remember leaving the house or much of what happened after that." She shivered. "Take me home, Dominic."

"Do you think that's a good idea?"

"I don't know. I don't care. I just want to be in my own house, sleep in my own bed." She looked up at him, her eyes haunted. "You'll stay with me, won't you? I don't want to be alone."

He nodded. He could understand her need to go home, to be surrounded by things that were familiar and reassuring. Whether they were at his place or hers, he intended to stay close to her.

At home, Maddy went upstairs. She felt unclean, somehow, as if she had been in the presence of evil. And perhaps she had. She made the water as hot as she could stand, added a healthy amount of bubble bath, and stepped into the tub.

Dominic sat on the sofa, his head cocked to the side as he listened to Maddy fill the tub. He heard the soft whisper of cloth against skin as she undressed, the faint splash as she slid into the tub, a sigh as the water closed over her. She'd been through hell, he thought, and although he wasn't to blame for Claret's actions, he felt guilty just the same.

He frowned when the doorbell rang. What the hell was Ava doing here? Thinking there might be trouble, he opened the door and stepped out on the porch. "What's up? I just left a few minutes ago."

"I know, but we need to talk."

"You could have called." When her gaze slid away from his, he asked, "Is something bothering you?"

"In a way." She folded her arms, her expression somber. "I've been thinking it might be time for us to leave New Orleans."

"What?"

"Now that Claret's had a taste of you, she's not going to be happy until she gets her hands on you again."

Dominic nodded. He'd thought of that, of course.

"Your life is in danger here. For that matter, so is Maddy's as long as you're around. I think it would be best for all concerned if you and I went home. Your father can send someone else to take your place here."

"I'm not leaving the country," he said adamantly. "Not without Maddy."

"Then we'll go to my place in Oregon and take her with us."

"Ava . . ."

"This isn't open for discussion!" she snapped.

Dominic reared back as her power slammed into him. "Dammit, woman, what the hell are you doing?"

"Reminding you of who's in charge here."

Throwing up his arms in a gesture of surrender, he said, "All right, all right. I get the message. I'll discuss it with Maddy tomorrow. I didn't know you had a place in Oregon," he said with a disarming smile.

Chapter 28

Claret bit out an oath as she stared at the cage and the two bodies sprawled inside. "Damn fools," she muttered. Not that she could fault them for trying. A taste of Dominic's blood was worth the risk. But that was neither here nor there. The only thing that mattered now was that Dominic was gone. No telling if or when she would ever be lucky enough to have him in her clutches again. More's the pity.

With a rueful shake of her head, she left the house. Had her vampires survived Dominic's escape, they would have been just as dead for daring to lay their hands on what was hers and hers alone.

Only they would have met their end by her hand instead of his.

Chapter 29

Maddy woke late. Feeling slightly disoriented, she lay there a moment, staring up at the ceiling. Her memory of what had happened was vague. She remembered waking up in a strange place. Feeling lethargic. There'd been two men. Or two creatures who had once been men. Had she performed magic? She seemed to recall trying to mesmerize them. Compelling them to let her go. She remembered walking down an unfamiliar street with no idea where she was or where to go. And then Ava had pulled up and taken her home.

She thought Dominic had communicated with her somehow. She seemed to recall his voice in her mind. And then he had been there. It had all been so bizarre. She could almost believe she had dreamed the whole thing.

Moving like a zombie herself, Maddy forced herself to get out of bed. She tiptoed down the hall, opened the door to the guest room, and peeked inside to see if Dominic had stayed the night. For a moment, she just stood there, staring at him, her emotions dangerously close to the surface.

With a sigh, she quietly closed the door and shuffled into the kitchen. Maybe a cup of black coffee would clear her head.

Jasper stared at the cage that had held Quill's son. A cage that now held only the ashes of two Transylvanian vampires. And knew that his life was over. He risked a glance at the Elder Knight and shuddered. Gregory's face was red with rage.

"Can. You. Explain. This?" The Elder Knight spat out each word.

Slowly, Jasper shook his head. "He was here. I saw him. I can still smell him."

Screaming, "He's not here now!" the Elder Knight wrapped his hands around the warlock's throat. "You have failed me for the last time, you bloody, ignorant, inept fool!"

"My lord," Jasper squeaked. "Wait . . . please. You might yet . . . have need . . . of me."

"For what, pray tell, you useless, spineless toad."

Magic shimmered in the air. Jasper let out a horrified cry as he fell from the Elder Knight's grip.

And croaked when he hit the floor.

The Elder Knight cackled. "Perhaps you can find a princess to kiss your ugly face and break the spell."

Still laughing, Gregory 73 transported himself back to the Knights' stronghold.

Chapter 30

It was late afternoon when Dominic rose. Opening his senses, he searched the house for Maddy, knew a moment of relief when he located her in the living room.

His gaze moved over her as he sauntered into the room. He knew just by looking at her that she was still experiencing the aftereffects of Claret's spell.

She smiled faintly when she looked up and saw him standing there. "Hi."

"Hi, yourself. How are you feeling?"

"Like I was drugged."

"I guess you were, in a way. Do you hurt anywhere?"

"No."

Closing the distance between them, he sat beside her, his arm sliding around her shoulders as his gaze searched hers. She looked tired, her face pale.

"I feel so weird," she confessed.

"That's understandable," he said, "considering all you've been through."

"I guess. It's just all so mixed up in my head, I don't know what was real and what wasn't."

"Near as I can tell, Claret worked some kind of vampire

voodoo on you. Magic that you managed to overcome. No small feat, I might add. Claret's an old vampire."

"How did you escape?"

"Just lucky, I guess. Two of the members of her coven tried to take my blood. I had other ideas."

Resting her head on his shoulder, she said, "I'm glad you got away. Glad we both got away. Do you think she'll keep trying?"

"I'm afraid so. That's why we're leaving town."

"You're leaving?" Sitting back, she looked up at him. "Where are you going? How long will you be gone?"

"Ava has a place in Oregon. We're going there. I'm not sure for how long."

"I'll miss you."

"I'd miss you, too, which is why I'm wondering if you'd consider coming with us."

"I'd love to."

Dominic blew out a sigh. He'd been afraid she might say no, in which case he was prepared to insist, because there was no way he was leaving her here alone as long as Claret and the Knights were a threat.

"How soon are you leaving?"

"I'm not sure. Probably in a day or two. After all that's happened, Ava's anxious to get out of town." It galled him to leave, but Ava was right—as long as he was in New Orleans, Maddy's life was in danger.

"I'll have to let my parents know. And shut up the house."

"That shouldn't take long. Once we're settled in Oregon, Ava will be able to help you explore your magical abilities without a lot of distractions."

"I guess so. It's just hard to believe that I'll ever be any good at it. I mean, I'm not really a witch. Am I?"

"Only time will tell," he murmured, drawing her back into his arms. "Until then, I can think of a wonderful way to pass the time."

"Can you?" Anticipation thrummed through her. "What did you have in mind?"

"This." Lowering his head to hers, he brushed his lips over hers before claiming them in a long, slow kiss that made her toes curl with pleasure. "And this." He kissed her longer, deeper, until she was breathless, every nerve quivering with longing.

Dominic groaned low in his throat. Damn, she was dynamite in his arms. Reluctantly, he lifted his head and put a little space between them.

Maddy looked up at him, wondering why he had stopped, until she saw the faint red glow in his eyes. Remembering what he'd said, about his hunger being roused by desire, she scooted a little further away.

He flashed her a wry grin. "Smart girl."

She nodded uncertainly.

"Hey, not to worry. I'm not out of control, but damn, Maddy, I want you like I've never wanted anything else in my life."

She nodded again, not knowing what to say, wondering how much danger she would actually be in if he ever lost control. It was something to think about.

"I think I'd better go."

"All right." She lifted her head for his kiss, glad that the red had faded from his eyes. Even though she knew he was a vampire, it was disconcerting to see proof of it.

He kissed her quickly. "I'll see you later." After he'd

fed, he thought, when he had his hunger and his desire in check.

"Okay." She walked him to the door, watched him descend the porch stairs. And disappear into the darkness.

Brow furrowed, Maddy hurried back inside and closed and locked the door. Her life had turned upside down in a remarkably short time, she mused. She had met vampires and witches, good and bad. Both fascinated and frightened her. And now, she possessed a small degree of magic herself, all because of Ava's spell. That, too, was both fascinating and frightening. It would probably be wise to learn exactly what she could and couldn't do, for her own safety and that of those around her.

But the real question was, did she want to pursue something so exciting? Something so powerful and potentially dangerous?

It was a sobering question that lingered in her mind, one for which she had no ready answer.

The next two days were busy ones for Maddy. She called her parents and let them know she was taking a vacation with a friend. She cleaned the house from top to bottom, paused the utilities, paid the gardener a month in advance. Her parents had put a hold on the mail when they left, so she didn't have to worry about that.

She spent an hour or two deciding what clothes to pack. Grabbed a couple of books. And she was ready to go.

* * *

Ava's place in Portland looked like a dollhouse, quaint and lovely and surrounded by flowers and a swath of emerald lawn. The inside was just as amazing. Maddy shook her head as she glanced around, thinking she had never been in a house that seemed almost alive; there was a strong undercurrent of magic that made her skin tingle.

The downstairs held a living room, a small kitchen and dining room, and a tiny bathroom. There were three bedrooms upstairs—one large and two smaller ones. The larger one was Ava's, of course. It looked like something out of an old English castle, with expensive rugs on the floor and tapestries on the wall.

Ava assigned Maddy to a room done in shades of pink and mauve. A single window overlooked the backyard, which reminded Maddy of a forest in fairyland, filled with ferns and flowers and a small pond.

Dominic's room was across the hall. Maddy wondered if Ava had decorated it for him, as it was all done up in brown and beige. The window was covered with a heavy drape to block the sun's light.

"What's on the third floor?" Maddy asked as they returned to the living room.

"It's where I practice my magic." Ava fixed her and Dominic with a stern look. "Neither of you are to venture inside unless I'm with you."

"Better listen to her," Dominic said. "No telling what skeletons she has behind that door."

Maddy stared at him, wide-eyed. Was he joking?

Ava glared at him. "I'm hungry. Let's have lunch."

"You two go ahead," Dominic said. "I'm going upstairs

to rest awhile." He winked at Maddy. "Call me if you need me."

Maddy stared after him, wondering if he was warning her, or simply assuring her that he would heed her call.

Looking annoyed, Ava rolled her eyes. "Don't listen to Dom. You're in no danger from me or anyone else while you're here. What would you like for lunch?"

"Anything is fine," Maddy said. She followed Ava into the dining room, took the chair the witch indicated. A few words from Ava set the table. A wave of her hand produced a platter of sandwiches, one bowl of macaroni salad and another of potato chips. Two bottles of water and two cans of soda came next.

Maddy blinked in astonishment. "I guess you never have to cook."

Ava grinned at her. "Oh, I prepare a meal now and then, but this is so much faster. And easier."

With some trepidation, Maddy reached for a sandwich. It was one thing to summon an apple to her hand, quite another to produce a meal out of thin air. "Do you think I really have magic? That it wasn't just a fluke of some kind?"

"Oh, you have it, my dear. I can feel it inside you, trying to get out. But, as I said, it remains to be seen how strong it is. There are those who believe everyone is blessed with some degree of magic. Some look for it. A few find it. Some never do. For all you know, you may have a distant ancestor who had the gift."

"It's possible, I suppose." She'd never been interested in genealogy. For all she knew, she could have kings and queens and witches somewhere in her ancestry.

"One thing I've learned," Ava said, filling her glass with soda, "is that anything is possible.

"There are many types of magic," Ava went on. "Ceremonial magic is used to summon spirits. White magic summons angels. Dark magic can be used to summon demons to do a witch's bidding. However, I don't advise it. There's fire magic and air magic and water magic."

"And food magic," Maddy said, gesturing at the table.

Ava laughed. "Indeed. Later tonight, if you like, I'll lend you my Book of Shadows."

"What's that?"

"Many witches keep them to record information or spells from other witches, or to jot down their own favorite spells, what works and what doesn't, symbols, invocations, and runes, that sort of thing. I've recorded a number of enchantments and rituals in mine. You might think about starting a book of your own."

Dominic woke with the setting sun. He listened to the sounds of the house, sensed that it had rained earlier, caught the scent of damp earth, listened to the whisper of the wind in the trees.

Rising, he transported himself into the city to satisfy his hunger, then returned to Ava's. He found the women in the living room, bent over a leather-bound book laid open on the coffee table.

"Well, what a cozy coven," he remarked, dropping down on the chair across from the sofa. "Got room for one more?"

"We always have room for you," Ava said with a smile.

He jerked his chin toward the book. "What's that?"

"It's a Book of Shadows," Ava replied. "Sort of like a witch's diary."

"I see. So, I broke in on a class in Witchcraft 101."

Maddy grinned at him. "It's all so fascinating!" she exclaimed. "I had no idea anything like this even existed. I mean, Ava is amazing. She knows so much!"

"Yeah," Dominic agreed. "Sometimes I think she knows too much."

"I know your parents are worried about you," Ava retorted. "Your mother wants you to come home."

Dominic shook his head. "No way."

"She knew you'd say that. Your father is thinking of coming here, because we don't seem to be making any progress in finding the Knights' new stronghold."

Dominic muttered an oath under his breath.

"Don't worry, I talked him out of it," Ava said. "At least for now. We've been going about this all wrong. Jasper is working for the Knights. He's a powerful wizard, but deep inside he's a coward. We need to find Jasper and convince him that it's in his best interest to tell us the location of the stronghold. I don't know why I didn't think of it before."

Dominic grunted softly. Ava was right, he thought with a wry grin. But then, she usually was.

The rest of the evening passed pleasantly enough. Dominic sat back in his chair, content to watch Ava instruct Maddy in a few simple spells. He was amazed at how quickly Maddy mastered them. Not as quickly as his sister, but then, Lily had been born a witch, so it was only natural that her magic came more readily. Still, he was impressed with Maddy's ability. He watched her hands, so expressive, as she wove a simple spell. He liked the way her eyes glowed with excitement, her unabashed sense of accomplishment when she succeeded.

At ten o'clock, Ava closed the book. "I think that's enough for tonight. I'll see you two in the morning." Bending down to kiss Dominic's cheek, she whispered, "Behave yourself," before going upstairs.

Dominic stared after her. She was something else, he thought.

"Did we bore you to death?" Maddy asked.

"What? No. It was pretty entertaining, actually. Especially when you tried to conjure a cat and got a rat instead."

"Hey, it could have happened to anyone."

"If you say so. Seriously, I'm impressed with your talent."

"Really?"

"Really. Enough shop talk," he said. Moving to sit on the sofa beside her, he slipped his arm around her shoulders. "Let's talk about us."

"What about us?"

"You know I love you. I know you love me." He caressed her cheek with his fingertips. "I want you. You want me." His gaze moved over her face. "If I asked you to marry me, what would you say?"

"Are you asking?"

"I think so."

"Well, when you know for sure, ask me again."

"Will you marry me, Maddy?"

With tears of joy shining in her eyes, she murmured, "Yes, Dominic, I'll marry you."

"Maddy!" Pulling her close, he kissed her ever so gently.

He had kissed her before, she thought dreamily, but never like this. It was warm and tender, filled with a promise of love and forever.

Maddy was still thinking about forever later that night in bed. Dominic could live for another century or more. And no matter how long he lived, he would always look much the same as he did now. What would happen when he didn't age and she did? If they had children, they would all outlive her. That just didn't seem right.

Among my people, there are ways to prolong human life. She heard Dominic's words whisper provocatively through the back of her mind. When she had asked how it was done, he'd said he didn't know how, just that it was possible. Would she have to become a vampire? The thought chilled her. She had no problem with Dominic's being one. He had been born that way. For him, it was natural.

How did the Hungarian vampires prolong a human life? Some kind of antiaging serum? A dose of their blood? Magic?

The thought kept her awake until dawn, when she finally fell into a restless sleep.

* * *

Ava woke to a quiet house. Slipping out of bed, she pulled on her favorite fluffy robe and padded up the stairs to the third floor. A wave of her hand unlocked the door. Stepping into the room, she closed and locked the door behind her.

It was here that she kept the tools of her trade—a cauldron, a scrying mirror, a variety of incense and oils, a wrought-iron candlestick, a number of candles of various colors, a jeweled dagger, a silver pentacle, and a wand made of ebony, numerous vials filled with herbs, and other, less ordinary things.

She had nothing of Jasper's, which would make summoning him difficult. She tried several different spells. All failed.

Was he dead? That was the only logical answer. Still, she tried one more incantation, one that had never failed. Until now.

Brow furrowed, she left the room and locked the door behind her.

Had she done something wrong? Was Maddy's burgeoning magic somehow interfering with her own? Ava thrust the thought aside as unlikely. The girl's powers were no match for her own. There was only one answer that made sense—Jasper had met an untimely end, likely at the hands of the Elder Knight.

Chapter 31

Jasper took refuge under a pile of discarded boxes behind a tattoo parlor. He had thought being a vulture was the worst thing that had ever happened to him, but being a toad was far worse. The vulture had been a bird of prey. The toad *was* prey. Had he been able, he would have screamed his rage against the Elder Knight, but all that emerged from his throat was a weak croak.

For a time, he had considered trying to hop to the stronghold in hopes that the Knight would remove the spell, but after encountering dogs, cats, and a snake in the first mile, he had decided his chances of making it that far alive were less than zero.

His only other hope was Claret, and that was a slim hope at best.

He waited until dark, then hopped toward the city. With luck, he would find the vampire in her favorite haunt. But even if he found her, how was he going to identify himself before she stepped on him? Or tossed him through a window? He had no concept of time, but it seemed to take hours before he reached the Crimson Rose.

All he had to do now was wait for someone to open the damn door.

Claret was in the midst of feeding on a rather handsome man she had picked up when she was distracted by a croak that seemed to come from under the table. Curious, she released the man from her thrall and sent him on his way, then bent down to see what was causing the noise. And came face-to-face with a large, ugly, brown frog. She was about to kick it out of the way when she noticed its eyes. They were not the eyes of a toad, but human eyes. Eyes she had seen before. "Jasper! What the hell?"

Reaching down, she picked up the ugly creature, then slid out of the booth and left the tavern.

At home, she set the toad on a chair. Focusing her power, she picked up the scent of witchcraft. So, who had the wizard angered this time?

"Who did this to you, Jasper? Was it the Elder Knight?"

The toad's head bobbed up and down.

Well, that made sense. She knew Jasper had been playing her against the Knight.

Jasper croaked, the noise sounding like a plea for help.

"Sorry, I can't help you. I don't have that kind of power. You need a witch."

His head bobbed again.

"The only witch I know is Ava. Unfortunately for you, she seems to have left town," Claret said with a shrug. "And I don't know where she's gone." And then she smiled. "But I know how to find her. And I will take you to her on one condition. If she breaks the spell, you will swear allegiance to me and no one else. Do we have a deal?"

Once again, the frog signaled his agreement.

Chapter 32

Maddy woke with a smile on her face. She was getting married! To Dominic. What would her parents think when they learned she was marrying a man they had never met? If she wanted them at the wedding, she and Dominic would have to wait a while; her folks weren't due home for another few months. Perhaps she should call her mom and let her know she was engaged before she announced she was getting married.

What would Ava say?

What would Dominic's parents say?

Throwing the covers aside, she swung her legs over the edge of the bed, then sat there, unable to stop smiling. Mrs. Dominic Falconer. Maddy Falconer. Dominic's woman.

Humming "Here Comes the Bride," she waltzed into the bathroom to shower.

Sitting at the table in the kitchen, Ava blew out a sigh. "Here Comes the Bride" indeed. What was Dominic thinking? He had just met the girl a short while ago. Did Maddy have any idea what she was getting into? Dominic wasn't just any vampire. He was the son of Hungarian vampire royalty. She knew she should call home and let his parents know but decided against it. They would likely blame her for not keeping his mind on what they had been sent here to do.

And then she frowned. Why had his parents sent Dominic to New Orleans, of all places? The Knights' last stronghold had been up on the Canadian border. Did Quill really think the Brotherhood would move to Louisiana, a place known for the large number of Transylvanian vampires? True, the Knights killed Transylvanian vampires if any crossed their path, but their main goal was to wipe out Quill's people. And there were only a handful of Hungarian vampires in Louisiana.

It didn't make sense. But then, few things in the paranormal world did. Like Maddy having magic.

Ava sighed. She had known Maddy and Dominic were fated to meet. She tapped her fingers on the edge of the table. Had Callie known it, too? Was that why they had sent Dominic to New Orleans? To meet his mate? Had hunting the Knights been a red herring, with the real objective making sure that Maddy and Dominic fell in love?

Ava shook her head. What was she thinking? That was just too far-fetched to consider. And yet, the more she thought about it, the more sense it made.

Laughing softly, she magicked a cup of hot chocolate and a blueberry muffin. Then, hearing Maddy's footsteps on the stairs, she magicked another cup of cocoa and a scone for her future great-granddaughter.

Maddy smiled at Ava as she scuffed into the kitchen.

Had Dominic already told her about their engagement? If not, should she mention it?

"Good morning," Ava said brightly. "Won't you join me?"

"Thanks."

Ava pushed a cup of hot chocolate toward her. "Would you prefer a muffin or a scone?"

"A scone, please."

"You look very happy this morning," Ava remarked, hiding a smile of her own.

"Do I?"

"Any particular reason?"

Maddy sipped her chocolate to avoid answering right away. To tell or not to tell?

"Congratulations, dear," Ava said. "I'm happy for both of you."

"You don't mind?"

"I'll admit I think it's a little soon, but if Dominic is happy, I'm happy." Reaching across the table, Ava patted her hand. "Of course, I want you to be happy, too."

"Oh, I am. And I know it's kind of sudden, but, after all, you're the one who encouraged us to date in the first place. Brought us together in the first place."

"So I did," Ava murmured. "So I did." How had Callie managed that?

"Have you ever been married?"

"Twice. My first husband was a Knight of the Dark Wood."

"A knight? Like swords and castles?"

"Not quite. Has Dominic never mentioned the Knights?"

"No. But you did. I remember now. You said their sole purpose in life was to destroy vampires like Dominic. But you never said why."

"Unlike Transylvanian vampires, Dominic's people are able to procreate with human females. The Brotherhood considers that an abomination. They also have no fondness for Transylvanian vampires, or witches, but their main focus is the destruction of Dominic and those like him."

Maddy stared at Ava. It sounded like some kind of ancient cult.

"Dominic and I came here hoping to find information on the new leader of the Knights and the location of their stronghold. So far, we haven't had much luck. I know you love Dom," Ava said. "But are you brave enough to share your life with him?"

"I don't know. Tell me about his parents."

"I met his father, Quill, many years ago. I might have loved him, but when we met, I knew he was destined to belong to my granddaughter, Callie. I'd seen them quite clearly in a vision. When Callie grew up, I kept an eye on her. The two of them faced many challenges when they met. The Knights were determined to destroy Quill. I was working for the Knights at the time. Of course, I couldn't let them destroy Quill. Soon after Dominic and Lily were born, the family went home to Savaria.

"We lived there quite peacefully. And then Quill and his father, Andras, learned of the deaths of some of our people in New Orleans and decided to send Dominic to the States to look into it. His task was to find out all he could about the new leader of the Knights of the Dark Wood, and what the Brotherhood's intentions were, without revealing his parentage. As I said, we haven't had much luck. And then Dominic met you, and I'm afraid he got sidetracked."

Maddy shook her head. Knights and witches and a

mysterious Brotherhood. What had she gotten herself into? It wasn't just a few men trying to kill Dominic. It was a war that had been going on for decades, perhaps centuries. If Dominic killed the Elder Knight or, heaven forbid, the Elder Knight killed Dominic, it would just add fuel to the fire.

And then there was that sexy female vampire, Claret. She didn't want Dominic dead. She just wanted his blood.

When would it all end? Would it ever end? Would any of them even survive?

Dominic sensed Maddy's distress when he rose that evening. What could have caused it? Last night, she had agreed to marry him. Now she was beset by doubts. Why?

He found the women of the house in the kitchen, Ava's grimoire open between them. They turned in unison to look at him. Ava smiled. Maddy's gaze slid away from his.

Dominic propped his shoulder against the doorjamb. "All right, one of you had better tell me what's going on. Ava?"

"I told Maddy about the Brotherhood and the Dark Knights."

A muscle twitched in his jaw. "I see."

"She has a right to know everything, Dom. It's not fair to keep her in the dark."

Well, that explained Maddy's state of mind.

Ava was right, of course, but he would have liked to have told Maddy in his own time, in his own way.

Ava glanced from Dominic to Maddy and back again.

Without a word, Ava removed her apron and marched out the back door.

The silence in the kitchen was deafening.

Maddy stared after Ava, wondering at the sudden tension between Dominic and his great-grandmother.

Jaw clenched, Dominic turned on his heel and left the house, afraid his anger at Ava might spill over onto Maddy. Stalking the dark streets, he cursed Ava, cursed himself for what he was, cursed his parents for giving him life. Cursed everyone but the woman he loved. Thanks to Ava, Maddy was having doubts again. Not that he could blame her. Violence and death were a part of his life and always would be. Maybe it was too much to expect Maddy to accept it the way his mother had.

He was so angry, it took him a moment to realize he was being followed. With a growl, he spun around. For a moment, the two Knights following him froze. And then, as if pulled by the same string, they lunged toward him.

Ordinarily, he would have vanished from their sight. But not tonight. Tonight, he was looking for a fight. He wrested the dagger from the first Knight, slammed the man's back against the side of a building, and drove the blade into his heart. Spinning on his heel, he ducked to the side, barely avoiding the second hunter's weapon.

With a low growl, Dominic feinted left, darted right, and grabbed the man around the neck. The Knight struggled valiantly, his heart beating a wild tattoo as he realized death was imminent.

Dominic paused. Took a deep breath. And ripped the medallion from around the Knight's neck and tossed it aside. Forcing the man to face him, Dominic mesmerized him with a look, then transported the two of them to the third floor of Ava's house. Next to the room where she practiced her magic, there was a small closet. He shoved the man inside.

"Where do the Knights make their stronghold?"

The man stared at him, eyes blazing with defiance.

"You will tell me what I want to know."

The Knight shuddered as Dominic's power washed over him. "I can't. The Elder Knight will kill me."

Dominic grinned at the man, displaying his fangs. "I've not yet fed."

The Knight's face paled. Wide-eyed, he stared at Dominic, whose eyes had gone red.

"Don't. Please."

Dominic licked his lips. "This is your last chance."

"Connecticut," the man gasped. "The stronghold is in the Dark Entry Forest in Cornwall, Connecticut."

Dominic's gaze bored into his. "You will stay here until I release you," he said. "Do you understand?"

When the man nodded, Dominic closed the door.

Ava looked up when he entered the room. Seeing the expression on his face, she glanced at Maddy. "Would you mind making me a cup of tea the old-fashioned way?"

They wanted her out of the room, Maddy thought, when all she wanted to do was talk to Dominic, ask why he'd left so abruptly. Instead, her voice laced with sarcasm, she said, "Of course not. I wouldn't want to forget how to brew a cup of tea the old-fashioned way."

"And perhaps some toast with jelly?" Ava waited until Maddy was out of the room before asking, "What's wrong?"

"Two of the Knights attacked me tonight," he said, his

voice pitched for her ears alone. "I killed one. The other is upstairs. He told me the Knights' stronghold is in the Dark Entry Forest in Cornwall, Connecticut."

Ava stared at him in disbelief. "Are you sure that's what he said?"

"Yeah? What's the big deal? A forest is a forest."

"You've never heard of this one?"

"No, why?"

"Well, for one thing, it's rumored to be haunted."

"Haunted?"

"Indeed. It started out as a small settlement around 1740. In the eighteenth century, it was known as Owlsbury. It was a popular place until folks started reporting odd sightings and strange happenings. Animals started disappearing and people began to believe the forest was haunted. By the twentieth century, all the inhabitants had died or moved away. The forest sits in the dark shadows of three mountains, hence the name."

"Sounds like the perfect place for the Knights of the Dark Wood," Dominic muttered.

"I suppose so, although I'm not sure I want to go there."

"You afraid?"

"Not afraid, exactly. Wary, perhaps. There are stories of people being possessed by demons, something I try to avoid. So, what's our next move? Do we go there, just the two of us?"

He shrugged. "All right by me."

"What are you going to do with the Knight you brought home?"

"I'll take him back where I found him later tonight."

"I know the Elder Knight by reputation," Ava remarked. "He's a powerful wizard."

"What about Jasper?" Dominic asked. "Whose side is he on?"

"I don't think we have to worry about him anymore," Ava remarked. "I think he's dead, perhaps by the hand of the Elder Knight. Perhaps it was Claret's doing. All I know is, I can't locate him anywhere. What about Maddy? We can't leave her here alone. . . ."

Ava cleared her throat as Maddy entered the room, a cup in one hand, a plate in the other. "Thank you, dear."

Maddy glanced from Ava to Dominic. "Were you talking about me?"

"I was just telling Dom how pleased I am that the two of you found each other," Ava said smoothly. "Have you set a date for the wedding?"

That night, after Ava and Maddy had gone to bed, Dominic questioned the Knight again. He needed to know how many men were at the stronghold, if they had a new witch, how many Knights guarded the entrance. It was common knowledge that there were only thirteen active Knights at any one time, but they had members in training in just about every big city across the country, and others waiting in reserve that could be called up at a moment's notice, if necessary. When he had all the answers he needed, he wiped the memory of what had happened from the man's mind and sent him on his way. He just hoped he wouldn't regret it later.

He paused on his way downstairs to look in on Maddy. She slept on her side, one hand tucked beneath her cheek, one bare foot peeking out from under the covers. His heart swelled with love as he bent down to brush a kiss across her brow.

Her eyelids fluttered open. “Dominic?”

“Yes, love. Go back to sleep.”

When he turned to leave, she reached for his hand. “Are you mad at me? You left so abruptly tonight. I was afraid . . .”

“It had nothing to do with you. It’s Ava. Sometimes she . . . never mind, sweetheart.”

“What were you and Ava whispering about when she sent me into the kitchen?”

“Nothing you need to worry about right now.” And maybe never, he hoped.

“You’re keeping something from me. I know it.”

“I discovered the location of the Knights’ stronghold.”

Eyes wide, she sat up. “You’re not thinking of going there? Dominic, tell me you’re not!”

“It’s the reason I came here in the first place.”

“But . . . that’s madness. They’re hunting you. You can’t just walk in there.”

“When I’m ready to go, I won’t be alone.”

“Oh? Do you have an army somewhere I don’t know about?”

“No.” He grinned in spite of himself. “Just Ava.”

Maddy stared at him. He had to be kidding! Wasn’t he?

Chapter 33

Finding Dominic had been all too easy, Claret mused. She had finally realized his witchy mother had cast some sort of protection spell around him so that her kind couldn't find him after tasting his blood. And she had to admit it was a masterful spell. But his mother's enchantment didn't prevent Claret from following the trail of her own blood. And the only vampire who had bitten her recently was Dominic. She could have followed the scent of her own blood blindfolded. Why hadn't she thought of it before?

The house was dark, protected by a double layer of wards erected by both witch and vampire. Barring an invitation, there was no way for anyone—mortal, witch, or vampire—to cross the threshold.

She glanced at the small wire cage that held Jasper. In his present form, the toad could get inside with no problem at all. But in this form, he was also useless. What would his fate be if he slipped inside? There was no love lost between Jasper and Ava. Would the witch take pity on him and return him to his mortal form? Or destroy him?

She didn't really care what happened to Jasper. Her main interest in seeing him restored to his human self was to help her thwart the Elder Knight and thereby keep Dominic alive. She was determined to have Dominic at her mercy again, to be able to glut herself on his blood—and his power—whenever she wished. And she feared she might need Jasper's help to accomplish it.

Muttering, "Good luck," she opened the little cage. "Remember your promise."

He croaked once as he hopped out of the box.

"Fail me and I'll make soup out of you," Claret vowed. A wave of her hand and she disappeared into the darkness.

Jasper stared at the place where she had stood, then turned and hopped toward the house, wondering what fate awaited him there.

Chapter 34

Maddy woke early. Wandering into the kitchen, she fixed a cup of hot chocolate, added a generous helping of marshmallows, and carried the cup outside. It was a beautiful day, the sky above clear, though gray clouds hovered in the distance.

Sitting on a wicker chair on the front porch, she let her mind wander. For better or worse, she was going to marry Dominic. She refused to let a few lingering doubts and fears change her mind. She had to believe he had been joking when he said Ava was his only backup. There were other Hungarian vampires in the country. Surely he could call on them for help, if needed. And then there was his family. If they were as powerful as Ava claimed, wouldn't they come to their son's aid?

With a sigh, she put her cup on the little table beside her chair, let out a gasp of surprise when a large brown toad tried to jump in her lap and missed. She stared down at the ugly little creature, thinking it was the strangest-looking frog she had ever seen.

Gazing up at her, it croaked softly. Almost, it sounded sad, she thought, and then rolled her eyes. Whoever heard of a sad frog? But there was something in its eyes, something almost human.

The story of the princess and the frog rose in the back of her mind. Maybe this wasn't a frog at all, but an enchanted prince searching for a princess to bestow love's kiss and release him from a wicked witch's spell.

Maddy shook her head. She'd always had a rather wild imagination, but this was the wildest notion of all, she thought. And then she frowned. Ava was a witch quite capable of turning a man into a frog. . . . She shook the idea away, thinking she'd been spending too much time with witches and vampires.

She reached toward the toad, thinking she would take it into the backyard and turn it loose by the little pond when the screen door flew open and Ava cried, "Don't touch it!"

Startled, Maddy almost fell out of her chair.

The toad croaked loudly and took refuge behind a flowerpot.

"Is it poisonous or something?" Maddy asked, regaining her seat.

"Worse."

"I don't understand."

"It's not an ordinary toad."

"How do you know?"

"It's Jasper. He's under an enchantment of some kind."

"Who's Jasper?"

"An evil wizard I once turned into a vulture."

Maddy's eyes widened. "Why?"

"He has a knack for aligning himself with the wrong side. First Claret, and now the Knights of the Dark Wood.

Many years ago, he put my granddaughter's life in danger, as well as Quill's. Fool that he is, he thought he was more powerful than I." Ava smiled at the memory. "But I stole his magic and transformed him into a huge, ugly vulture. Sadly, the new Elder Knight released him from my spell." Her laughter filled the air. "But apparently he ran afoul of the new Elder Knight as well." A wave of her hand drew the toad out of his hiding place. "I wonder what brings him here now?" Lifting her head, she closed her eyes and drew in a deep breath. "Claret!" She hissed the name as her eyes flew open.

"The vampire is here?" Maddy glanced around, even though she knew the creature couldn't be out in the light of day.

"She was here last night." Ava muttered a very unladylike oath. "She must have followed her link to Dominic. But why did she bring Jasper?"

The toad croaked pitifully.

Ava sat on the porch, eyes narrowed as she regarded the creature. "Did she think I would set you free?" she wondered aloud. "To what end?" Placing her hand on the toad's head, she chanted softly.

The words were foreign to Maddy. She shivered as the air around them grew cold. Ever so slowly, ghostlike figures gathered around the frog. Maddy recognized the vampire queen. Was the other figure Jasper? They were speaking to each other, but she couldn't hear the words.

A few moments later, the figures dissolved. The air lost its chill.

Ava blew out a breath as she regained her feet. "Well, that explains it. Claret brought him here on the condition that if I returned him to his human form, he would swear allegiance to her and no one else. She also wants Dominic in captivity again, and Jasper's help in thwarting the Elder Knight."

"What are you going to do?"

"I haven't decided." Bending down, she conjured a cage around the toad. "For now, we'll keep him here, where he can't cause any trouble."

Maddy stared at the helpless creature. What would it be like, to be transformed into an animal? Or, in this case, a toad? Was he aware of his human life? Did he understand what was being said? He had been turned into a vulture before. Though she wouldn't wish to be either, of the two, she thought being a bird of prey would be less odious. After all, most people dreamed of being able to fly. She didn't know anyone who wanted to be an ugly, brown toad.

Dominic stared at the cage sitting on the coffee table, frowned when he saw a large, brown toad inside. He glanced at his great-grandmother, one brow raised. "Practicing a new spell that requires frog legs?"

With a sigh of exasperation, Ava said, "It's Jasper."

"The wizard? No shit."

"Language, Dominic, we have a guest."

"Sorry, love."

Maddy pressed a hand to her mouth to keep from laughing at Dominic's expression, which hovered between embarrassment and annoyance.

"So, what are you going to do with him?" Dominic asked.

"I'm not sure," Ava said. "My instinct tells me to destroy him."

"But?" Dominic sat on the sofa next to Maddy and took her hand in his.

"I keep thinking he might come in handy, although I can't imagine any scenario in which he would."

"Me either."

"You can't just kill him," Maddy exclaimed. "I mean, it's none of my business but . . . it's murder. Isn't it?"

Maddy felt a chill when Dominic and Ava exchanged glances.

"She's right," Dominic agreed reluctantly. "Toad or man, you can't just kill him in cold blood."

Ava blew out an exaggerated sigh. And then she looked at Dominic, and they both burst out laughing. "I'm sorry, Maddy," she said. "We were just pulling your chain. I'd never kill him or anyone else without a damn good reason."

"Language, Ava," Dominic said with a grin.

This time, Maddy joined in the laughter. But deep down, something told her that doing away with Jasper wouldn't have bothered Ava at all.

The three of them were sitting down to dinner later that evening when Dominic went suddenly still. A wave of preternatural power raised the hair on Maddy's arms. A moment later, the candles in the center of the table flickered and went out.

"She's here." Dominic's voice was ice cold.

Maddy knew without asking he meant the vampire, Claret. "What does she want?"

"Me. Or, to be more exact, my blood."

Of course. She remembered how he'd told her that the Transylvanian vampires craved the blood of his kind. Fear skittered down her spine. The vampire had trapped both of them once before. It was an experience that still gave her nightmares, one she didn't want to endure again.

Some of her fear left her when Dominic took her hand. "Don't worry, love. She can't come inside."

Maddy let out a startled cry when she saw the vampire's face at the window.

A wave of Ava's hand closed the drapes. A moment later, Maddy heard the vampire let out a screech as the sprinklers came on.

"If only she was the Wicked Witch of the West," Ava remarked with a broad grin. "We'd be rid of her for good."

Later that night, after Ava and Maddy had gone to bed, Dominic left the house. Standing on the front porch, he said, "Show yourself, vampire. I know you're out there."

She materialized out of the shadows. As usual, she wore a long dress that outlined every luscious curve. This one was the color of plums, formfitting as always, with a deep V-neck. "I knew you'd come out."

"Did you?"

She glided toward the porch, hips swaying provocatively.

"What do you want?"

"You know very well what I want." She stared up at him, dark eyes glittering in the light of the moon.

"Why did you bring the wizard here?"

"I was hoping the witch would dissolve the spell that binds him."

Dominic snorted. "Why the devil would she do that?"

She brushed the question aside with a wave of her hand. "We can help each other, you and I."

"Yeah? How so?"

"The Elder Knight wants your head. All I want is a little of your blood now and then."

"Now and then?" he asked skeptically. "Is that why you locked me in a cage?"

"That wouldn't be necessary if you'd just give it to me willingly."

"What's in it for me if I agree?"

"Jasper and I will help you defeat the Elder Knight."

"What makes you think I can't do it on my own?"

"What makes you think you can?" she retorted.

Dominic grinned. In spite of his instincts and his good sense, he found himself liking the vampire queen. And maybe she had a point. Vampires gained strength as they aged. And while he had inherited much of his power from his father, he was still a young vampire. He wasn't sure how old Claret was, but he guessed she was well over a hundred, maybe closer to two. With vampires and witches, there was really no way to tell.

She tilted her head to the side, her eyes narrowed as she waited for his decision.

"Do you know why he wants me dead? I mean, other than the fact that that's what the Knights do? His targeting me seems more personal than that, even though I've never met him."

"Sadly, no. Do we have a deal?"

"Let me think about it."

"Any chance you'd give me a taste before I leave?"

He considered it for a moment. He knew what it was like to crave something, how it could become an obsession. Allowing her a small drink cost him nothing. "Just one." Cloaking himself in power, he descended the stairs and held out his arm. "More than one sip," he warned, "and I'll break your neck."

She smiled up at him, her fangs ghostly white in the darkness. Grasping his arm in both hands, she bit into his wrist, took one long swallow, and released him. "I'll be waiting for your answer," she purred, and vanished from his sight.

When Dominic turned back toward the porch, Ava was standing on the bottom step, waiting for him.

"What the hell are you doing?" she exclaimed. "Have you lost your mind?"

"She just wanted to talk."

"Really? I didn't see much conversation going on."

"She wants to make a deal—my blood for her help in defeating the Elder Knight. Oh, and she wants you to release Jasper from whatever spell he's under."

"Forget it. We don't need her. Or him."

"She said the Knight wants my head in particular. Why?"

"It's what they do, remember? He doesn't need any other reason."

"But there is one, isn't there?"

Ava's gaze slid away from his.

"What the hell's going on?"

"Your father killed the Elder Knight's father."

Comprehension dawned in Dominic's eyes.

"It was in self-defense, and it happened decades ago," Ava went on. "I recently learned that Gregory's father,

Frederick, was a vampire hunter. To my knowledge, Quill had no idea that Frederick was the Elder Knight's father. Of course, Gregory 73 wasn't the Elder Knight back then. Your father still doesn't know about the relationship between Gregory and Frederick. I don't know how Gregory found out about Quill."

"But you knew. That's why you insisted on coming to the States with me."

"Indeed. Gregory 73 is powerful, but not as powerful as he thinks. As for Jasper . . ." She shrugged. "Alone, he's no real threat."

"And Claret?"

"Trust me, you shouldn't believe a word she says. If you're smart, you'll be on your guard whenever she's around."

"I don't need you to tell me that."

"But?"

He shrugged. "I don't trust her, but in spite of everything, I can't help liking her."

Ava shook her head in disgust. "I wonder how much you'll like her when she's got you locked up again," she muttered as she returned to the house and slammed the door.

Dominic blew out a sigh. She was right, of course. But then, she usually was.

Chapter 35

Maddy gazed into Ava's scrying mirror. Try as she might, she couldn't summon an image of her parents.

"Stop thinking about Dominic and concentrate," Ava said. "If you want to see your parents, you have to concentrate on them. Maybe it would be easier to focus on just one of them. Try again."

Maddy shook the image of Dominic from her mind and summoned an image of her mother. She held her breath as shadows moved below the mirror's surface, writhing and shifting until the ghostly figures cleared and the image of her mother rose to the surface. She was standing at the ship's rail, and as Maddy watched, her father came up beside her and slipped his arm around her mother's shoulders. Maddy blinked back a tear when they smiled at each other.

When she heard the sound of a car backfiring out on the street, it broke her concentration, and the image vanished.

"Well done," Ava said. "I knew you could do it. It will be easier next time."

Maddy grinned inwardly. If she'd been alone, she would have tried to summon an image of Dominic, sleeping.

"Now," Ava said, "I think it's time you tried casting a spell."

"What kind of spell?"

Ava picked up a water bottle and poured the contents into a cup. "One of my granddaughter's first spells was turning water into chocolate milk." Opening her grimoire, she flipped through the pages. "This is the incantation she used."

Maddy read the instructions, then frowned. "It says I need a wand."

"Wands are mainly used to focus power. It's a simple spell. I think you can do it. But you might need a wand for some of the more complicated spells. We'll see about making you one if you like."

It was near dark when Ava closed the grimoire. "You did well today. Are you sure there aren't any witches in your family?" she asked as they left the third-floor room and made their way down the stairs to the kitchen.

"None that I ever heard of," Maddy said. "I guess I could ask my mother next time I talk to her."

"I wouldn't be surprised to find a witch or two way back in your ancestry somewhere. What shall we have for dinner?"

Dominic woke to the tantalizing aroma of Ava's homemade spaghetti sauce. He could hear his great-grandmother and Maddy talking about the ins and outs of magic wands in the kitchen.

"What's yours made of?" Maddy asked.

"Ebony. But hazel and ash both make good ones, as do hawthorn and cherry. But for you, I think apple would be best. Apple wands have the qualities of youth, beauty, and love." Ava smiled. "Perfect for someone young and in love. And, as it happens, there's an apple tree in the backyard."

Dominic grinned as he made his way downstairs. Youth and beauty described his Maddy to a T. As for love, he intended to see she was never without it.

"Sauce smells good," he said as he kissed Ava on the cheek. "How did you know I wanted spaghetti for dinner?"

"I'm a witch, remember? Besides, it's been your favorite dish since you were a boy."

"I guess I'll have to learn her recipe," Maddy said as Dominic pulled her into his embrace.

They kept the conversation light at dinner. There was no mention of knights and the Brotherhood, or of wizards, or Claret.

Until Jasper croaked.

They all turned to stare at the toad.

"Maybe you should just turn him loose," Dominic said. "Or at least feed him once in a while."

"Sad to say, I'm all out of flies, crickets, and spiders," Ava retorted.

"How long are you going to keep him like that?"

"Feeling sorry for him, are you, Dominic?" Ava asked. "I can't imagine why, considering he'd be more than happy to deliver you to Claret—or the Elder Knight—depending on which he's more afraid of at the moment."

"Then kill him and put him out of his misery."

The toad began hopping up and down and back and

forth. It was obvious he understood what was being said, Maddy thought. And just as obvious that he was terrified.

"I don't mean to stick my nose in where it doesn't belong," Maddy said. "But I think Dominic's right. Keeping Jasper like this is cruel."

Silence fell over the table. Maddy clenched her hands in her lap, wishing she'd kept her mouth shut.

She risked a glance at Dominic, surprised to find him smiling at her.

"If you want to release him from the spell," Ava said, "do it."

"Me?" Maddy exclaimed. "I'm not powerful enough to do that."

"How do you know?"

"Because . . . because I know. I barely managed to summon an image of my parents, and then only for a moment. Besides, this is someone else's spell. I wouldn't even know where to begin."

Pushing away from the table, Ava picked up the cage and set it in front of Maddy. "I give him to you. Do with him as you will."

Maddy stared at Ava, her thoughts chaotic. How could she possibly return Jasper to his own form? So far, all her magic consisted of summoning small objects, turning water into hot chocolate, and basic scrying. Hardly the kind of talent she needed to undo a spell cast by a powerful wizard who had years of practice in the Dark Arts.

The toad croaked softly. Maddy stared at the helpless creature, who stared back at her. Was it her imagination or were its eyes filled with sadness?

Later that night, after Ava had gone to bed and Dominic had gone hunting, Maddy carried the toad into the backyard and set the cage in a patch of weeds alongside the house. With luck, he might catch a bug or two.

Wary of being alone outside after dark, she moved to stand in the kitchen doorway. Gazing up at the stars, she wished she could see into the future. What would her life be like when she married Dominic? Where would they live? Would they always have to be wary of vampire hunters and the Knights of the Dark Wood? Would his parents like her? Would hers like him? What was his sister like?

"So many questions."

Maddy glanced over her shoulder to see Dominic standing behind her. "Reading my mind?"

"Guilty as charged," he admitted as he came to stand at the door beside her. Jerking his chin toward the cage, he asked, "What are you going to do with him?"

"I don't know. Turn him loose, maybe?"

Dominic grunted softly as he stepped outside. Hunkering down on the grass, he dug a hole, pulled out a couple of fat, wiggly worms, and dropped them inside the cage. "I'm not sure that's a good idea."

Maddy grimaced as the toad quickly devoured his dinner.

"Have you tried revoking the spell?"

"I wouldn't know where to begin."

"Maybe you could borrow Ava's grimoire."

"Maybe." She shivered as the air turned suddenly cool.

A moment later, Claret materialized beside Dominic.

He rose fluidly to his feet and moved between the vampire and Maddy. "What the hell are you doing here?"

"I came to check on Jasper. I was hoping Ava had revoked the spell."

"It's not gonna happen," Dominic said. "So why don't you take him and get out of here?"

"I thought you might like to know the Elder Knight is in New Orleans. He's searching for you high and low."

"I'm aware of that."

"Why does he want you so badly? I wonder," Claret mused.

Dominic shrugged. Picking up the cage, he thrust it toward her. "Don't come here again."

"We should be allies, Dominic, not enemies."

"I'm not crazy enough to trust you. Go home, Claret. There's nothing for you here."

Before she could reply, Dominic pulled Maddy into his arms, stepped into the house, and shut the door.

Claret stared after them, her eyes narrowed with rage. "You'll rue the day you rejected my help, Dominic Falconer," she hissed, then turned her attention to Jasper. Opening the cage door, she dumped the frog onto the ground and dropped the cage beside him. "As for you, Jasper, you'll stay out of my way if you know what's good for you," she warned, and vanished from sight.

"He's gone?" Ava stared at Maddy across the breakfast table the next morning. "What did you do with him?"

"I didn't do anything," Maddy said defensively. "After dinner last night, I took him outside to get him something to eat. Dominic joined me and dug up a couple of worms for him. And the next thing I knew, Claret was there. She had a few words with Dominic, and he as much as told her to go to hell. The next thing I knew, we were in the house. I don't know what happened to the toad."

Ava heaved an aggravated sigh. “I should have just killed him.”

“Why didn’t you?”

“Because you wouldn’t have approved,” Ava admitted. “If Claret took Jasper with her . . .” Her voice trailed off and she shook her head. “Jasper has the devil’s own luck. No matter what predicament he gets himself into, he always manages to see the better side of it.”

“What do you think he’ll do now?”

“I can’t imagine. If the Elder Knight is still in New Orleans, maybe we should go back and confront him, put an end to this once and for all.”

“If Dominic defeated him, would that be the end of it?”

“Sadly, no. The Brotherhood would just find a new Elder Knight. I’m not sure anything, short of wiping them out completely, will ever stop them.”

“There must be something you can do. A truce of some kind?”

“A truce,” Ava murmured. She stared into the distance. Or a spell. One that would erase their inherent protocol to destroy the Hungarian vampires and replace it with a new directive. Perhaps one that would set them against the Transylvanian vampires, who were, after all, a far greater threat to humanity than Dominic’s people had ever been. The ability to impregnate human females was in no way a danger to the population. The number of Hungarian vampires who had married human females over the centuries was nothing compared to the number of mortals killed by Claret’s kind.

Would it be possible to concoct a spell that powerful? One that would last indefinitely and affect every member of the Brotherhood? Her breakfast forgotten, she hurried up to the third floor.

Maddy stared after her. She had called Ava's name three times and gotten no response. Had Ava gone into some kind of trance?

Puzzled by the witch's odd behavior, she finished her orange juice and cleared the table. So, what to do with the rest of the day? Ava would likely be upstairs for who knew how long. Dominic was at rest, most likely until late afternoon.

Grabbing a book, she read for an hour. Practiced a new spell Ava had taught her. Watched an old comedy on Netflix. And it was only noon. Picking up Ava's grimoire from the coffee table, Maddy wandered out into the backyard. And almost stepped on Jasper.

She was surprised when the toad followed her to a wooden bench set under a tree. When she sat down, the toad squatted at her feet.

"I guess you're bored, too. And probably tired of being a frog." She couldn't help feeling sorry for him. It was beyond cruel to leave him as he was. Maybe she could turn him into something less odious—a dog or a cat perhaps. "Well, let's look in Ava's book and see what we can come up with."

Chapter 36

Maddy had just fixed a fresh pot of coffee when Ava entered the kitchen. "Smells good," she said appreciatively.

"I'll fix you a cup," Maddy offered. She pulled two cups from a shelf, filled them, and handed one to Ava before taking the seat across from her. She had hardly seen Dominic's great-grandmother since she'd hurried up to the attic hours before.

Ava let out a sigh of sheer pleasure as she picked up her cup and took a sip. "Just what I needed. So, you found Jasper again," she said with her customary prescience. "Did you have any luck removing the spell?"

Maddy shook her head. "I tried several of the spells I found in your grimoire, but none of them worked."

"Perhaps it's time to make you that wand," Ava said. "Let me get a refill and some clippers and then we'll go out back and you can find a branch that pleases you."

Maddy felt a rush of excitement. A wand of her own. Maybe she would feel more like a real witch if she had one.

* * *

Outside, Maddy looked at the apple tree. Was it a coincidence that Ava had chosen an apple tree for her when summoning an apple was the first bit of magic she had ever done? She moved beneath the tree and looked up, wondering which branch to use.

"It will work better if you can find a small branch that's fallen from the tree. If not, you need to ask the tree's permission before you take one."

"Oh? Why?"

"It's the polite thing to do," Ava said with a grin. "Seriously, it's believed that a branch taken without permission will not be effective."

"How do I ask a tree for permission?" Maddy asked.

"Simply close your eyes and mentally make your request. If you feel peace afterward, you're good to go."

Feeling a little foolish, Maddy closed her eyes. *Apple tree, may I please use one of your branches?* She waited for several moments and then, to her astonishment, she knew in her heart it was all right.

Smiling faintly, she cut a long, slender branch from the tree.

They spent the rest of the afternoon shaping and sanding the wand.

"You can decorate it or paint it," Ava remarked. "You can carve designs into the wood, or just leave it plain. Whatever makes it feel like your own."

Maddy held the wand in her hand and closed her eyes. She liked the feel of it, the weight of it. She smiled as it warmed in her hand. She had thought to decorate it with stars or half-moons, but in the end, she left it plain, with only a light coat of varnish to protect the wood.

When it was dry, Maddy ran her fingertips over the

wand. She shivered as she felt a trace of magic flow through her.

Ava smiled her approval. "Excellent. With time and practice, you're going to be a powerful witch."

"As good as you?"

"Well, I don't know about that," Ava said with a teasing grin. "It does take time to master one's craft. Most witches tend to possess one particular area of expertise, whether it's earth, wind, fire, or water. Some rare ones possess the power to call on all four of them. Dominic's mother is one of those, as am I."

"How will I know which power is mine?"

"That knowledge will come to you in time. You must be patient," Ava said. Then, changing the subject, she asked, "Have you seen Jasper?"

"No. When I didn't have any luck returning him to his own form, he hopped away. I don't know where he is now."

"If we're lucky, a predator got him."

Maddy grimaced, unsettled by the image of a snake or some large bird dining on the toad.

The Elder Knight paced the floor of his bedroom, his anger and frustration fanning his fury. His rage summoned the wind, and it blew through the stronghold, toppling trees and tearing the roof off one of the buildings. Try as he might, he could find no trace of the Hungarian vampire, though Jasper had mentioned that a Transylvanian vampire known as Claret was also interested in Falconer. Odd, he thought. Why would she want Dominic? The two types of vampire were known to be enemies. Was she also after his head?

Perhaps he needed to locate this Claret. Perhaps she could tell him where to find Dominic.

As he prepared to transport himself back to New Orleans, he wondered, briefly, about Jasper's fate.

Claret lifted her head from her prey's neck as dark magic rippled through the misty night air. She thrust her prey aside as a man clad in black materialized beside her. Before she could vanish, that same magic moved over her, rendering her immobile and helpless.

"You are Claret, are you not?" he asked imperiously.

She nodded.

"You are familiar with Dominic Falconer?"

She nodded again.

"Where is he?"

"I don't know. He's left the city."

His power drove her to her knees. "Do not lie to me!" he roared as he pulled a sword from the air and laid the glittering blade against the side of her neck.

"He's in Oregon."

"Where in Oregon?"

She tried not to answer, but the words were pulled from her throat. "In Portland."

"I am told you want him," he said, eyes narrowed. "Why?"

"His blood. I crave it."

"Ah, yes. I've heard it is like catnip to your kind."

She stared up at him. She had rarely been afraid of anything since being turned, but this man—this warlock—terrified her. There was no mercy in his eyes, no shred of pity or kindness.

Only darkness.

And death. Her death.

Dominic. Help me. She choked back a cry as the stranger ran the point of the blade along both of her cheeks. Razor sharp, it opened long, narrow gashes from the corner of her eyes to her jaw.

"My thanks for your help," the Elder Knight said with mock courtesy.

Claret let out a cry of denial as he raised the blade for the killing blow, gasped as strong arms wrapped around her and whisked her out of harm's way.

"What the hell!" Ava stared at Dominic in disbelief as he appeared on the front porch with Claret in his arms.

Dominic set the vampire on her feet. "If anyone kills her, it's going to be me, not that crazy Elder Knight."

A slow smile spread over Claret's face. "I knew you cared."

Dominic snorted. Truth be told, he didn't know why he had saved her from the Knight. Claret wanted his blood. The Knight wanted his head. But, of the two, Claret was the lesser evil. "You're out of danger for the moment. Now, be gone."

"As you wish," she murmured. And vanished from sight.

Ava shook her head in exasperation. "I hope you don't live to regret that."

"Yeah," Dominic muttered. "Me too."

* * *

Claret materialized in her lair deep in the bowels of an old, abandoned church. No one else knew where it was, not even members of her coven. She had warded it against any and all intruders, be they vampires, witches, werewolves, or humans. And then she had hired a witch to do the same, thereby insuring a double layer of protection.

But after her encounter with the Elder Knight, she no longer felt safe. Damn the man, he was the scariest thing she had ever encountered. No wonder Jasper was afraid of him.

Collapsing on the sofa, she closed her eyes. Not long ago, she had intended to trap Dominic one way or another. She had been willing to kill his great-grandmother and his girlfriend if necessary. Anything to ensure that she could savor his blood at her leisure.

But no more. She owed Dominic Falconer her life.

And as soon as she worked up the courage to leave the security of her lair, she would seek him out and tell him so.

Chapter 37

Maddy glanced at the grandfather clock across from the sofa. Dominic would be rising soon. He had been unusually quiet the last two nights, his thoughts turned inward. Ava, too, had been reticent. Knowing he had a lot on his mind, Maddy hadn't pressed him for answers. Instead, she had spent the time practicing her magic. The wand made all the difference in the world. Day by day, she could feel her magic growing stronger, becoming an integral part of her. It was exhilarating. And a little frightening.

She had mastered all the simpler spells in Ava's grimoire, her confidence growing with each success. Ava applauded her efforts, although she often seemed distracted. Maddy suddenly wished Jasper was still around. She would have loved to have another try at restoring his humanity.

She smiled at Dominic when he entered the living room that evening, then frowned when he merely nodded in return.

Rising, she moved toward him. "Okay, what's going on? Are you mad at me? Changed your mind about the wedding? What is it? You've hardly said a word to me in days."

"I know," he said quietly, and took her in his arms. "I'm going after the Elder Knight."

"What? When? Why?"

"It's time to end this. He found Claret in New Orleans. He was about to destroy her when she called for me."

"What?"

"I couldn't let him kill her. . . ."

Maddy leaned back so she could see his face. "After what she did to us? She locked you in a cage. She put some kind of sleeping spell on me! She might have killed us both! I should think you'd be glad to see the last of her."

"You'd think so, wouldn't you?" He couldn't say he understood his actions either.

"Is there something going on between the two of you? Something I should know about?"

"No! No, nothing like that, love. But in spite of everything, I just couldn't let her be destroyed."

"I know what that everything is," she retorted. "Thirty-six, twenty-six, thirty-six." Maddy glared at him when he threw back his head and laughed.

"You've got nothing to be jealous of, sweetheart." His hand stroked up and down her back. "Ava and I will be leaving tomorrow night, now that I know where the Knights' stronghold is located."

"Don't you mean you and Ava and me?"

"No. I don't want you anywhere near the place."

"I think that's my decision, isn't it? Not yours."

"Maddy, use your head. We're going to battle. I won't have time to look after you."

"I can look after myself!" she exclaimed, eyes flashing with indignation.

"Honey, you've never been in a battle of any kind in your whole life, much less one like this."

Refusing to admit he was right, she asked, "Where is this mysterious stronghold?"

"And just why do you need to know?"

"Why won't you tell me? Afraid I'll follow you?"

"Exactly."

"I'm a witch, remember? And I've tasted your blood. I can find you anywhere."

Shit. He hadn't thought of that. Although it wasn't precisely true. He could always block her if he chose to do so.

"Tell me," she coaxed.

"Connecticut," he muttered. "But you've got to promise me that you won't come after us." His gaze bored into hers. "Do I have your word?"

She opened her mouth to argue, then thought better of it. After all, he was right. She had no fighting experience. He wouldn't be able to concentrate if he was worrying about her.

"All right, I promise." But even as she spoke the words, she wondered how she could watch Dominic and Ava go off to fight who knew what while she stayed safely at home.

Dominic stood outside later that night, after Ava and Maddy had gone to bed. He hoped like hell he was doing the right thing in going to confront the Brotherhood. But something had to be done. The Knights had been hunting his people with renewed enthusiasm ever since the new Elder Knight took over.

Dominic blew out a sigh. The Elder Knight had a personal vendetta against Quill for killing his father. And Dominic's father wasn't available, so there was a good chance the Knight had decided to avenge himself on his enemy's son. Perhaps if he met the man one-on-one, they could come to some sort of an understanding, although Dominic thought the odds of that happening were a million to one. He considered calling his father for help but quickly thrust the thought aside. Quill was needed at home, more now than ever, while Andras had gone to Montenegro to settle a dispute between two warring families.

Dominic shook his head as he caught a familiar scent. Moments later, Claret sashayed toward him, her midnight-blue silk gown swishing around her ankles. "Lovely night."

"What are you doing here?"

"I came to thank you for saving my life. And to help you defeat the Brotherhood."

He arched one brow. "Is that right?"

"You and Ava can't do it alone."

"Are you sure about that?"

"No. But no man threatens me and gets away with it."

"What makes you think I'd ever trust you to have my back?"

"Like I said, you saved me. I owe you a life debt."

"And once it's paid?"

She smiled, showing a hint of fang. "A small taste of your blood to show your appreciation for my help would be welcome."

She was incorrigible, he thought.

"Perhaps you would give it to me before the fight? It would make me stronger."

"Perhaps. I'll talk it over with Ava. We're leaving tomorrow around midnight."

"I'll be here." With an airy wave, Claret turned and walked away, hips swaying provocatively, until she was lost in the darkness.

She was something else, Dominic mused as he returned to the house. And hoped like hell he could trust her. Because he was afraid she was right. It might take more than two of them to bring the Brotherhood down.

Later that night, when they were alone upstairs, Maddy clung to Dominic. She knew arguing with him was useless. He was determined to confront the Brotherhood with only Ava and Claret at his back. She couldn't believe he trusted the vampire. Or that two vampires and a witch could defeat the Elder Knight and the members of the Brotherhood. She had overheard Ava mention that the Elder Knight was also a warlock, though it wasn't common knowledge.

"Maddy, relax," Dominic murmured. "I'll be fine."

"You don't know that."

"Trust me, love. I will always come back to you." Cupping her face in his hands, he kissed her lightly. It had been meant as a token of his love and assurance, but as soon as his mouth covered hers, desire exploded between them. She clutched his shoulders, her body yearning toward his.

With a low growl, he carried her to bed and tucked her

beneath him. His mouth ravaged hers while she writhed against him.

"Dominic . . ." She moaned as his tongue dueled with hers, fanning the fire between them. A few magical words and their clothing disappeared.

Dominic lifted his head, a glint in his eyes. And then he claimed her lips once more while his hands—those clever hands—aroused her until she gasped, "Now, Dominic!"

He thrust into her, carrying her over the edge, felt her shudder with pleasure before his own release came.

He rolled onto his side, carrying her with him.

Maddy snuggled against him. Sighed deeply. And fell asleep in his arms.

He held her close for a few moments, then tucked her into bed before going to his lair. He closed his eyes and smiled as every breath carried the scent of their love-making. He was still smiling when the sun cleared the horizon and the dark sleep carried him away.

Chapter 38

Dominic rose earlier than usual in the morning so he could spend as much time as possible with Maddy before he left.

He found the women in the kitchen cleaning up the breakfast dishes as only witches could. Standing in the doorway, he grinned as plates and cups and flatware were miraculously washed and put away.

"Dominic, you're up early," Maddy said, a blush warming her cheeks when she remembered the night past. "Can I fix you anything to eat?"

His gaze moved to her throat and lingered there for the space of a heartbeat.

"I was thinking of something a little more traditional," she remarked, "but if you need it . . ."

"Maybe later." Closing the distance between them, he drew her into his arms. "How would you like to go for a drive, or take a walk?"

"Either one sounds good."

Dominic glanced at Ava. "Do you mind?"

"I'd appreciate some time alone. There are a few spells I'd like to review before we leave."

Releasing Maddy, he kissed Ava on the cheek. "We won't be gone long."

It was a beautiful day. It had rained during the night, just enough to clear the air. Dominic drove to a secluded beach. After parking the car, he led Maddy down a winding footpath to the sand.

"We should have brought a blanket," Dominic remarked. "The sand is still damp from the rain."

"Not to worry," Maddy said. A few murmured words, a few intricate motions with her hands, and a blanket appeared.

"Like my father always said, it pays to have a witch in the family."

Sitting cross-legged on the blanket, she smiled up at him. "Remember that."

"Oh, I will," he said, dropping down beside her. "I never intend to go anywhere without one."

"Except to Connecticut."

"Maddy . . ."

"I know, I know. I'm sorry." She gazed out at the ocean, thinking how beautiful and peaceful it looked with the sun silvering the waves. Hard to believe in just a few hours, Dominic would be fighting for his life. "You will be careful."

"I promise." He drew her up against him, her back against his chest, his arms wrapping around her waist, his legs on either side of hers. "I love you, Maddy," he murmured, his breath warm against the side of her neck. "You're the best thing that ever happened to me. Nothing will keep me from coming home to you."

She sighed as she leaned back against him. With the sun shining down on them like a blessing, it was hard to imagine that anything could go wrong.

Maddy fidgeted during dinner, too nervous to sit still or eat much. Sensing her distress, Ava started reminiscing about her second husband. "His name was Will. He was a wonderful man, very down to earth, but so very sweet. I never told him I was a witch."

"Never?" Maddy exclaimed. "Why not?"

"He wouldn't have understood. He'd been brought up by very strict parents who believed that all witches were demons. I just couldn't bring myself to tell him. I was always careful to keep my magic under wraps, so to speak. We had a wonderful life together. He died shortly after Callie's mother was born." A faint smile curved her lips. "My first husband, John, was more understanding about my magic. I think I told you, he was a Knight of the Dark Wood."

Maddy nodded.

"Members of the Brotherhood are forbidden to marry unless they leave the Order. He offered to renounce his vows, but I couldn't let him do that. I knew how much being a Knight meant to him. And he knew I could never give up my magic. We were very young and madly in love and we married in secret. I promised I'd never betray the Brotherhood and he vowed he'd never tell anyone I was a witch. It wasn't safe to be a witch in those days. Back then, people tended to be suspicious of anyone who was different. Actually, that hasn't changed much."

"I never knew you were married to a Knight," Dominic remarked.

"It's not common knowledge. I trust you will both keep my secret."

"Sure," Dominic said. He glanced at Maddy, who looked a little pale.

"Of course," she said agreeably.

Dominic frowned. "You've been single a long time, Grams. How is it that you never married again?"

"I've been too busy," she said. "First raising my own children, then looking after your mother and father. And now keeping an eye on you and Lily."

"Would you like to get married again?" Maddy asked.

"Perhaps," Ava said with a shrug. "If the right man came along." She glanced at the clock over the mantel. "I'm going upstairs to do a little research on the Dark Entry Forest and then rest for a few hours."

Dominic sent a sideways glance at Maddy, hoping she'd missed the reference to the Dark Entry Forest, but her expression revealed nothing.

"She isn't going up to rest, is she?" Maddy asked.

"No. She's just giving us a little more time alone to say goodbye."

Dominic slipped his arm around Maddy's shoulders and leaned in for a kiss. In spite of the reassuring words he'd given Maddy earlier, he had his own doubts about their success.

Claret arrived on the stroke of midnight.

Ava glanced at Dominic. "Are you sure taking her along is a good idea?"

Dominic shrugged. "We need all the help we can get."

"I don't like you either, witch," Claret said with a sneer. "But I like the Brotherhood even less."

Ava snorted. "So the enemy of my enemy is my friend? Is that it?"

"Like he said, you need all the help you can get."

Ava frowned thoughtfully. And then she smiled. She'd been wondering how to get inside the stronghold. Claret's presence would solve the problem. "You're welcome to join us, as long as you do as I say, when I say it."

"Fine."

Due to the time change between Portland and Connecticut, it was a little after three a.m. when they arrived on the outskirts of the forest. No animals stirred in the underbrush. Night birds were eerily silent. Dark clouds covered the moon and the stars. An overpowering sense of danger and evil rode the wings of the night.

"Can you feel it?" Ava whispered. "That sense of evil?"

Dominic nodded as he scanned their surroundings. The air felt heavy, oppressive. "A lot of people have died here. This place reeks of death and fear and old blood."

"That's true of most places," Claret muttered. "How do we find the stronghold?"

"Leave that to me," Ava said. "We need to find a safe place for you to spend the day first. If you go up in smoke when the sun rises, you're liable to start a forest fire."

Claret glared at her. "That's not remotely funny. And you needn't worry about me. I'll go to ground before dawn."

Ava shuddered at the thought of the vampire burrowing into the earth to spend the day.

Claret smiled at Dominic. "A little of your blood would help me rest better."

She had a one-track mind, he thought with wry amusement. "Maybe tonight."

"No harm in asking," she replied.

"All right, you two, that's enough." Chanting softly, Ava waved her hand over a deadfall. A moment later, the wood was transformed into a square table. Lifting the bag she carried with her, Ava reached inside.

Dominic watched as she withdrew a cauldron, a dagger, several small jars filled with pungent herbs, four black candles, and her wand.

She set them out carefully—the cauldron in the middle of the table, the candles around it at the points of the compass. She placed the dagger at one end of the table, with the blade pointing toward the cauldron, and the jars at the other end.

A flick of her fingers lit the candles.

Chanting softly, she poured the contents of the jars into the cauldron. There was a hissing sound as the herbs caught fire. A plume of blue-gray smoke rose from the container, hovered in the still air for a moment, and then slowly drifted to the ground.

Dominic watched in amazement as the smoke took on the shape of a Knight.

"The stronghold is to the north," Ava said, her voice deep and sounding disembodied.

Dominic darted forward as her face paled, his arm snaking around her waist to hold her steady. "What the hell!"

With a shake of her head, she murmured, "I'm all right." Smiling, she pointed at the ground. "Look."

Dominic and Claret both looked downward. A faintly glowing path cut through the forest, heading toward the north.

Ava quickly replaced her implements in the bag and tucked it under the table. "Let's go," she said briskly. "We don't have much time before dawn."

Maddy stared out the window. Dominic, Claret, and Ava had left hours ago. She had tried to get some sleep, but it was no use. It was so unfair! They had taken that horrible vampire Claret with them but left her behind. So, she wasn't a vampire and she wasn't a powerful witch like Ava, but she might have been able to help in some small way. Sitting here, waiting for their return, was driving her crazy.

Taking up Ava's grimoire, she turned the pages, looking for a spell that would transport her to Connecticut. Sadly, she didn't have the nerve to try any of the invocations in the book. But what she did have was a credit card.

Picking up her cell phone, she called the airport. Thirty minutes later, she had a flight to Cornwall, Connecticut.

The rising sun was painting the sky with glowing shades of pink, orange, and lavender when Claret went to ground.

Ava shuddered as the dirt closed over the vampire. "Have you ever done that?"

"Not yet."

"It's like being buried alive," Ava muttered. "Although technically she's not alive."

Dominic glanced around. Deep in the shadow of three mountains, the forest received little sunlight. "I'm going to get some rest," he said as he sat down, his back against a tree. "Are you going to be all right?"

"There's no one else around. I'll conjure a protective spell around us. It'll be safe enough." Chanting softly, she made several gestures with her hands. A moment later, her table and the bag holding her magical implements appeared. "Don't worry about me. I'm working on a new spell."

With a nod, he closed his eyes and surrendered to the darkness, his last conscious thought of Maddy.

Maddy yawned as she stepped off the plane, small suitcase in hand. The flight had been uneventful, for which she was grateful. She hated flying and nothing less than her love for Dominic and her concern for his safety had given her the nerve to get on a plane and fly across the country.

After renting a car, she drove to the nearest restaurant for breakfast. Thanks to Ava's slip of the tongue, she knew where the three were headed. Waiting for her order, she picked up her cell phone, called up Google, and asked for directions to the Dark Forest. She only hoped that once she arrived, she would be able to use her magic to find Dominic and the others.

She thanked the waitress who brought her breakfast, frowned when it occurred to her that Dominic and Claret would likely be at rest at this time of the day. She hoped

Ava would be awake and happy to see her—assuming she could even find the witch.

And that Dominic wouldn't be angry with her for following him.

Dominic jackknifed to a sitting position, nostrils flaring as he glanced around.

"What's wrong?" Ava asked.

"Maddy's here!"

"What?"

Gaining his feet, he lifted his head. "How the hell did she get here?"

"How should I know?"

He turned around as Maddy's scent grew closer, along with the faint scuff of her tentative footsteps.

A moment later, she rounded a bend in the road, then came to an abrupt halt when she saw the look on Dominic's face. He wasn't glad to see her. Ava looked amused. Claret was nowhere in sight.

Eyes narrowed, Dominic said, "You promised me that you'd stay home."

"I know."

"So what are you doing here?"

"And how did you find us?" Ava asked.

"From you," Dominic said.

Ava frowned at him and then said, "Oh. I let it slip, didn't I?"

"How did you find this place?" Dominic asked.

"I booked a flight to the nearest city, and when the plane landed, I rented a car. Once I got here, I followed the lingering signature of Ava's magic on the path and . . ." Maddy shrugged one shoulder. "And here I am."

"Well done," Ava said with a grin.

"Well done, indeed," Dominic muttered.

"Where's Claret?" Maddy asked, looking around.

"She's resting," Ava said. Then, glancing at Dominic, she added, "Don't just stand there, boy. Give the girl a hug."

Muttering under his breath, Dominic closed the distance between himself and Maddy and drew her into his arms. "I'm still mad at you."

"I know." Smiling, she went up on her tiptoes and kissed him. "But you won't stay mad, will you?"

"Not with you in my arms."

Ava rolled her eyes. "All right, people, can we get back to the matter at hand?"

When Claret joined them that evening, Ava laid out her plan.

"Are you crazy?" Claret exclaimed. "Last time I saw the Elder Knight, he almost took my head."

"You're the one who wanted in on this," Ava reminded her. "And don't worry, I'll have your back."

Claret snorted. "That's not very comforting."

"If you want out, just say so. We'll think of something else."

"All right, I'm in. But only if Dominic lets me drink from him before I go."

"Fine," he said. "As long as you stop when I tell you to."

"Wait a minute," Ava said. "I think you should let her drink enough that it actually weakens you a little. The

Elder Knight will be able to sense it. It might help explain how she got you here."

Claret grinned as she folded her hands over Dominic's shoulders and bent her head to his neck.

Maddy tried to look away but couldn't. There was something almost sensual in Claret's expression as she drank. And drank. She cast an anxious glance at Ava when Dominic's skin paled.

"Enough!" Ava said. And when Claret refused to stop, Ava made a fist, then quickly opened her hand, unleashing a flame of fire that singed the vampire's skin.

Claret screeched and reared back, her eyes as red as Dominic's blood.

"It's time to go," Ava said and began to chant, her voice pitched low. When she held out her hand, a pair of silver shackles materialized in her palm.

Dominic hissed with pain as she locked them in place.

Another bit of magic put a pair of thick gloves on Claret's hands.

"How do I explain knowing the exact location of the stronghold?" Claret asked.

"Just tell him a black witch gave you a magical amulet. Like this one," Ava said, as she dropped a gold chain that held a large, clear stone around the vampire's neck.

"What am I supposed to do?" Maddy asked.

"I want you to follow us, but stay out of sight. I may need to call on your power for backup if the Elder Knight's magic proves too strong."

Dominic, Maddy, and Claret followed Ava through the thick darkness, a darkness that seemed to grow more impenetrable with each footstep. Although Dominic couldn't see anything other than the looming silhouettes of trees on every side, he could sense the dark magic hovering in the air, threatening to smother him. He quietly cursed Claret for taking so much blood. It had, indeed, weakened him, as did the shackles burning the skin on his wrists. But his main worry was for Maddy. They shouldn't have let her come along. The scent of her blood tickled his nostrils, increasing the hunger rising within him.

A few miles later, Ava whispered a magical incantation that revealed the outer walls of the stronghold. Made of dark gray stone, it resembled a medieval castle, complete with turrets.

"Not so big as the old one," Ava whispered. "Maddy, stay back."

"So what do we do now?" Dominic asked. "Knock on the door?"

"It won't be necessary," Ava said, and vanished from sight.

Her words still hung in the air when one of the double doors swung open and a Knight appeared, a lantern in one hand, a sword in the other. Surprise flickered in his eyes when he saw Claret and Dominic. "What the hell!"

"I demand to see the Elder Knight," Claret said imperiously. "I've brought him a gift."

"Follow me."

Dominic glanced around as they trailed the Knight into the center of a large, open area paved with stones. Twelve Knights were gathered there, some standing, some sitting on wooden benches. Torches burned at intervals, casting flickering shadows on the faces of the men.

There was a shift in the air as the Elder Knight stepped

out of a doorway to Dominic's left. If he was surprised to see them, it didn't show. "Claret, isn't it?" He strode toward her, eyes glittering. "How did you find this place?"

"It wasn't easy," Claret replied with a toss of her head. "First, I had to capture his woman and then I had to convince him that I would slowly drain her dry if he refused to cooperate with me. Once I knew what state you were in, I found a witch I could trust." The amulet around her neck glowed softly when she touched it. "She gave me this to guide me the rest of the way. Of course, I have no intention of letting the girl live," she said with a wolfish grin. "She'll be a tasty treat when I get back home."

Dominic growled low in his throat.

The Elder Knight's gaze flicked to him briefly, then back to Claret. "You must want something of me, else you would not be here. What is it?"

She lifted one shoulder in a negligent shrug. "I was hoping for an exchange of favors."

"Indeed?"

"I've grown rather fond of Jasper. I was hoping you would remove the spell and return him to his own form. In exchange, I'll give you the vampire, as long as you let me take his blood before he dies."

"And what's to stop me from destroying you both here and now?"

A wave of dark magic flooded the area.

Claret smiled as all the Knights suddenly collapsed.

All but the Elder Knight, who appeared momentarily stunned. To Claret's amazement, he shook it off and then reached for her. She danced out of his way as a sword appeared in Dominic's hand. In a blur of movement, he drove the blade through the Elder Knight's heart.

For a moment, the Elder Knight stood there, his mouth open in a silent scream of pain and surprise before the light went out of his eyes and he toppled to the ground.

Ava appeared at Dominic's side. A word dissolved the shackles that bound him. "Well, that was easier than I thought it would be. Are you all right?"

He nodded, his eyes going red as he stared at the crimson stream leaking from the Elder Knight's chest. Dead blood, but still warm. Fueled by the violence and the scent of hot, fresh blood, his hunger roared to life, clawing at his vitals, hot and swift and undeniable.

He was reaching for the Knight when Maddy came running toward him. "Oh, Dominic, I'm so glad . . ."

The words died in her throat when he caught her in his arms.

Ava screamed, "No!" as he sank his fangs into Maddy's neck.

But he was beyond hearing, beyond caring, as his preternatural blood lust burned out of control. Only when Maddy's heartbeat slowed and became erratic did he realize what he'd done.

But by then, it was too late.

Chapter 39

With Maddy still in his arms, Dominic dropped to the ground as the horror of what he'd done—what he had always feared he would do—became a reality.

Kneeling beside him, Ava laid a tentative hand on his shoulder. "Dominic. Dominic! Look at me."

He stared at her, his eyes red and haunted.

"She's not gone yet. There's still time to save her." Ava held out her arm. "Drink quickly. Are you listening to me? There's still time to save her."

"What if she doesn't want this?"

"We don't have time to worry about that now. Drink!"

Moving woodenly, he took hold of Ava's arm and bit into her wrist. Witch blood. Family or not, it was always bitter. He took only a little, then bit into his own wrist and held the bleeding wound to Maddy's lips. Voice thick with unshed tears, he whispered, "Drink, love. Drink and come back to me."

He watched as his blood dripped into her mouth, felt a wave of relief when she swallowed, once, twice, three times, before taking hold of his arm.

Dominic closed his eyes as she drank, hating himself

for what he'd done, praying she would forgive him in time.

As her heartbeat grew steady, her face less pale, he pulled his wrist away and took her into his arms. She sighed once and then tumbled into the dark sleep.

When she woke tomorrow night, she would no longer be wholly human, nor wholly vampire.

"Well," Claret said, "I didn't see that coming." She glanced at the Knights, still trapped in Ava's spell. "What are you going to do with them?"

"I'm going to erase their oath to hunt and destroy Dominic and his people and replace it with another directive."

Claret's eyes narrowed. "Such as?"

"What do you think?"

"You wouldn't! Isn't it bad enough that ordinary hunters are constantly after us?"

"It won't change much. The Knights already destroy your kind when they find them. At the moment, it's just a sideline. In the future, killing your kind will be their main focus."

Claret snorted. "You can't work your magic on every Knight in the country."

"That's true. But I've chosen a new Elder Knight from this group. He'll instruct the others."

Screaming her rage, Claret lunged at Ava with murder in her eyes, let out a shriek as the witch summoned a sharp wooden stake to her hand.

Before Ava could strike, Dominic was there. Wresting the stake from Ava, he shoved Claret out of the way. "Enough!" he roared. His gaze darted from witch to vampire and back again. "I won't have you kill her.

I've had enough of death and destruction. I'm calling a truce between the three of us. Claret, you will never again destroy my kind or imprison them for your sustenance. And you . . ." He turned his angry gaze on Ava. "You will alter your directive and forbid the Knights to hunt in New Orleans because our kind are also there. Agreed?"

Witch and vampire glared at each other, their hatred a palpable presence.

Jaw clenched, Claret nodded sullenly.

"Agreed," Ava muttered.

Without another word, Dominic gathered Maddy in his arms and transported the two of them to Ava's house in Portland.

Dominic looked up when Ava entered the bedroom a few hours later.

"Is she going to be all right?" Ava asked.

"I think so, but there's no way to know for sure until tomorrow night. Did everything go as planned back at the stronghold?"

"Yes. I appointed a new Elder Knight, Jeremy 26, a young man not dead set in the old ways of the Brotherhood. In the future, they will hunt only Transylvanian vampires, but not in New Orleans," she assured him. "You and the other Hungarian vampires will need to be careful for a while, because it will take some time for the new Elder Knight to inform all of his followers of their new directive."

She pursed her lips, her anger hovering around her like a dark cloud. "I can't believe you stopped me from destroying that despicable creature! What were you thinking?"

Dominic shook his head. "I don't know." He pictured Claret in his mind, an enigma in a red silk dress. She had killed indiscriminately. She had imprisoned Maddy and kept him locked in a cage like some wild animal. And yet he couldn't abide the thought of another death. Right or wrong, he understood her in ways Ava never would. He knew what the craving for blood was like, how hard it could be to resist taking what you wanted when you had no family to help you overcome the yearning. Claret was a stubborn creature who knew what she wanted and was willing to do whatever it took to get it. He had to admire her for that—even when it was his blood she craved.

"Dom? You need to feed." Ava shook his shoulder when he didn't respond. "Dominic."

"What?"

"You need to feed."

He looked at her blankly for a moment and then nodded.

"I'll stay with Maddy until you get back."

Feeling dead inside because of what had happened, he willed himself into downtown Portland. Late as it was, there were still people on the streets—homeless people, couples exiting a late-night movie, a man and a woman giggling like teenagers as they staggered out of a nightclub.

He called them both to him, drank as much as he dared from each, and sent them on their way.

For a long moment, he stood in the shadows, thinking about what he'd done to Maddy. But there was no going back. And when he thought about it dispassionately, her new life wouldn't really be so bad.

He just hoped she would agree.

* * *

It was dark when Maddy woke. Odd, she thought; it seemed she'd been asleep for days. Turning her head to the side, she saw Dominic propped on one elbow on the bed beside her. She frowned, wondering why he was looking at her so strangely. "What time is it?" she asked, sitting up.

"A little after seven."

"Seven?" She glanced at the window. "But . . . it's still dark out."

"It usually is after the sun goes down."

"I slept all day?" She frowned at him. "I don't think I've ever done that before."

"You probably won't do it again."

"Did I miss something?" She stared at him, confusion in her eyes.

"What do you remember of last night?"

"You went to the stronghold with Claret. There was a confrontation and you killed the Elder Knight. Ava dissolved the manacles that shackled you. I was so glad you were unhurt I ran toward you. . . ." Her voice trailed off as she lifted a hand to her throat. "I think you bit me."

"Yes."

"I don't remember anything after that. Why don't I? What happened?"

"I needed blood because I'd let Claret drink from me. When I killed the Knight, the violence and the scent of his blood triggered my thirst. . . ." He paused, his gaze sliding away from hers. "I almost killed you."

She stared at him, eyes wide.

"There are things I have to tell you." He sat up, hands clenched at his sides.

Sitting up, she looked out the window, certain that she didn't want to hear whatever he had to say.

"You were at the point of death," he said, his voice flat. "I couldn't let that happen. I gave you some of my blood."

Fear danced in the depths of her eyes as she waited for him to go on.

"It's going to change you."

"You didn't!" She shook her head in denial. "Tell me you didn't turn me into a vampire!"

"No. Not quite."

"Not quite?"

"Do you remember when I told you there were ways to extend human life?"

She didn't answer, simply stared at him, her face pale, her eyes wide and afraid.

He took a deep breath and blew it out in a long sigh. "You're still mostly human . . ."

"*Mostly* human? What does that mean?"

"A few times a year, you'll have a sudden craving for blood and you'll feel tired during the day. If you don't drink a little blood when you feel the urge, you'll age a little more quickly than normal. If you go without for an extended period of time, it could be fatal. When you turn thirty, you'll stop aging naturally. You won't get sick anymore, and you'll be stronger physically. That's about it, except for one thing."

"I'm part vampire?"

He nodded. "You'll get used to it, in time."

She couldn't believe what he had told her. How could

she be *part* vampire? Either you were one, or you weren't. It was impossible, and she refused to believe a word of it.

Until she doubled over with pain. *Lord*, she thought, *I'm dying*.

Dominic slipped his arm around her. "Try to relax."

"What's wrong with me?" she gasped.

"You need blood."

She glanced at him over her shoulder, her gaze lingering on his throat.

"Any blood will do. You can drink from me, if you like. Or I can get a bag out of the refrigerator."

Dominic's blood. In the midst of pain and doubt, she remembered how pleasant it had been to taste him.

"From you," she said, her voice little more than a whisper.

He bit into his wrist and held it out to her.

Maddy stared at the dark red blood oozing from the two tiny punctures and thought she'd never wanted anything more in her life. Feeling suddenly embarrassed, she lowered her head and lapped it up, felt it sizzle through her, instantly relieving the pain and filling her with a warm, sensual pleasure.

Dominic closed his eyes as she drank from him. Maybe she wouldn't hate him after all.

That hope died when she lifted her head and he saw the expression on her face.

"I'm going home," she said. "Alone."

He didn't argue, didn't beg for her forgiveness or ask her to stay. He simply nodded. "I'll have Ava take you."

* * *

Silent tears tracked down Maddy's cheeks as she watched Dominic leave the room. She felt numb inside, as if every emotion had been leeched from her soul, leaving nothing behind but an empty shell. She was part vampire. She needed blood or she would age more rapidly. If she abstained, she would die. The thought was terrifying.

She cried while she packed her few belongings. Cried for what Dominic had done to her. Cried because, in spite of everything, she was going to miss him. She told herself leaving was for the best. She didn't really want to marry a vampire or be a witch. She just wanted to go home and forget any of this had happened, go back to her nice, quiet, safe life. Except she couldn't. She would be reminded of what she'd become several times a year, when she would have a sudden craving for blood. And if she ignored it. . . . Suddenly chilled inside and out, she thrust the thought from her mind. If only she had stayed home where she belonged, none of this would have happened.

After asking his great-grandmother to see Maddy safely back to New Orleans, Dominic left the house. With no destination in mind, he wandered the streets of Portland, his thoughts as dismal as the gray clouds overhead. He had lost Maddy. He had killed the Elder Knight. Ava had given the Brotherhood a new goal. As for Jasper, no one knew—or cared—what had become of him.

All in all, he wished he had stayed in Hungary.

Chapter 40

"We need to go to New Orleans"

Quill Falconer stared across the dinner table at his wife. "Now?" They'd been living in Hungary ever since the birth of the twins.

"Dominic's unhappy."

"Well, who can blame him? He's supposed to be hunting the Knights of the Dark Wood in New Orleans," Quill said, and then shook his head. "Don't tell me—there's a girl involved."

"Yes, and he's deeply in love with her."

"So, what's the problem?"

"I can't see everything clearly," Callie said. "All I know is that it has something to do with him killing Gregory 73."

Quill's lips twitched in a wry grin. "Mission accomplished. Good for him."

"Not so good. Somehow, killing the Knight brought out Dom's bloodlust and he attacked the girl—Maddy, her name is. And then, because she was close to death, he panicked and gave her his blood. A lot of his blood."

Understanding dawned in Quill's eyes. "So, she's not too happy about it."

"Apparently not."

"What do you know about the girl? Have they been intimate?"

"Only that she's young. And yes," she said with a sigh, "they've slept together."

Quill grunted softly. "Sex always makes things more complicated."

"Tell me about it," she said with an impish grin. "Anyway, she doesn't want any more to do with him. Oh! I almost forgot—it seems she has a bit of a talent for magic."

"Nowhere as strong as yours, I'm guessing. How's Ava?"

"Same as always. But she's worried about Dom. He hasn't been himself since the girl left him."

"He'll get over it." But even as he said the words, Quill had his doubts. Had he lost Callie . . . He shook his head. It didn't bear thinking about.

Reaching across the table, Callie took his hand in hers. "Will he?"

Quill stared out the dining room window. There was snow on the mountains, the sky dark with clouds and the promise of more rain before nightfall. "He's a grown man," he said, at last. "Do you think he'd appreciate us showing up?"

Callie pondered that for a moment. Dominic was much like his father—handsome, proud, and independent. Quill was right, as usual, but she wasn't happy about it. No matter that Dom was his own man now.. He was still her little boy and always would be. But it would be wrong to go to him now. He wouldn't like it at all.

"Glad you see things my way," Quill remarked.

"I guess you're right," she admitted. "We shouldn't go. We'll send Lily instead."

"Do you know where Dominic is?"

"No. Try as I might, I can't find him. He's closed his mind to me."

"Yeah," Quill said ruefully. "Me too. Not a good sign."

"Sooner or later, Liliana will find him," Callie said confidently.

"Are you sure it's safe to send her on her own?"

"Ava will look after her."

"I guess it's settled, then. Come on, let's go find our girl and tell her to pack a suitcase. She's going to America."

Chapter 41

Being part vampire wasn't as bad as Maddy had feared. She didn't have a constant craving for blood. She slept just fine, although there were occasional nightmares in which she re-lived what had happened in the Knights' stronghold—the savage expression on Dominic's face when he attacked her, the horror she'd felt when he bit her—but those times grew farther apart with each passing day. Hopefully, they would eventually fade from her memory altogether.

She found a part-time job at the local library, just to have something to do. She rather enjoyed working there, returning books to the stacks, reading to a group of children a couple of times a week, and occasionally working at the front desk. She felt the need to be surrounded by people who weren't vampires or witches, just normal human beings.

Nights were the worst. No matter how she tried, she couldn't stop thinking about Dominic. All she had to do was close her eyes and his image sprang to life—tall and dark and devastatingly handsome. Sometimes she could almost hear his voice calling her name. It never failed to bring tears to her eyes. Perhaps she shouldn't have left him. And yet, how could she stay? What if he had another overwhelming urge to feed on her again? What if the next time he couldn't stop?

Ava had decided to stay in New Orleans after seeing Maddy home. She called from time to time, usually just a brief *hello, how are you doing?* Maddy appreciated Ava's concern, but her calls always led to memories of Dominic.

Memories she would rather forget. Honesty forced her to admit that what had happened was as much her fault as his. If only she had listened to him and stayed in Portland instead of following him to Cornwall.

Maddy had been home for almost three weeks when Ava called and invited her over for tea.

"I don't think so," Maddy said. "Maybe in a week or so."

"Please, change your mind," Ava coaxed. "I've been where you are. It's never easy moving on from a failed relationship. But there's someone here who would like to see you."

Maddy's heart skipped a beat. Was it Dominic?

"Shall we say three o'clock?"

Maddy bit down on her lower lip. What if it was Dominic? Was she ready to see him again? Knowing she'd regret it if she refused, she said, "All right. I'll be there."

Maddy's nerves were on edge when she arrived at Ava's house and rang the bell.

Ava answered the door a moment later, a smile of welcome on her face. "It's so good to see you," she said, "although you're looking a little flushed. Are you feeling all right?"

"I'm fine." Maddy glanced past Ava, hoping to see Dominic. Swallowing her disappointment, she followed Ava into the living room.

Ava gestured toward the sofa. "Sit down, dear."

Maddy perched on the edge of the couch, her pulse racing at the sound of footsteps. Only it wasn't Dominic who entered the room carrying a tea tray, but a lovely young woman who could only be his twin. The same black hair, the same dark gray eyes, the same features, except softer and more feminine.

"Maddy, this is Dominic's sister, Liliana."

The girl smiled at Maddy as she set the tray on the coffee table. "I'm so happy to meet you," Lily said.

"And I, you," Maddy replied.

"Lily's come here hoping to find Dominic," Ava said, filling three china cups with tea.

"Find him? I don't understand. Is he missing?"

"In a way," Lily said. "He's blocked the whole family from communicating with him. My parents are worried, of course. But if anyone can find him, it's me. After all, being twins, we share a bond stronger than most. I can usually get in touch with him even when nobody else can. But I'm not having any luck so far. If he's in New Orleans, I can't locate him."

"How long has he been missing?"

"Since you left him," Ava said, a faint note of accusation in her tone.

Maddy felt a twinge of guilt. If anything happened to

him . . . She thrust the thought from her mind. He was a vampire. He could take care of himself and anyone who crossed his path.

"My brother loves you," Lily said. "My parents are worried about him, because he's never been in love before. He doesn't always respond well to strong emotions."

"You don't think anything's happened to him, do you?" Maddy asked anxiously.

"No. But this is the first time he's shut us out completely. Naturally we're all concerned."

"Naturally," Maddy agreed. "But I have no idea where he might be."

"If you were to try to contact him, he might answer."

"I'll try," Maddy said and reached for her phone.

"Not that way." Lily tapped her temple with her forefinger. "Telepathically. Blood to blood."

"Oh." Taking a deep breath, Maddy closed her eyes and thought about Dominic, the deep tenor of his voice, the wonder of his touch, the excitement of his kisses. *Dominic? Dominic, where are you? Please answer me.*

Maddy, what's wrong?

Your sister is here. She's worried about you.

Maddy felt his disappointment as if it were her own. *Dominic, are you there?*

Tell Lily I'm fine.

Are you?

Why do you care?

His words sliced into her heart like a dagger.

And then he was gone.

When she opened her eyes, Lily and Ava were both staring at her.

"Well?" Ava said. "Did he reply? What did he say?"

"He said to tell Lily he's fine."

"That's all he said?" Lily asked. "Where is he?"

"He didn't say. I . . . I asked how he was and he asked why I cared." She blinked back her tears. "And then there was just, I don't know, emptiness."

"Well, at least we know he's still alive," Ava remarked, blinking back a few tears of her own.

"Why did you leave him?" Lily asked.

"Why?" Maddy stared at her in disbelief. "Why? He almost killed me."

"I don't believe it."

"Well, it's true!" Maddy retorted. "He told me so himself. Not only that, but he made me a . . . I don't know what."

"So, you no longer care for him? Just like that?"

To avoid answering, Maddy sipped her tea. How *did* she feel about Dominic? For weeks, she'd told herself she didn't care anymore. But if that was true, why had her heart skipped a beat at the first sound of his voice in her mind?

"You were going to be married," Ava said over the rim of her teacup. "You must have loved him."

"I thought I did."

"He gave you a rare gift," Lily said quietly. "There are many people who would love to have what you now have, to know they'll live a long, healthy life, that they'll never be sick and that they might live for hundreds of years with a man who loves them. It wasn't just his blood that Dominic gave you, but the blood of generations of our people. Not to mention Ava's and my mother's."

"I never thought of that." Ava frowned thoughtfully,

and then a slow smile spread across her face. "No wonder you suddenly had magic. You tasted Dominic's blood several times, didn't you? Long before he bit you this last time."

Maddy arched her brow in disbelief. "Are you saying that because I tasted his blood, I have some of his mother's magic?"

"Callie is a very powerful witch. I should know. She gets it from me. And you, too, have my blood in your veins through Dominic."

Maddy looked from Ava to Lily and back again. Was it possible? Feeling a sudden need to be alone with her thoughts, she rose abruptly. "It was nice to meet you, Lily. Ava, thank you for the tea."

Before either of them could respond, she fled the house.

At home, she paced the floor. Deny it though she might, she was afraid Lily was right. In drinking Dominic's blood, she had consumed the blood of centuries of Hungarian vampires, as well as the blood of several powerful witches.

She sank down in a chair. Almost without conscious thought, a cup of hot chocolate and a blueberry muffin appeared on the table beside her. Feeling suddenly daring, she focused on the hearth and twitched her nose. And a fire crackled to life.

"Who's a witch? I'm a witch," she murmured, and swallowed a burst of hysterical laughter, afraid if she gave into it, she would dissolve into tears. Not only was she a bona fide witch, but, thanks to the dark mist that had hovered over her during Ava's spell, she could feel dark magic inside her, something she found as intriguing as it was terrifying. She had never discussed it with Dominic, but she knew he was aware of it, as was Ava.

Standing in the shadows outside Maddy's house, Dominic breathed in her scent, though he refused to admit that he had missed it—and her—more than he had thought possible. He missed her smile, her laughter, the taste of her kisses, the feel of her body pressed intimately to his, her sweet spirit and caring heart. He had tried to stay away from her, but to no avail. Night after night, he found himself lingering on the front porch hoping to catch a glimpse of her, inhale her warm, sweet scent as he remembered how right it had felt to hold her in his arms.

He wondered if he went down on his knees and begged, whether she would forgive him for what he'd done. Take pity on him and let him call her once in a while just to hear the sound of her voice.

Lost in memories of Maddy, he didn't realize she had stepped out onto the porch until he heard her gasp of surprise.

"Dominic!"

His gaze moved over her. She was as lovely as he remembered, although her eyes were tinged with sadness, and she seemed thinner. Dared he hope she'd been missing him half as much as he missed her?

"What are you doing here?" she asked, her voice little more than a whisper.

"I've been coming here every night since you got home," he confessed.

Waiting for an explanation, she searched his gaze.

"I miss you," he said simply. "I know you'll never forgive me for what I did. I have no excuse."

"I may have overreacted a little," she murmured. "But I'd never seen you quite like that, so . . . so out of control. I've never been so scared in my whole life."

"Yeah, well, it scared the hell out of me, too. I've never experienced blood hunger like that before. Or since." He shrugged. "I just didn't know how to handle it."

"I'm sorry, Dominic."

It sounded like goodbye, he thought. But what did he expect?

"I love you," he said. "I always will. Okay if I kiss you one last time before I go?"

At her nod, he closed the distance between them, cupped her face in his palms, and kissed her lightly.

Unable to resist being closer, she leaned into him.

He slipped his arm around her waist.

She clasped her hands behind his neck.

Desire flamed between them, hotter than a thousand suns. There was no need for words. Dominic swung her up into his arms, carried her inside, and kicked the door shut behind them. They made it as far as the living room floor before they were both naked and locked in each other's arms, their mouths fused together.

"Don't ever leave me again," she gasped. "No matter what I say."

"Never." He showered her with kisses as his hands rediscovered the silk of her hair, the satin of her skin.

She wrapped her legs around his waist when he rose

over her, his eyes dark with desire as he claimed her for his own.

Curled up on the sofa in Ava's house, Lily and her great-grandmother smiled as they exchanged knowing glances.

"Well, Granny, it seems they've kissed and made up," Lily remarked.

Ava laughed softly. "Yes, indeed. And none too soon."

Chapter 42

Dominic woke abruptly. He frowned when he rolled over and found that Maddy wasn't beside him. He had carried her upstairs last night, he recalled with a smile, and they had slept locked in each other's arms.

When the noise came again, he tossed the blankets aside and padded into the bathroom, muttering, "What the hell!" when he saw her leaning over the toilet.

Maddy glanced over her shoulder. "Go away."

"Are you sick?" She couldn't be sick, he thought. Not with his blood in her veins. But something was definitely wrong.

"I don't think so. Maybe it was something I ate." She made a shooing motion with her hand. "Get out of here."

"No way." Going to the sink, he ran a washcloth under the cool water, then filled a glass and handed it to her.

Embarrassed that he had seen her throwing up, Maddy rinsed her mouth.

When she was done, he took the glass and handed her the cloth.

"Thanks." She wiped her face, grasped the hand he offered, and let him pull her to her feet.

"Are you feeling better?" he asked.

"Better than I did, but still kind of queasy," she said, tossing the washcloth into the sink. "I thought you said I wouldn't get sick anymore."

Shrugging, he placed his hand on her brow. "You don't have a fever." What the hell could be wrong?

His gaze ran over her from head to foot. She looked healthy, her heartbeat was strong and steady, her pulse normal. He was about to suggest they go to see Ava when his cell phone rang.

Striding into the bedroom, he picked it up and barked, "Hello."

"Hello to you, too," his great-grandmother said dryly. "What are you growling about?"

"There's something wrong with Maddy. I was about to bring her over to see you. She shouldn't be getting sick."

"What do you mean?"

"She's been throwing up."

Lily's laughter sounded in the background.

"What's so damn funny?" he asked, his patience growing thin.

"Doesn't Maddy know what's wrong?" Ava asked, sounding amused.

"If she did, don't you think she'd tell me?"

"I don't know. Some women like to keep it a secret for a while."

"What are you talking about?"

"Basic biology, Dominic."

"Congratulations, brother," Lily said, her voice filled with laughter.

Dominic stared at the phone. Looked at Maddy, who was standing in the bathroom doorway, a towel wrapped around her nakedness, her eyes wide. "Do you know what they're talking about?"

She nodded, her face flushed.

"Well, I wish to hell somebody would tell me!"

"Hang up, Dominic," Maddy said. "We need to talk."

He didn't bother to tell Ava goodbye, just ended the call. "All right, what the devil's going on?"

"Do you love me?"

"What kind of fool question is that?" he asked irritably. "Didn't I prove it to you last night? Twice?"

"Do you still want to marry me?"

"Just name the day."

"What should we name the baby?"

He stared at her, feeling as if someone had just punched him in the gut. "You're pregnant? How?"

"The usual way," Maddy said, and burst out laughing. "I wish you could see your face."

"Pregnant." He said the word as if he'd just heard it for the first time. "Pregnant." A slow smile spread across his face as he went to Maddy and drew her gently into his arms. "Why didn't you tell me sooner?"

"I didn't know until Lily said congratulations and everything clicked into place." Her gaze searched his. "Does it change anything between us?"

"Damn right," he said, his knuckles caressing her cheek. "It makes me love you even more."

Wrapping her arms around his neck, she whispered, "Show me."

"Any time, my love."

She giggled as he swept her off her feet and carried her back to bed.

* * *

With a sigh, Dominic cradled Maddy in his arms. "Are you happy about the baby?" he asked.

"Yes, but . . ."

"But what?"

"Well, are baby vampires like regular babies?"

"I guess so."

"I won't have to give him blood instead of milk, will I?"

"No," he said, stifling a grin. "It's like I told you, our young are human until puberty."

"And all our children will be boys," she murmured.

He heard the disappointment in her voice. Not that he could blame her. Like most women, she probably wanted a daughter. "Is that a game changer?"

"No," she said slowly. "There's no guarantee that I'd have a daughter, no matter who I married."

Giving her shoulders a squeeze, Dominic brushed a kiss across her cheek. "If you want a little girl, we can always adopt one."

"You'd do that?"

"You must know I'd do anything for you."

With a sigh, she snuggled against him. A baby. She was going to have a baby. "Oh! What am I going to tell my parents?"

"The truth?"

"That my husband is a vampire and I'm carrying his baby?"

"We can get married tomorrow and then pretend the baby came a little early."

"What about the vampire thing? Will my mom and dad be able to tell what you are?"

"You couldn't. Neither will they. Will your parents be upset if they miss the wedding?"

"Better upset than disappointed in me." Maddy shook her head. "I was going to be the 'good' daughter and not get pregnant out of wedlock like my sister. I'll never hear the end of it from Fran."

"If your parents say anything, you can tell them we were so much in love, we just couldn't wait a minute longer."

"It's sort of the truth," Maddy said with a grin. "I couldn't wait any longer."

"It's settled, then. I'll have Ava make the arrangements. The two of you can conjure a wedding gown. And tomorrow, you'll be Mrs. Dominic Falconer."

Maddy smiled. And then she frowned. "What about *your* parents?"

"If I know Lily, they're already on their way."

Maddy shivered at the thought of meeting his mother and father. One was a powerful vampire, the other a powerful witch. What if they didn't like her? What if they disapproved of their son's marriage? What if they had someone else in mind for him?

"Stop worrying, love," Dominic said. "They'll be as crazy about you as I am."

"I knew we never should have sent Ava to the States with Dominic," Callie said as she dropped her cell phone on the coffee table. "Some chaperone she turned out to be."

Quill grinned. "Darlin', all the chaperones in the world wouldn't have done any good. Dominic's a young, healthy male."

"He's marrying a girl we haven't even met! A girl who's already pregnant!"

"Lily likes Maddy. You'll probably like her, too. And just think, you'll have another daughter to love."

"That's true," she said with a smile.

"And if I recall right," he said, waggling his eyebrows, "we didn't wait for the wedding either."

A slow smile spread over Callie's face. "You Falconer men," she muttered. "You're just too darn sexy to resist."

Maddy didn't know how Ava managed to find a church and arrange for the wedding to take place the following night. Magic, she supposed.

While Dominic went hunting, Ava and Lily came over to keep her company. Ava conjured a bridal magazine, and the three of them spent an hour looking at wedding gowns before Maddy found one she loved. Ava taught her the necessary incantation and in a matter of minutes, the loveliest wedding gown she had ever seen appeared in a shower of stardust.

She ran her hands over the floor-length skirt, which was a froth of lace and silk. The sleeves were long, the neckline square.

"Let's see how it looks on you," Lily said.

A moment later, Maddy was looking at herself in a full-length mirror conjured by Lily. "It's beautiful," Maddy exclaimed softly.

"And you look beautiful in it." A murmured word by Ava produced a shoulder-length veil in one hand and a longer one in the other. "Which will it be?"

"The short one, I think," Maddy decided.

With a nod, Ava set it in place.

"I can't wait to get married," Lily said as she took the

unwanted veil and placed it on her own head. "Just so I can wear a dress like that and a veil like this."

Ava looked at her sharply. "Is there something we should know?"

"What?" With a laugh, Lily shrugged. "No. I haven't met anyone I'd even consider marrying."

"Well, that's a relief."

"I don't think so," Lily said with a pout. "I'm an old maid."

"Child, you don't know what old is."

"I know I'm twenty five and I don't even have a boyfriend."

Maddy grinned as she listened to Lily and Ava, relieved that she liked Dominic's sister and his great-grandmother. She just hoped she would like his parents as much. And earnestly prayed they would like her.

Maddy woke before sunrise the next morning. Heart pounding, she glanced at Dominic, asleep beside her. Tonight, he would be her husband. The thought sent a thrill of excitement skating down her spine, along with a bit of doubt. Everything was happening so fast. It was like living life on speed—meet Dominic, meet Ava, fall in love, discover he's a vampire, Ava a witch and that, she herself is a witch, meet Lily, learn she's pregnant, get married. Maybe they should have waited a while to tie the knot. And they would have, she thought, except for the baby. She couldn't let her child, an innocent, be born out of wedlock.

"Second thoughts?" Dominic asked, his eyes still closed.

"Yes. And no."

"We can wait if you want." He sat up when she didn't say anything. "Have you changed your mind, Maddy? If so, just tell me. I'll support you and the baby no matter what you decide."

Maddy sighed. What had she ever done to deserve such a man? She would be crazy to let him go. Reaching for him, she pulled him down beside her. "I haven't changed my mind. Just a touch of wedding jitters, I guess."

"Understandable. We haven't known each other very long and yet, in some ways, I feel like I've been waiting for you my whole life."

She was melting inside, Maddy thought as he captured her lips with his in a long, searing kiss that threatened to melt her bones, even as it erased every last doubt from her mind.

Chapter 43

"Maddy? Maddy, wake up."

"I'm too tired, Dominic. Let me sleep a little longer." Eyes still closed, she frowned. "What are you doing up so early anyway?"

"My parents are here."

"Oh. That's nice." She bolted upright. "Your parents! They're here? Now?"

"Yeah. And anxious to meet their future daughter-in-law."

Maddy clutched the blankets to her chest. "But I'm not ready."

"Maddy, love, there's no need to be afraid."

She started to say she wasn't afraid, but it was true. Dominic was a vampire, but his father was a *vampire* and had been one for centuries. And his mother—Ava had spoken of Callie, of how powerful she was.

Dominic sat on the edge of the bed. "What are you so worried about?"

"I feel so . . . small. So inadequate in comparison with your mother, not to mention Ava and Lily."

"Hey. My mother didn't come into her magic until

she was about your age. And believe me, you're plenty powerful right now. Don't forget, you've got the blood of two witches and centuries of ancient vampire blood in your veins. You're the equal of anybody in the family. Well, except maybe my grandfather. And even if you weren't, none of that matters. What matters is that I love you. And so will they." He kissed her lightly. "You don't want them to think you're a coward, do you?"

"What? Of course not."

"I'll tell you a secret. I think my mother was a little hesitant to meet her in-laws, too. Now, come on. Get dressed. We're getting married in a few hours, remember?"

Maddy inhaled deeply several times as she took a last look in the mirror. Was her dress too short? Did her hair look all right? With a toss of her head, she marched down the stairs to meet Dominic's parents.

They both stood when she entered the room. His mother was lovely, with honey-gold hair and deep blue eyes. Maddy couldn't help staring when she saw his father. He and Dominic could have been brothers, they looked so much alike. The only difference was that Dominic's hair was black while his father's was a dark, dark brown.

Dominic took her hand in his. "Maddy, this is my mother, Callie."

His mother hurried toward her. "Maddy!" she exclaimed, giving her a hug. "I'm so glad to meet you. You're even lovelier than Dom said."

"I'm happy to meet you, too," Maddy said, hating the tremor in her voice.

"And this is my father, Quill."

Maddy flushed when her future father-in-law kissed her on the cheek.

"Welcome to the family," he said, his gray eyes twinkling. "It's not often we gain a daughter and a grandson at the same time."

Maddy glared at Dominic.

"Don't be mad at Dominic," Quill said, a twinkle in his eye. "It was Lily who let the cat out of the bag, so to speak."

"Please, sit down," Maddy said. Dominic settled into the easy chair across from the sofa, and Maddy perched on the arm. "Can I get you anything?"

"No, thank you," Callie said. "This is all so exciting, the wedding and the baby. Dominic told us your parents are away. I know you must be sorry they can't be here. I am, too. I was hoping to meet them."

Maddy nodded. "I know they'll be disappointed, but with the baby coming, I don't want to wait."

"Completely understandable," Quill said.

"I'm just so glad we could be here." Callie glanced at her son. "Do you know where you're going to live?"

"We haven't made up our minds yet," he replied, "but I think Maddy wants to be near her mother, with the baby coming and all."

"Of course." Callie glanced at her watch. "Quill, we need to go. I need to change clothes, and I'm sure Maddy has a lot to do."

"That wasn't so bad, was it?" Dominic asked when his parents had taken their leave.

"No. Your mom and dad are very nice. I didn't expect them to be so accepting. Especially about the baby."

"Yeah, I'm gonna kill Lily. That was news I wanted to share myself."

"I don't blame you for being upset," Maddy remarked, one hand resting on her belly. "But to tell you the truth, I'm glad the secret's out."

"Yeah, well, even if Lily hadn't snitched, my mother probably would have sensed it when she hugged you. Come on, love, we'd better go upstairs and get ready. We don't want to be late."

The church Ava had found was small and quaint, with lovely stained-glass windows. The interior was lit by candles, the pews made of dark wood. Dominic's parents sat in the front pew on one side of the narrow aisle, Ava and Lily sat in the opposite row.

Maddy knew a moment of regret that her parents weren't there, that her father wasn't beside her as she walked down the aisle. Her heart pounded nervously as she took her place at the altar beside Dominic. She felt an odd tremor in the air when the clergyman entered the chapel—a tall, spare man with iron-gray hair and sharp, brown eyes.

He smiled at Dominic's family before turning his attention to Maddy and Dominic. "We are gathered here today for this most solemn occasion, the joining of this man and this woman. Marriage is a sacred covenant, instituted by our Maker, and not to be entered into lightly. I understand the bride and groom have written their own vows. You may proceed."

Maddy took a deep breath as she reached for Dominic's hand and slipped a wedding band on his finger. "Dominic, I promise to love you and only you all the days of my life. I promise to support you and always stand by your side in good times and bad. I will try my best to be the woman you deserve and, hopefully, to bear your children and grow old beside you."

As he slipped a matching wedding band on her finger, Dominic murmured, "Maddy, I will love you and only you from this night forward and throughout eternity. I will cherish you and protect you. I promise to be the best husband I can, to always listen to your concerns and to put your wants and your needs above my own."

The clergyman nodded as he looked from one to the other. "By the power vested in me, I now pronounce you man and wife. Dominic, you may kiss your bride."

Dominic carefully lifted her veil before drawing her into his arms. "Forever," he whispered as he claimed his first kiss as her husband.

Maddy forgot they weren't alone as he deepened the kiss. He was hers, she thought, hers for as long as she lived.

A discreet cough from the front row brought a flush to her cheeks. "Dominic."

"Forget about them," he said with a wink and kissed her again.

This time, when he let her go, the family gathered around them.

"I always wanted a sister!" Lily exclaimed with a broad smile as she took Maddy's hands in hers. "Welcome to the family."

"Thank you, Lily."

"Be happy, both of you." Blinking a tear from her eye, Ava said, "I knew you were meant to be together the first time I saw you."

"I'm so glad you were right." Maddy bit down on her lower lip when Quill came toward her.

"We have two daughters now," he said, his voice deep. "We will love you as our own." Leaning down, he kissed her cheek. "Be happy, Maddy. And if you ever need anything, don't hesitate to call us. We'll always be there for you."

"Thank you, Mr. Falconer."

"I hope, when you know me better, you'll call me 'Father.'"

She nodded, her heart swelling with emotion.

"My turn," Callie said, after elbowing Quill out of the way. "I'm so glad Dominic found you. I admit, I had my doubts when I discovered you'd only known each other a short time, but I can see how much he loves you, and how much you love him. I wish you all the best. And as Quill said, if you ever need us, we'll be there."

Maddy smiled, her throat thick with unshed tears.

"Well, we'd better go," Ava said. "There's a perfectly good dinner waiting for us at the best restaurant in town!"

Chapter 44

Jasper stood in the shadows outside the church, his anger growing stronger with every passing moment. So, Dominic had married the girl and now they were all just one, big, happy family. No doubt they hadn't given him a thought since Portland, while he'd thought of nothing else but the shabby, thoughtless way they'd treated him.

Well, he intended to make them pay for every day he'd been trapped in that toad's hideous body, for every disgusting thing he'd had to eat to survive—bugs and worms and flies. He could still taste the loathsome things, doubted he would ever forget.

He supposed he owed Dominic a word of thanks. With the Elder Knight's death, the enchantment that had trapped him in the body of a toad had been broken, thereby freeing him from the Knight's revolting spell. But he didn't feel grateful, only angry and jealous.

And bent on vengeance. Not so much against Dominic, but against the witch who had refused to release him from the Knight's enchantment. The same witch who had turned him into a vulture over twenty-five years ago.

And heaven help anyone who tried to stop him.

Chapter 45

The restaurant was lovely. Ava had ordered a lavish dinner, complete with wine for the vampires and champagne for the witches.

While they waited for dinner, Callie reached into her large handbag and withdrew two small packages wrapped in wedding paper. Handing the smaller of the two to Maddy, she said, "This one is from Andras and Mirella, Dominic's grandparents. They said to tell you both they were sorry they couldn't attend the wedding, but there was some serious trouble that only Andras could settle."

Wondering what it could be, Maddy carefully unwrapped the gift. Inside, she found a check for a hundred thousand dollars. Speechless, she handed it to Dominic.

"Well, damn," he exclaimed softly. "I never expected anything like this."

Quill laughed. "It's for a down payment on a house. Your grandfather had a feeling you might want to stay in the States for a while."

"He knows me all too well," Dominic said.

"Yeah. Well, it comes with a contingency."

"We have to go home for a visit at least once a year," Dominic said with a wry grin.

"Right the first time."

"This is from us," Callie said, and offered Maddy the second package.

This one held plane tickets and an all-expenses paid trip to Italy.

"For your honeymoon," Callie said. "Or whenever."

"And this is from me," Ava said, producing a package wrapped with colorful ribbons. "Although it's really for Dominic."

Curious, Maddy unwrapped the package. Feeling a blush rise in her cheeks, she lifted a long, white nightgown from the box. It was lighter than air and shimmered like starlight.

"Thanks, Grams," Dominic said, grinning. "I love it."

"That's not my only gift, although the second one is really for me. I'd like to decorate the nursery when the time comes."

"Of course," Maddy said with a smile.

"This is from me for Dominic," Lily said, handing a small bag to her brother. "Although it's really for Maddy."

Dominic removed the tissue paper, glanced into the bag, and lifted one brow as he looked at his sister.

"What is it?" Maddy asked.

With a shake of his head, Dominic pulled a pair of black bikini briefs out of the bag.

Quill laughed, Callie rolled her eyes, Ava snickered, and Maddy blushed.

* * *

It was late when the party broke up. After numerous hugs and kisses and promises to stay in touch, Dominic's parents left for home.

Lily decided to stay and spend more time with Ava and her brother and new sister-in-law.

When they reached Maddy's home, Dominic swung her into his arms and carried her over the threshold. Shutting the door, he slowly lowered her to her feet. "I love you, Maddy. I hope I never let you down."

Maddy smiled at him, then took him by the hand and led him upstairs to her bedroom.

When they reached the bed, she pushed him down on the mattress. Then, feeling suddenly bold, she began to undress, ever so slowly—removing first her veil, then her shoes, followed by a seductive striptease that elicited a low whistle of appreciation from Dominic.

A moment later, she was flat on her back on the bed and a fully aroused male was hovering over her, his dark eyes burning into hers as he lowered his head and claimed her lips with his in a long, searing kiss that left her breathless and panting with need.

Throwing her head back, she cried his name as he thrust into her, carrying her over the edge into paradise.

Maddy woke slowly, her body aching in places it had never hurt before. Turning her head to the side, she smiled when she saw Dominic sleeping beside her. "Husband," she whispered. "What a wonderful word."

They had made love before and it had been wonderful, but last night . . . last night he had made her forever his in a way she couldn't explain but had felt in every fiber of her being.

With a sigh, she placed her hand on her belly. His child was growing inside her. She had little experience with babies. What kind of mother would she be? She traced Dominic's lower lip with her fingertips. What kind of father would he be?

Knowing Dominic would likely sleep at least until afternoon, she slipped out of bed, threw on a robe, and padded downstairs. They'd have to find a place to live soon, she thought, because her parents would be home in two months. Her parents! She needed to call them to tell them the news.

As she'd feared, the news of her so-called spur-of-the-moment wedding didn't go over well with her parents, especially with her mother.

"How could you get married without us or your sister being there?" her mother asked.

"I'm sorry, Mom. I knew you'd be disappointed, but we just couldn't wait to be together. I know you'll understand when you meet Dominic. I love him so much. Please try to be happy for me."

With a sob, her mother said, "Your father wants to speak to you."

"I love you, Mom," Maddy said, but her only answer was more sniffles.

Her father was a little more understanding. "I can't say I'm not disappointed," he said, "but I still remember what it was like to be young and in love. What does he do for a living? I think you might have told me, but I forgot."

"He's in business with his father and grandfather," Maddy said. "His family is very close."

"I can't wait to meet him. And don't worry about your mother. She'll get over it. Everything all right at the house?"

"Yes, fine. Dominic's father gave us money for a down payment on a place of our own."

"Really? Well, I guess his business must be doing well. We'll call you when we're on our way home."

"Thanks, Dad. I love you."

"Love you, too, Maddy girl."

Feeling better, Maddy ended the call.

Thirty minutes later, she headed for the kitchen in search of coffee and nourishment. After all, she was eating for two now.

Sitting at the table, she ate a leisurely breakfast. They needed to find a house pretty quickly, she thought. They hadn't really talked about where they wanted to live. Originally, she'd thought she wanted to stay in New Orleans, but there were too many bad memories in Louisiana. Florida maybe? Or California? Anywhere but Connecticut. Still, her parents were here, and now that she was expecting a baby . . . She smiled as she placed her hand on her belly. With the baby coming, it might be nice to have her mother nearby. But it didn't really matter where they lived, she thought, as long as Dominic was beside her.

Picking up her cell phone, she searched online for houses for sale. So many choices. One story or two? Big lot, or something smaller and easier to maintain? Pool or no pool? Close to the city or not? How would Dominic feel about getting a puppy?

She frowned as a new thought occurred to her. Thanks to Quill's generosity, they had a sizable down payment, but that was just the beginning. She had no idea how much Dominic made working for his father, or whether he would still be getting paid if they remained in the States.

Deciding it was a discussion for later, she poured herself another cup of coffee and went back to house-hunting. An hour later, she found one that she loved. Brimming with excitement, she kept watching the clock, tapping her foot impatiently as she waited for Dominic to rise.

Maddy's bubbling excitement penetrated the dark sleep. Throwing the blankets aside, Dominic pulled on a pair of sweatpants and sauntered into the living room. "Did you win the lottery or what?" he asked, joining her on the sofa.

"You're up early."

"How could I sleep with you practically bouncing off the walls? What's up?"

"I found a house!" She tapped a few keys, then thrust her phone under his nose. "Look!"

He had to admit it was a good-looking house. A white, two-story home with a wraparound porch, a red-brick chimney, and dark green trim situated on a swath of well-kept lawn. He scrolled down to read the details: three bedrooms, two bathrooms, living room, kitchen, den, bonus room. Even a pool. "Metairie," he said. "That's what, about eight miles from here?"

"Too close to my parents?" Maddy asked.

"I doubt if it will be a problem for me if it's not for you."

"Can we go look at it?"

"Sure. Let me take a shower and get dressed."

"It's perfect!" Maddy exclaimed.

"You've only seen one room," Dominic said. One quick glance at the Realtor's face and he knew the guy was already figuring out his commission. "Come on, let's go see the rest."

Dominic had to admit the place was darn near perfect. The paint and carpets—all done in subtle earth tones—were new, the yard well-taken care of, the pool immaculate, the rooms good-size with lots of closets and cupboards, something Maddy had insisted on.

"Well?" she asked impatiently. "What do you think? Can we afford it?"

"Not to worry, love." Glancing over his shoulder at the agent, Dominic said, "We'll take it."

Never had time passed so slowly. Maddy counted the days until escrow would be complete. She had hoped for a thirty-day escrow, but had to settle for sixty. She didn't know how she could possibly wait that long.

A week after discovering she was pregnant, she went to the doctor for an exam. She was three months pregnant, he informed her, a month further along than she'd thought. She left his office with a number of pamphlets for new mothers, a suggestion to watch her weight and exercise, as well as a prescription for prenatal vitamins.

She quit her job at the library the next day. Sixty days seemed like forever. She passed the time shopping, making a second visit to the doctor, looking at paint samples and carpet swatches. Dominic had told her money wasn't an issue and she took him at his word. She discovered a fondness for mission-style furniture. Fortunately, Dominic liked it, too, and they arranged to have the pieces she'd chosen delivered the morning they were scheduled to take possession of the house.

At last, the day arrived when they could move in.

Dominic swung her up into his arms and carried her over the threshold. "Welcome home, love." Setting her on her feet, he drew her into his embrace and kissed her.

"I can't believe it," she said, eyes shining with happiness. "A home of our own."

"And a baby on the way."

"I was thinking about our honeymoon," Maddy said. "Would you mind if we postponed it until after the baby comes?"

"Whatever you want is fine with me."

She glanced around the living room, mentally arranging the furniture. They'd bought only the necessities—a sofa and a love seat, end tables, a bedroom set, a big-screen TV, a dining table and six chairs, kitchen appliances, dishes, a few pots, silverware, towels for the bathroom and the kitchen.

As she decided where she wanted things, Dominic moved them. Having a vampire for a husband was a handy thing, she mused, as he easily put the bed frame together and lifted the mattress and box springs into place. It took him less than an hour.

"I was thinking I'd call Ava and ask if now would be a good time to decorate the nursery."

"I'm sure she's just been waiting for your call."

Ava answered on the first ring. "Maddy! How's married life?"

"Wonderful! Are you busy?"

"No, why?"

"Is tomorrow morning a good time to decorate the nursery?"

"It's perfect."

"Not too early. I'm still feeling a little queasy first thing in the morning."

"How about eleven?"

"I'll see you then." Humming softly, Maddy ended the call. Life was perfect, she thought as she headed outside to water the flowers. She had a lovely home, a sexy, caring husband, and a baby on the way. What else could she ask for?

Maddy had expected it to take days to decorate the nursery, but with Ava in charge, it took only hours. Ava made suggestions and when Maddy approved, they appeared as if by, well, magic. Pale blue walls. Puffy white clouds on the ceiling. A cartoon knight in shining armor fighting a fiery dragon rode boldly across one wall. A vampire who looked suspiciously like Dominic appeared on another. A word and the wave of a hand conjured a crib, a changing table, a padded rocking chair, a lamp in the shape of a unicorn, pleated curtains at the window.

Maddy could only shake her head as she admired the finished project. “I don’t know how to thank you.”

“Just make sure to let me babysit once in a while.” Ava laid her hand on the swell of Maddy’s belly. “I can’t wait to hold him.”

“Me either. Do you think he’ll look like Dominic?”

“It wouldn’t surprise me. The Falconer genes are very strong.”

“And so are the Falconer men,” Dominic remarked as he came into the room.

“What do you think?” Maddy asked, gesturing at the mural as he slipped his arm around her waist.

“Looks good. Especially the vampire,” he said, winking at Ava.

“I knew you’d like it,” she said. “Well, I’m off. Lily and I are going shopping. Walk me out, Dom?”

“Sure.” He kissed the top of Maddy’s head. “Be right back.” Out on the porch, with the front door closed behind them, he asked, “What’s bothering you, Ava?”

“I’m not sure. I have this nagging feeling that something bad is about to happen, but I don’t know what it is. Have you sensed anything?”

Dominic shook his head. “The Elder Knight is dead. You’ve changed their main directive. Jasper is hopping around somewhere, if some predator hasn’t eaten him. Maddy’s healthy.”

“Maybe I’m just worrying for nothing,” Ava said with a shrug. “I always get nervous when there’s a baby on the way. See you soon.”

After Ava left, Dominic opened his preternatural senses but found nothing to alarm him. No scent of vampires or witches or hunters. Only the fragrance of trees and grass and flowers.

And chocolate chip cookies.

Grinning, he hurried into the kitchen to grab one before they cooled off.

Chapter 46

Maddy glanced at herself in the mirror as she stepped out of the shower. No doubt about it, she was getting fat. Well, not fat, she amended. But she was six months along now and definitely looked pregnant. The last few weeks had flown by, with every day better than the last. Her morning sickness had passed and she felt wonderful.

She loved married life, loved Dominic more with every passing day. He took such good care of her, soothed her fears when she thought about actually delivering the baby, went out in the middle of the night when she had a sudden craving for watermelon, rubbed her back when it ached.

Sometimes she sat in the rocking chair in the nursery, imagining what it would be like to hold her son in her arms. She had little experience with babies and couldn't wait to hold him close, to suckle him and bathe him and change his diapers. To watch him take his first steps, hear his first word, accompany him to school on his first day at kindergarten.

Lily and Ava came to visit two or three times a week, and she welcomed their company. Ava often brought gifts for the baby—a little brown-and-white-stuffed teddy bear, a cloth book of nursery rhymes, a windup car, a musical mobile for over his crib. Lily, too, brought gifts—a pillow in the shape of a unicorn, a pair of cowboy boots, shirts and socks and shoes. Maddy grinned, thinking she had enough onesies and booties for a dozen babies.

Her parents had come by several times since getting home. She had been nervous at the thought of introducing them to Dominic, but he had turned on the charm, and by the time her mom and dad went home that night, whatever qualms they might have entertained were gone. Both were thrilled at the prospect of having another grandchild. And life was good.

Humming a lullaby, she dressed, grabbed a hat and a book, and stepped outside to read while she waited for Dominic to wake up. It was a lovely day, the sky a bright blue. She moved one of the chairs into the sun, thinking she could read and work on her tan at the same time.

She was halfway through the book when she heard footsteps behind her. She smiled, thinking it was Dominic, let out a yelp when something stabbed her in the arm. Before she could turn around, the world began to spin. She cried Dominic's name before darkness swept her away.

Dominic woke with a start. Certain he had heard Maddy call his name, he glanced around the room, but she wasn't there. Thinking he must have imagined it, he stretched out on the bed, intending to rest for a few more minutes. But first he opened his senses to see what his bride was up to.

Sitting up, he expanded his senses, searching for the

link that bound them, but there was nothing there, only emptiness.

Rising, he pulled on a pair of jeans and searched the house, then stepped out into the backyard. The book she'd been reading lay on the grass beside her chair. He sensed she had been there only moments ago. Where was she now?

He lifted his head, nostrils flared. And cursed when he caught a familiar scent.

Jasper! What the hell? The warlock had been a toad the last time he'd seen him. Had someone released him from the spell? he wondered. And then he frowned. Of course, the Elder Knight's curse would have been broken with his death.

Dammit! Why hadn't he thought of that sooner? Why hadn't Ava?

And what the hell was he going to do now?

Chapter 47

Maddy regained consciousness slowly. Her head felt stuffed with cotton, and when she tried to sit up, she couldn't. A single candle flickered across the room. The dim light hurt her eyes.

Fear spiked through her when a man stepped out of the shadows in the corner. "Who are you? What do you want with me?"

"Don't you recognize me? Perhaps if I hopped around the room?"

Jasper! She fought the wave of panic that swept through her when she saw the malevolent expression on his face. She tried to speak but couldn't form the words.

"This is how it's going to be," he said, his voice as cold as the grave. "I'm going to allow you to call the vampire. You're to say exactly what I tell you and nothing more. Do you understand?"

Maddy nodded.

"Don't try any tricks. He won't be able to locate you, so trying to keep him on the phone won't do any good." He grinned wolfishly. "I learned a lot from the Elder

Knight. Neither the witch nor the vampire will be able to set you free."

She cringed when his hands grasped her shoulders and pulled her into a sitting position. He muttered some words in a language she didn't understand, and breathed a sigh of relief as part of whatever spell he had put her under dissolved.

"Call the vampire," he said, thrusting his cell phone into her hand. "I'll tell you what to say."

Dominic grabbed his phone on the first ring, hoping it was Maddy, but he didn't recognize the number. He was about to ignore the call when something prompted him to answer it. "Hello?"

"Dominic, I'm with Jasper."

"Maddy! Are you all right?"

"He's going to kill me unless you bring Ava to him," she said, her voice wooden.

She was under some sort of spell. The thought angered him almost as much as it worried him.

"The witch's hands are to be shackled behind her back," she went on in the same flat tone. "Her head must be covered. And she's to drink the potion Jasper left on the front porch of my parents' house before you bring her. Don't try to locate me. He's done something to block our bond. The directions to where I am are in the box with the potion. If you're not here by midnight, don't bother coming."

"Maddy!"

But it was too late. The call ended. When he tried to

call her back, there was no response. Apparently Jasper had destroyed the phone.

Shit! Pulling on a shirt and his boots, Dominic headed for Maddy's parents' place, where he found a plastic bag. A look inside showed a small black box. A thought took him to Ava's house.

She was waiting for Dominic on the porch when he arrived.

"Jasper's got Maddy," he said curtly.

"I know."

"How?"

Stepping back, she said, "We can't discuss it out here."

Dominic followed her into the living room. Too agitated to sit, he paced the floor in front of the fireplace as he relayed Maddy's message. "What has he done to her?"

"I don't know, but one thing is certain—he's used dark magic on her."

"Can you block it or break it?" he asked anxiously.

"Perhaps."

Dominic swore under his breath. "Where the hell did he learn dark magic?"

"Most likely from the Elder Knight."

He gestured at the bag, which reeked of dark magic. "Did Jasper use that same kind of magic on Maddy?"

"I doubt if he used anything so strong," Ava said thoughtfully. "Open the bag."

Dominic removed the box from the bag. As soon as he lifted the lid, the skin on his fingers blistered.

"Dark magic," Ava murmured as she lifted a small bottle from inside. It was filled with a clear liquid. Slipping on a pair of heavy gloves, she took Dominic's hands in hers. Eyes closed, she began to chant softly in Hungarian.

After several moments, the blisters on his hands dried up and disappeared.

"Thanks."

Still wearing the gloves, Ava uncorked the bottle, took a whiff, and quickly sealed it again.

"What is it?"

"More dark magic. It's an old and powerful spell concocted by a black witch a thousand years ago. It's been used on kings and queens through the ages by those who wanted to steal power. One drink and I'll be a zombie for twenty-four hours, compelled to do whatever Jasper says."

"Dammit, I can't let you drink that stuff. You'd be powerless against him. There's got to be another way!"

"What way would that be, Dom? Are you going to let him kill Maddy? He doesn't want her. He wants revenge for the years he spent as a vulture, and because I refused to undo the Elder Knight's enchantment."

"I don't give a damn what his reasons are, or what he wants. He's got my wife and my child. I can't just sit here and do nothing!"

"Calm down and listen to me. We're going to need Lily's help."

"Lily!" Dominic exclaimed. "He's already got my wife. I'm not giving him my sister, too!"

"Relax," Ava said as she grabbed her cell phone. "I have a plan and Lily's part of it. With luck, we'll all see the better side of this yet."

At five minutes to midnight, Dominic transported himself, Lily, and Ava to the address they had found inside the box with the potion. The house had recently been in a fire. The outside walls were charred; the stink of smoke lingered in the air.

Lily stayed out of sight as they approached the place.

The potion Ava had consumed left her with a strange kind of lassitude. As instructed, Dominic had shackled her hands behind her back and dropped a hood over her head. He carried her to the front door, held her close while he knocked, then set her on her feet, his arm around her waist to hold her up.

The door opened a crack and Jasper peered out.

"I've done what you wanted," Dominic said. "Give me Maddy."

"Not yet."

"Then let me see her."

Jasper opened the door a little wider.

Maddy was seated on a wrought-iron bench in the middle of the room, her hands and feet bound to the metal, her head lowered. She didn't look up, didn't move or indicate that she'd heard—or recognized—his voice.

"We had a deal," Dominic said, his voice tight with rage. "Ava for Maddy."

"Once I've finished with the witch, I'll turn the girl loose. She's my insurance that you won't try anything until the witch is dead."

A muscle twitched in Dominic's jaw. "I'm not leaving without my wife. So do what you intend to do and be quick about it."

In reply, Jasper grabbed Ava by the shoulders and dragged her inside, then kicked the door shut.

Hands clenched, Dominic stood there for a moment

before striding down the sidewalk to where Lily waited. "Are you ready?"

Nudging him in the side with her elbow, she said, "What do you think?" as she opened the canvas bag slung over her shoulder.

"Put on the cloak so I can make sure it works."

"Fine." Reaching into the bag, Lily withdrew an invisibility cloak similar to those Ava had made for the Knights of the Dark Wood decades ago. After shaking it out, she draped it over her head. "Can you see me?"

"No. If the spell Ava gave you doesn't work, you get the hell out of here."

"Stop worrying, Dom. It's going to work. I'll take care of Ava. You grab Maddy."

Dominic nodded. "Here we go."

Maddy kept her head down. It had taken all her self-control not to react when she heard Dominic's voice. Whatever Jasper had injected her with had worn off, but she didn't want him to know that. Better to let him think she was still unconscious and helpless. Her only worry now was that whatever he'd injected her with might harm the baby.

She listened as Jasper moved around the room, muttering under his breath about what he was going to do to Ava before he slit her throat. He kicked her in the side once, but Ava didn't move, didn't make a sound. Engrossed in plotting his revenge, he didn't notice the faint silvery mist that slid down the chimney.

Maddy's heart skipped a beat as the mist drifted behind

her. *Don't move*. Dominic's voice whispered inside her head. She sensed him behind her, knew he had assumed his own shape, though he was masking his presence. She felt his hands brush her skin as he untied her hands and feet. Then, not caring how much noise he made, Dominic put his arms around her and transported the two of them out of the house.

As soon as Dom and Maddy were safely out of harm's way, Lily draped the invisibility cloak over her head, kicked open the door, and shouted the words of unmaking that would break Ava's enchantment and the shackles binding her wrists. Dashing forward, Lily covered Ava with the cloak as well. Hand in hand, they ran out the front door.

Screaming his anger and frustration, Jasper darted out of the house. And ran headfirst into Maddy's spell, which transformed him from man into mouse in the blink of an eye.

Jasper let out a startled cry that quickly turned into a squeak—and then a squeal of raw terror as a cat darted out of the shadows beside the house. The mouse ran toward the bushes that grew near the street with the cat right behind it.

Maddy shuddered as a high-pitched wail that sounded eerily human punctuated the quiet of the night, testifying to the warlock's fate.

"No more than he deserves," Ava said as she removed the invisibility cloak and slipped her arm around Lily's waist. "Your mother would be proud of you, Liliana. And so am I. And you, Maddy; wherever did you learn that spell?"

"From your grimoire, of course," Maddy confessed. "Although I had no idea if it would work."

Dominic laughed as he gave Maddy's shoulders a squeeze. "Like my father always said, it's good to have a witch—or three or four—in the family. Come on, ladies. Let's go home."

Chapter 48

Maddy stayed close to home the next few weeks. Being kidnapped and turning Jasper into a rodent had left her badly shaken, even though everyone assured her his fate was no more than he deserved. On some primal level, she agreed. He had been a despicable creature, devoid of conscience. He had done horrible things. Had his plan succeeded, he would have killed Ava without a qualm. But that didn't ease her guilt. She had killed a man.

And although she hadn't mentioned it to Dominic, she'd had a horrible craving for blood since that night. Was it a punishment for what she'd done? Or had it been sparked by her violent act in taking a human life? Either way, she was too embarrassed to mention it.

She should have known she wouldn't be able to keep it a secret from Dominic for long.

Except for going out to hunt every few nights, as he was doing now, Dominic had stayed close to Maddy since the night of Jasper's death. He knew she was feeling guilty for what she'd done. It hadn't been part of their plan for Maddy to kill the warlock. Ava had intended to do that. Had wanted to do it. And so had Dominic.

But Maddy had reacted instinctively. Her enemy had come rushing out of the house with murder in his eyes and she had taken action without thought. It still amazed him that she had responded before anyone else.

Dominic fed quickly and willed himself back to the house. He found Maddy on the sofa in the living room, staring at the wall.

"Maddy?"

She looked at him blankly for a moment, then forced a smile. "You're back early."

"Yeah." Sitting beside her, he draped his arm around her shoulders. "Talk to me, love. Tell me what's bothering you."

"I killed a man. Shouldn't that bother me?"

"It was self-defense, done on the spur of the moment. And technically, he was killed by a cat. You had no way of knowing that would happen. You have no reason to feel guilty."

"But I do! And I'm . . ." She clapped a hand to her mouth.

"You're what?"

"Nothing."

She wasn't going to tell him, he thought. But he couldn't help her if he didn't know what was wrong. He let his mind brush hers, ever so lightly, and then grunted softly. He should have known what was troubling her. It was perfectly normal. For vampires.

"You need to feed. Why didn't you tell me?"

"I couldn't."

"Once you feed, the craving will pass. And you'll only

have to do it twice a year." Rolling up his sleeve, he said, "You'll feel better if you drink a little."

"Why am I feeling this way?"

"It's natural." His mind brushed her again. "Killing "Jasper aroused your hunting instincts, that's all."

"That's all!" she exclaimed. "It might be natural for you, but it's not for me!"

"I'm afraid it is now." Biting into his wrist, he offered her his arm.

And waited.

Maddy stared at the dark red blood. She craved it as nothing else, but still she hesitated.

Until the scent of it threatened to drive her crazy.

Taking hold of his arm, she drank. And drank. Why had she waited so long for this? The power of it spread through her, strengthening her bond with Dominic, filling her with a warm, sensual pleasure like no other. It chased away her doubts and eased her guilt.

Dominic brushed a kiss across the top of her head. "Don't take it all, darlin'," he murmured.

With a sigh, she lifted her head. "I love you."

"No more than I love you, Mrs. Falconer. Shall I show you how much?"

Anticipation unfurled deep within her when he wrapped his arms around her, his mouth covering hers, his tongue like a flame as he ravaged her lips. Holding her tight, their mouths still fused together, he walked her to the fireplace and drew her down on the rug. With a murmured word, their clothes disappeared. A wave of his hand brought the fire to life.

Maddy snuggled against him, basking in the warmth of the flames, which weren't nearly as hot as the fire that burned between them. His body was firm and well-muscled, and she reveled in running her fingertips along his arms, across his chest, down his hard, flat belly.

He growled low in his throat as he rolled over, carrying her with him, so that she was on top, her legs on either side of his. "Tell me," he said, his dark eyes alight with desire. "Tell me you want me."

"I want you." She gasped, her fingers digging into his shoulders as he thrust into her. He had made love to her before, sometimes slow and gentle, sometimes not so slow or so gentle, but never this masterfully, or this roughly. And she loved it. She raked her nails down his chest when he bit her. And then, for the first time, she bit him in return. And the fire between them blazed hotter and brighter until she felt she might melt in his arms.

And then, with one last thrust, he carried them both over the edge.

Maddy woke with a sigh, her legs tangled with Dominic's, her head pillowed on his shoulder. Just when she'd thought nothing would ever surprise her again, Dominic had taken her places she never knew existed. The second time they'd made love, he had opened the blood bond between them, and it had taken their lovemaking to a whole new level. She had experienced what he did, knew what he was thinking, feeling, as his body merged with hers. It had been the most amazing high she'd ever known. And the best part was, she had felt his love for her.

Had he experienced the same thing? Felt what she felt?

Known what she was thinking, how much she loved him? Needed him?

Smiling, she trailed her fingers across his chest, followed the line of dark hair down his belly . . . let out a shriek when he rolled over, carrying her with him, so she straddled his hips.

"You're playing with fire, girl," he said, dark eyes glinting red.

"I like fire," she said, her voice husky as her fingers delved into the hair at his nape. "Burn me up."

It was hours before Maddy woke again, sore and satisfied and smiling. She groaned softly as she eased away from Dominic, who was sleeping soundly. She spent a minute admiring his broad chest and shoulders, his strong arms and legs, his flat belly. She never tired of looking at him. Even now, a faint flicker of desire unfurled within her, and with it a strong sense of possession. He was hers, forever hers, and she would never let him go.

"It's thoughts like that that got you into trouble," he said, stifling a laugh.

"Go back to sleep, you big stud," she muttered, biting back a grin. "I need my rest."

Maddy was in the kitchen, wondering what to have for lunch, when the first pain hit. She wrapped her arms around her stomach, panic surging through her. It couldn't be the baby. She wasn't due for another month. She stood there, one hand pressed to her belly, waiting for the pain to pass.

When it did, she took a deep breath. Only to let out a low groan when it came again. She was about to call for Dominic when he appeared beside her.

"What is it? What's wrong?"

"I don't know . . . it hurts."

"Everything will be all right." Swearing softly, he gathered her in his arms and transported the two of them to the nearest hospital. Pushing his way through the emergency room doors, he shouted for a nurse.

Five minutes later, Maddy was on her way to an examination room.

Dominic paced the hallway. With his preternatural senses, he had no trouble hearing what was being said. She was in labor. The baby was coming too soon and way too fast.

Opening the link to his parents, he told them what was happening, then contacted Ava and Lily.

His great-grandmother and his sister arrived within minutes.

It took a little longer for the rest of the family.

And only moments to explain what had happened.

"She'll be all right," Callie said, squeezing his hand.

"The baby, too," Ava said. "Don't worry."

Don't worry, he thought. Don't worry when he could hear the anxiety in the voices of the doctor and the nurses, when he could feel their concern as they discussed whether it would be better to let the baby come naturally or perform a C-section.

Dominic cursed under his breath, wondering if whatever Jasper had given Maddy was to blame. Damn the man. If he'd still been alive, Dominic would have ripped him a new one.

He felt like he'd been pacing the floor for hours when the doctor finally appeared. "Mr. Falconer?" He hesitated as two men turned at the sound of his voice.

"Is she all right?" Dominic asked anxiously.

"She's going to be fine," the doctor said with a reassuring smile. "She's been moved to one of the rooms on the third floor."

"And the baby?"

"He's a bit premature. There seems to be an anomaly of some kind in his blood that we haven't been able to identify."

"Is it fatal?"

"I'm afraid I can't say until we've run a few more tests. We'll monitor his vital signs carefully for a few days."

"Can I see my wife?"

"Soon. A nurse will let you know when you can go up."

"Thanks, Doctor." Leaning close to Ava, Dominic whispered, "Do you think this has something to do with our side of the family? Something the baby inherited from me?"

"I don't know, but I doubt it. You and Lily are perfectly healthy." She laid a hand on his arm. "Let's not worry until we have something to worry about."

Yeah, he thought, like that was going to stop him.

"I can't wait to see the baby," Lily said. "I'll bet he looks just like all the men in our family."

"Dammit, I can't wait any longer," Dominic said, and before anyone could stop him, he dissolved into mist and materialized on the third floor. Striding down the hallway as if he belonged there, he followed Maddy's scent to room 312.

She was asleep, her face as pale as the pillowcase beneath her head. Bending down, he kissed her cheek lightly so as not to wake her. Never had she looked more beautiful. At the sound of voices outside the door, he dissolved into mist again as a nurse entered the room.

It took only moments to locate the Neonatal Intensive Care Unit. Still in mist form, Dominic bypassed the nurse on duty and drifted from bassinette to bassinette until he found his son. His heart swelled with love as he gazed at the tiny infant swaddled in a blue blanket, a blue cotton cap on his head. So small, he thought. So helpless. So perfect; how could anything be wrong with him?

When another nurse entered the room, he floated out the door. Later tonight, he would return and give Maddy a little of his blood to strengthen her.

And maybe the baby, too.

Maddy woke to the sound of a baby crying in the distance. *Who had a baby?* A quick glance around showed she wasn't at home. For a moment, panic engulfed her. Had Jasper found her again?

"Maddy."

Relief washed through her at the sound of Dominic's voice. She started to ask what was going on, but it all came rushing back—the pain, their haste to get to the hospital. "My baby?" She glanced frantically around the room. "Where is he?"

"He's going to be fine," Dominic said, giving her shoulder a reassuring squeeze. "And so are you, my love."

"I want to see him."

When she started to sit up, Dominic stayed her with a gentle hand on her shoulder. "He's in NICU, but he's going to be all right. How are you feeling?"

"I want to see my baby. Now."

"Relax, love. You had a rough time of it." Rolling up his shirt sleeve, he bit into his wrist. "I want you to drink from me."

She didn't hesitate. The scent of his blood called to something primal deep within her. As always, it filled her with a warm, sensual pleasure. But, this time, she could also feel his strength flowing into her, through her, easing the pain, calming her anxiety.

"That's enough, love."

"Are you sure he's all right? When can I see him?"

"Right now." Lifting her into his arms, he carried her down the hall to the neonatal unit. A nurse was changing the diaper of one of the babies. After masking their presence, Dominic set Maddy on her feet.

She watched in horror as he bit his arm again and let a few drops of his blood drip into the baby's mouth. It seemed indecent, somehow, to feed blood to a newborn baby. But her horror soon turned to wonder as her son's pale cheeks turned pink. His breathing came easier and he seemed to gain weight right in front of her eyes.

"He'll be fine now," Dominic whispered, wiping a bit of blood from the baby's lips. "Come on, I need to get you back into bed before you're missed."

"He's beautiful, isn't he?" she murmured as he carried

her back to her room. "Will you stay with me awhile?" she asked as he settled her under the covers.

"You know I will. Try to get some sleep."

His words fell on deaf ears. Smiling, he kissed her cheek, then sank down on the hard, plastic chair beside the bed. It was going to be a long night, he thought as he stretched his legs out in front of him. But he was right where he wanted to be.

Chapter 49

When Maddy woke late the next morning, the first thing she saw was Dominic sitting in the chair beside her bed, their son cradled in his arms. She blinked and then rubbed her eyes to make sure she wasn't dreaming.

Feeling her gaze, Dominic looked up, a smile on his face. "Our son is doing fine," he said, his voice thick with emotion. "His vitals are good. He gained a bit of weight overnight and he's breathing on his own." He grinned at her. "The doctors are quite amazed and completely at a loss to explain his overnight improvement. They tested and retested but could find nothing wrong."

Tears trickled down Maddy's cheeks as Dominic stood and placed the baby in her arms. He was beautiful, his hair thick and black, his skin smooth. Her breasts felt suddenly heavy. It took a moment for the baby to get the hang of nursing, but when he did, she was overcome with a feeling of love and devotion she'd never known before.

When she looked over at Dominic, she was surprised to see tears in his eyes. Blinking them away, he murmured, "I've never seen anything as beautiful as the two of you."

Cupping her face in his hands, he kissed her gently. "I love you, wife."

"I love you, my husband."

"Enough of that lovey-dovey stuff," Ava exclaimed, hurrying into the room. "Let me see my great-great-grandson."

"Great-grandfathers first," Andras decreed. "After all, I've come the farthest. And we haven't even met Maddy yet." Moving to Maddy's bedside, he laid his hand on her shoulder. "I'm Andras, Dominic's grandfather. I'm sorry we missed the wedding."

"I'm so glad to finally meet you," Maddy said, embarrassed by the tremor in her voice. But she couldn't help it. She had never been in the presence of so much power before, and it was a little intimidating.

"And this is my wife, Mirella," he said, introducing the lovely woman standing at his side.

Mirella leaned down to press a kiss to Maddy's cheek. "Welcome to the family."

"Thank you."

"My turn now?" Ava asked impatiently.

"Almost," Callie said as she moved closer to the bed. "The baby is adorable. May I hold him?"

"Of course," Maddy said, and felt an immediate loss as Dominic's mother lifted the baby from her arms.

The rest of the family gathered around Callie, oohing and aahing over the infant.

"He's so adorable," Lily remarked. "I think I'm going to start looking for a husband."

While the family laughed, Maddy studied the men in the room. It was amazing, she thought. Andras and Quill both looked thirty, even though they were decades apart in age. Looking at them, she could see how Dominic would look in a few years. His mother and great-grandmother also looked far younger than their years, thanks, no doubt, to the blood they received from their husbands. It truly was a most remarkable family, and she was part of it. The thought made her smile.

They had all brought presents for the baby—clothes and toys and blankets and diapers. And a thousand shares of Disney stock from Andras and Mirella.

"Now that you're a family, you'll need a bigger car," Quill said as he handed Dominic a set of keys. "It's parked downstairs, complete with the best car seat money can buy."

As the two men embraced, Maddy wondered again what kind of business Dominic's family was in. Whatever it was, it was obviously very profitable. Maybe one day she would ask him.

Dominic's family had no sooner left the room when her parents hurried in. They had been out to dinner with friends the night before and then gone to a play. By the time they got the news and arrived at the hospital, Maddy had been asleep.

Maddy smiled as her mother cradled the baby in her arms. "You darling little thing. He's just beautiful, Maddy dear. He's so tiny."

"Well, he came a little early," Maddy said.

"Quite a bit early, I should say," her father remarked. "Why didn't you tell us as soon as you knew? We would have come home earlier."

Maddy flushed.

"It doesn't matter," her mother said. "What matters is

that he's here and he's healthy, Grandpa. Here, hold your grandson."

James looked almost scared as he took the infant in his arms. "What are you going to call him?"

Maddy glanced at Dominic. "We haven't really discussed it. I was thinking of naming him after you."

Leaning down, Dominic whispered in her ear.

"I love you," she whispered back. "Dominic thinks we should name the baby James Dominic."

"I'd be honored." James looked at Dominic, his eyes shiny with unshed tears. "Thank you . . . son."

"We should let Maddy get some rest," her mother said.

"Yes, of course," James agreed as he placed the baby in Maddy's arms. "We'll see you soon. Oh, Fran said she'll call you tomorrow."

Maddy nodded.

"Thanks for coming," Dominic said.

"James Dominic," Maddy murmured, feathering a kiss on her son's brow. "We can call him J.D. for short."

"J. D. Falconer," Dominic mused. "I like it. Your mom's right, you know. You should get some rest now."

"I'm fine." She looked up at him, her eyes filled with love and wonder. To think, she had once had doubts about spending her life with a vampire. How grateful she was at this moment that she had followed her heart's desire. He had given her everything she had ever wanted and much, much more.

Warmth engulfed her when he bent down to kiss her, and with it the assurance that the future would be even more exciting and wonderful than the past.

Don't miss the exciting prequel to

ENCHANT THE DAWN,

available now!

New York Times Bestselling Author

AMANDA ASHLEY

***RT BOOK REVIEWS* Career Achievement winner**

in Paranormal Romance!

ENCHANT THE NIGHT

"A master of her craft."—Maggie Shayne

In the arms of a centuries-old vampire, a woman awakens to newfound passion— and magical powers of her own.

Hungarian vampires are born, not made—and can breed with mortal females. Being one of the oldest of his kind, Quill Falconer has honed his skills at hunting just the right kind of prey, which is why his latest victim confounds him. She shouldn't remember his drinking her blood. And he shouldn't still be craving more . . .

Callie Hathaway's life is as normal as it can be after the death of the beloved grandmother who raised her. Until one night, feeling foggy and fatigued, she realizes that a strangely sensual encounter with a dark, handsome man didn't occur only in her imagination.

As Callie and Quill's unique connection draws them together, an ancient Order of Knights seeks Quill's destruction. Being together puts Callie in mortal danger—until she uncovers a magical family legacy. Side by side they'll fight for survival, and for each other, as the Brotherhood of vampire hunters gather for one final showdown.

Prologue

Chanting softly, twelve bearded men sat around a small fire in the middle of the Dark Wood. All had taken a solemn oath to destroy the last of the Hungarian vampires. Reprehensible creatures who were born rather than made, they were an affront to all that was holy.

The twelve rose when the Elder Knight appeared. On this night, they had gathered under the light of a full moon to initiate the newest member of their Order. Shrouded in long, black, hooded cloaks and masks, they formed a circle around the initiate and the Elder Knight.

"This is a solemn occasion," the Elder Knight intoned, and though he did not shout, his voice rang in the darkness. "Do you understand the gravity of the Oath of Allegiance you are about to make?"

The initiate bowed his head and said, "Yes."

"From this night forward, you will be known as Ricardo 42. Our laws are simple. You will never reveal the names of those gathered here, nor will you ever reveal the location of our temple in the Dark Wood. You will never marry. From this night forward, your sole purpose in life will be to protect humanity from any and all supernatural creatures, even at the cost of your own life. To betray these laws is punishable by death. Will you now swear on your life to obey these laws?"

"I so swear."

The Elder Knight reached into his long black robe and withdrew a jeweled dagger. After piercing his own palm with the dagger, he did the same to each of the Knights, and to Ricardo 42 last of all. Then, one by one, each Knight pressed his bleeding palm to that of the initiate. When it was done, the cuts in their hands closed without a trace.

"You are now one of us, Ricardo 42."

A Knight bearing a robe came forward and presented it to the initiate, then stood back as Ricardo put it on.

A rush of wind stirred the trees and a woman in a long gray cloak appeared, the hood pulled down low to hide her face. She placed a medallion around his neck. "This will alert you to the presence of Hungarian vampires and protect you from falling under their compulsion." Reaching into the pocket of her robe, she withdrew a small package. "This cloak of invisibility will hide you from their sight. Use it wisely." And with that bit of advice, she vanished.

One by one, the Knights welcomed Ricardo 42 into their midst.

And then, one by one, they disbanded, each to seek out and destroy the last of the Hungarian vampires.